## He had the kind of body that could do real damage

Even under the circumstances, with a gun pointed at her, Peachy couldn't help but take in the space where the butt of the gun creased the fabric of his jeans. Her eyes traveled very slowly up the length of the rifle to where one of his callused hands gripped the metal.

"Can I do something for you, sugar?" the stranger asked.

But Peachy couldn't get any words out of her mouth. And as if in slow motion, she saw him lower his rifle and take a step forward.

Peachy drew in a deep breath as he closed the space between them. She knew she was in serious trouble. Instead of backing away, she leaned forward, meeting him halfway for a kiss that sent her reeling. He plunged his tongue deep between her lips and she felt a response so immediate that all her passion threatened to surge forth.

How could this magical, thoroughly inappropriate kiss seem so right? It was as if she knew every inch of him, as if she'd always had. Maybe it had happened...in her dreams.

Dear Reader,

You're about to behold a "Rising Star!"
Four of them, to be exact. This month, we're
launching into the galaxy of American Romance a
new constellation—the stars of tomorrow...four
authors brand-new to our series.

And they're just in time to celebrate with us the tenth
anniversary of American Romance. In honor of this
occasion, we've got a slew of surprises in store this
year. "Rising Star" is just the beginning!

Join me, then, and welcome Jule McBride to
American Romance.

When native West Virginian Jule McBride was little,
she kept her books inside her grandmother Helen's
carved oak cabinet, to which only Jule had a key.
Only later did she realize that the characters she
loved weren't real and that someone called a
"writer" conjured them. That's when she knew one
day she'd be a writer. Even today, reading a good
book reminds Jule of home and hearth and the many
relatives who read to her as a child.

Don't wait another minute. Turn the page and catch
a "Rising Star"!

Sincerely,

Debra Matteucci
Senior Editor & Editorial Coordinator
Harlequin
300 East 42nd St.
New York, NY 10017

# JULE McBRIDE
## WILD CARD WEDDING

# *Harlequin Books*

TORONTO • NEW YORK • LONDON
AMSTERDAM • PARIS • SYDNEY • HAMBURG
STOCKHOLM • ATHENS • TOKYO • MILAN
MADRID • WARSAW • BUDAPEST • AUCKLAND

This book is for my great-aunt Winnie, for all her love and support, and for my Grandma Moore who really lives on Smith Creek Road

Published August 1993

ISBN 0-373-16500-5

WILD CARD WEDDING

# *Prologue*

Petulia Lofton clutched the scented sheet of cream, navy-bordered stationery between two perfectly squared, manicured nails and perused the shocking note again.

Dear Mother,
Sorry, but I simply can't meet one more musician, caterer, or dressmaker's assistant. I can't shop for baby things when I'm not married yet, much less pregnant. Since planning's your forte, not mine, I leave my wedding—the best the city will ever see, I'm sure—to your supervision. But don't worry, I just need a breather. I *will* come back for my wedding. See you June 1!
XOXOXOXOX,
Love and Kisses,
Peachy

Hadn't her impetuous daughter considered that her marriage to Wellington Vanderlynden was not a regular marriage? Petulia had encouraged the romance precisely because Wellington's father owned every Happy's Hot Dog stand in the world. And although some ingenue might laugh at a name such as Pappy Happy, absolutely no one would laugh at his bank account. Or at the fact that he intended to merge his empire with the Lofton's Fancy Foods Corporation on June first.

Hearing her husband's footsteps, she shoved the note into the pocket of her nautically inspired Christian Lacroix pantsuit.

"Hello, Pet!" Charles Lofton stepped into the kitchen and kissed her cheek. "Where's Peachy?"

Petulia reached up, straightened his Brooks Brothers tie, and smiled brightly. Yes, just where *was* Peachy?

Her daughter was fortunate enough to have her own apartment in the family's Upper East Side brownstone. An unused service entrance functioned as her private doorway, and she stopped downstairs most mornings in hopes that Alva, their cook, would fix her breakfast.

Peachy, of course, had never learned to cook.

"Peachy and I did have coffee and a nice chat earlier," Petulia finally said. "But then the dear had to go. She had an appointment with Damion to have her hair trimmed."

"Hair," Charles echoed. He nodded vaguely, as if hair were akin to nuclear physics and far beyond his comprehension. "Well, I'm headed downtown. I'm having lunch with some Happy Hot Dog people."

Petulia's goodbye was pleasant, but as soon as he was gone, her smile vanished. She vowed she would find Peachy before Charles discovered her brazen disappearance. Even if Peachy and her sister already received income from and were to inherit Fancy Foods, with its one hundred and fifty hamburger outlets, the carefully manipulated merger with Happy was important.

If her husband knew, he would be as upset by Peachy's irresponsible behavior as he would be by the possible financial penalty. Already, he feared that Fancy's next quarter might adversely affect Happy's decision. Petulia, herself, had made sure the decisive meeting was scheduled for 1:00 p.m., June first, just two hours before Peachy and Wellington were to be married at Saint Patrick's. She was sure the mood of the day would influence the deal in their favor.

Now she tried not to think of her fourteen hundred wedding guests or of the excuses she would have to offer the Vanderlyndens. Why couldn't Peachy be like her younger sister Christine? Christine would never pull a stunt like this. And now she, Petulia, would just have to cover for Peachy until she could find her.

It was a beautiful spring day. Nonetheless, she knew if she were a more volatile woman, she would certainly consider committing hara-kiri on Madison Avenue or at least flinging herself from Trump Tower. The society wedding of the year was only five weeks away.

"Five weeks!" she exclaimed. How was she supposed to conduct final fittings for a gown when there was no bride? *Five weeks.* Quite a lot could happen in five weeks. For all Petulia knew, Peachy could fall in love with somebody else in that amount of time. Her daughter was certainly impulsive enough.

"Oh, where is Peachy?" she whispered. "That is the question."

# WEEK ONE

*Here comes the bride . . .*

# Chapter One

For a full, impatient fifteen minutes, Peachy Long Lofton had been lounging on her old, black, battle-scarred, multi-stickered trunk, using her Louis Vuitton suitcase for an armrest, one of her three hatboxes for a footstool, and her oversize alligator bag for a pillow. She would have been comfortable if her high heels—*high hells*, she mentally amended—hadn't made her feet feel as though they'd been folded in two.

Having had her share of looks in various airports that day, she knew she looked ridiculous enough to be arrested by the style police, if there really were such a thing. But she was hardly going to explain to anyone that the feather boa around her neck was a last-minute choice; if she had opened the trunk or suitcase to pack the boa, she'd never have gotten either shut again. Besides, as far as she knew, Loftons were never required to make excuses for themselves.

"About time," she said as an old-fashioned Checker cab wound up the last stretch of mountain road. Even though she was the only person outside the tiny Chuck Yeager International Airport in Charleston, West Virginia, Peachy couldn't help but shove her thumb and finger in her mouth, letting loose one of her fiercest taxi-hailing whistles.

Not that the whistle had any visible effect on the taxi. It crept through the parking lot now, as if the driver meant to arrive sometime in February. Still, what West Virginia already lacked in terms of customer services, it made up for in sheer beauty. The air was sweet backwoods mountain air and it made Peachy feel free. Yes, West Virginia would provide the ideal meditative retreat.

The taxi was now close enough that she could read the license plate lettering: Wild Wonderful West Virginia. She certainly hoped not! The last thing she needed was anything even resembling wild. Unfortunately, she was well aware that Patsy Cline was singing about cowboys and whiskey and lost love through the taxi's open windows, and that wasn't helping her serenity one bit. She truly hoped the music wasn't some sort of omen; everything from ticket agents to baggage clerks had portended badly today.

The taxi driver, of whom Peachy could see nothing but a baseball cap, now angled his cab slowly back and forth, pulling to the curb as though he were in a tight-fitting parallel situation. As far as Peachy could see, he was the only man on the road. He got out, slammed his door, and opened the trunk. Gray hair stuck out from beneath his cap, and he had a wise, weathered face etched with character lines.

"Ma'am, I hate to tell you this," he finally said. "But this here's a taxicab. Goes by the name of Bessie. A moving van she ain't."

Peachy stood, lifted her suitcase, then deposited it soundly beside a spare tire, with complete disregard for the fact that it was the most expensive suitcase on the market. "Where I'm from," she said, "everybody moves in taxis." She slung an end of the feather boa over her shoulder and continued loading her luggage.

The cabbie didn't budge. "And where might that be?"

"New York."

"New York," he repeated, looking her up and down.

The lousy luggage clerks came to mind then, as did the boarding-pass woman who had glared at her micro-miniskirt. "New York," she said, unable to control her risng temper. "It's a recognized geographical state. It is on the map. And if you'd be so kind as to help me with my hat-boxes, you might find that we New Yorkers earn our reputations as notoriously generous tippers."

The cabbie burst out laughing and extended his hand, which Peachy shook.

"Bernie," he said. "Pleased to make your acquaintance."

"Peachy." She suddenly smiled. The old man had the kind of deep sparkle in his eyes that could light up a whole town.

Once she was safely ensconced in the back seat with the remainder of her luggage, she said, "We're going to the sweet little country house nearest the—" She reached in her alligator bag, which was difficult since it was scrunched next to her other belongings. There was barely room for her body in the back seat, much less for moving it, but she found the slip of paper and finished, "The Mountainside Interdenominational Church on Smith Creek Road, out toward Davis Creek. It's a few miles past Rock Lake Village."

"That's a fur piece," Bernie said, pulling out of the lot.

Illogically, she thought of the fur piece in her trunk—it was mink—and then realized that "fur" was a term of distance for Bernie. For an instant, she pondered the fact that he'd brought the fur. After all, it was only April and she hardly meant to spend the winter here. She reminded herself that she always overpacked.

For the first time she wondered what her great-aunt Helena's place would be like. Undoubtedly, a huge, rambling white house with freshly painted black shutters and crisp green ivy vines curling into the eaves. There would be the mandatory, white-railed upstairs veranda and a hanging swing on the wide front porch.

Not that she had ever actually seen the house, of course. In fact, she'd never even met her great-aunt. She'd slipped the elderly widow money over the years, when she herself wasn't between dividend checks, as she was now. Still, n matter what the old family black sheep was like, she owe Peachy, and Peachy wasn't above calling in her debts.

Since no one would ever expect to find Peachy—queen o the Upper East Side nightlife—in the heart of subdued Wes Virginia, where, she was sure, nothing ever happened Peachy knew she'd just pulled off one of her most brillian coups.

The place would be quiet, with no parties and absolutel no discussions about hot dogs. That was all her husband-to be in five weeks liked to talk about. Bagel bun, onion bun guacamole on beef-pork blend... She suddenly thought, "I divorce is good enough for Liz Taylor, it's good enough fo me, and..."

She caught herself, midthought, and told herself not t give in to those predictable premarital jitters. She wa headed for a glorious wedding at Saint Patrick's, a month long honeymoon tour in Europe, and then for a safe, prac tical, and very wonderful life.

"Hmm?" She snapped to attention, realizing that he foot was tapping, as if against her mind's will, to the taut twangy radio music. The song unsettled her in the way tha songs about lost love and broken hearts always did.

"I said, did the cat get your tongue?" Bernie's eyes me hers in the rearview mirror. "You look a little down. You'r not brokenhearted yourself, are ya, little lady?"

"Of course not," Peachy said almost curtly, half-angry at the cabbie for cutting into her reverie. "I'm engaged.' She also did not think his was a very polite line of question ing. Not every bride liked to discuss her nuptials ad nau seam.

"Well, congratulations!" Bernie exclaimed. He wound the car around a curve on the narrow, pine-lined road "What's the feller like?"

"Blond, blue-eyed, cleft chin, permanent suntan. Grea job, money, affiliated with a company that'll pull my fa

ther's business back into complete financial recovery...
he's perfect.''

And he was. Everyone adored Wellington, her heaven-
made match, especially her younger sister, Christine. He was
the son her father had always wanted and had never had,
even if he'd long ago turned Peachy into a sort of son. Not
that her education had made her much but a suitable part-
ner for business beaus such as Wellington. Still, she was
sassy and strong-willed, with a good mind for business, like
her father. It was he, after all, who had taught her her
trademark whistle.

''Well, honey,'' Bernie finally said. ''Nothing'll bore the
pants off you faster than perfection.''

She only nodded absently in response, suddenly feeling
anxious. Her lone reservation about the choice to hide in
West Virginia was the gossipy and sometimes unfortunately
disparaging stories that circulated about her deceased uncle, Kyle Lofton.

She supposed that every family deserved one skeleton,
even if it was difficult to imagine any relation on her father's side—the conservative Lofton side—even being
vaguely eccentric. Nonetheless, her father had once received an odd letter from Kyle; Kyle claimed he'd with-
drawn his money from banks, changed it to gold, and had
begun to work on a shelter stocked with food.

Kyle, convinced that another thirties-style depression was
on the way, had also suggested that Charles Lofton ''get out
of the Wall Street racket and do the same.'' The letter had
been the source of quite a few family jokes. And nothing
more, Peachy told herself now.

A pothole sent her bouncing in the seat and the hatbox in
her lap bumped her chin. She really hoped this uncomfortable ride would end quickly. As soon as she reached her
great-aunt's house, she'd relax in a hot, sudsy tub. Before
she even began to think about how not to become the kind
of wife her own mother was—a pretty appendage—per-

haps she would treat herself to a facial with her very favor ite clay mask.

BERNIE SHOVED the gear into park, singing along with yet another love song in his baritone. Peachy wasn't sure, but thought the vocalist was Loretta Lynn. "Well," he said when the notes ended, "this must be it."

Snatches of white paint winked through the trees. Bits of color—yellow, violet and red—glinted in the late afternoon sunlight. A disorderly array of glorious spring flowers nestled in the grass and blew in the breeze.

"Why, you lucky dog, you," Bernie continued. "It's a dream house, all right."

Peachy glanced back at the Mountainside Interdenominational Church. A small building that probably served as a community house was separate. The church itself was a small one-room affair. The large, imposing structure of Saint Patrick's leaped to her mind, and she felt a sudden surge of gratitude. In only five weeks, she would be marching down its impressive center aisle, with fourteen hundred pairs of eyes riveted on her.

Her attention reverted to the lovely country house as Bernie stepped onto the road's shoulder. A small footbridge crossed a creek and beyond that lay the well-maintained lawn. Rough-hewn, handmade flower boxes in the windows sparkled with recently watered flowers, and there was a willow tree, too, its fingerlike branches just grazing the creek's surface.

"It's smaller than I'd imagined . . . and it could use some paint." Peachy turned to look at Bernie. "I mean, the paint looks fine," she qualified, "but a fresh, new coat would really gleam. And those will have to go."

She pointed past a dividing fence and up a hill, directing Bernie's gaze to two old ramshackle outbuildings in the distance. There was a large, brownish structure that had probably once been a barn and another shed-like structure that, before modernization, had perhaps been an outhouse.

Bernie shrugged. "People build new 'round these parts, but don't ever tear down the old. Best thing to do would be to torch 'em. Just burn them down."

"Torch them," Peachy repeated, liking the sound of it. It would feel good, as if she were burning her old life down to ashes, for just one moment, before starting anew. And indeed, the new Peachy was going to be more responsible. She was going to put her hoity-toity education, which she'd frittered away for the past eight years, to use. She was going to be a tough-minded businessperson, just like her father. An image of a phoenix rising from the ashes flew through her mind. Yes, she'd do her great-aunt a favor and burn down the unused outbuildings, as a sort of hostess gift.

"Want to go say a big hello while I get your bags?" Bernie hiked his pant leg and propped his boot on Bessie's back fender, as if their next move required deep discussion.

"No," said Peachy. "Let's tiptoe. I want to surprise my aunt." She'd spoken to Helena, of course, but hadn't known the exact time of her arrival. She could already see the pleased, excited expression on the elderly woman's face.

Within a few minutes, the two managed to silently transfer the luggage to the wide front porch. Unfortunately, there was no upstairs veranda and the porch swing squeaked when Peachy tested it. Nonetheless, she was sure a can of oil would remedy the problem. Glancing around, she saw there were other small projects—some hedge trimming, a new flag needed for the mailbox—but otherwise, the place was pleasant enough.

"Best of luck to you, ma'am," Bernie said when she followed him back to the taxi for her last hatbox.

"And to you, too," Peachy said. Impulsively she leaned and shook his hand again. Then she dug deeply into her alligator bag, found some wadded bills, and tipped him as generously as she possibly could. With a sinking feeling, she admitted she was more cash poor than she'd thought. She certainly hoped she had saved enough for her return ticket. Why had she decided to take off on a jaunt between dividend checks?

She felt a gut-level twinge of sadness when Bernie got back inside Bessie and slammed the door. It was the kind of melancholic loneliness that marked the end of a long journey, the fear, however unwarranted, about what lay ahead. Bernie pulled out of the drive, singing some new country tune in his fine baritone. She waved and ran to the porch.

Looking over her shoulder, she realized Bernie had pulled into the church lot. Undoubtedly, he was waiting for his next fare call, but she hoped Helena didn't see him. It would ruin her splashy little dropped-out-of-the-sky effect. She stepped over her luggage, smoothed her clothes, squared her shoulders, and took a deep breath. Then she rang the bell.

A loud ka-boom answered. And it wasn't a car backfire. It sounded like a gunshot. An expletive followed, spoken by a man's deep, almost bass, voice. She froze, then steadied her nerves and glanced around. What was happening? She almost felt compelled to run for cover.

But that was ridiculous! Maniacs with guns belonged in the city. Smith Creek Road was hardly Manhattan. She listened as a screen door slammed somewhere in the house. Heavy boots lumbered across the wooden-sounding floors inside. Then the screen of the front door swung open so quickly that she inadvertently took a fast, self-protective step backward.

It was pointed at the sky, but it was aimed far too close to her head for comfort. Her eyes followed the long barrel of the rifle right down to the butt of the gun, which wedged against the outside of a very solid-looking, jeans-clad thigh.

Even under the circumstances, Peachy couldn't help but take in the space where the butt of the gun creased the fabric of his jeans. Half with fear and half with an excitement she immediately repressed, she thought, *Now there's the kind of body that could do real damage.*

She quickly twisted the engagement ring on her finger, as if for reassurance. Nonetheless, her eyes trailed very slowly back up the length of the rifle to where one of his large, wide, callused hands gripped the steel. His other free hand rested on his hip. His thumb was hooked loosely through a belt loop, so that it rested against the hand-tooled leather of his thick belt.

"Can I do something for you, sugar?" *Now here's a real piece of work.* Bronson West's gaze trailed over the luggage that littered his front porch.

His voice was every bit as terse-sounding as the tight line of his lips would have indicated. Her glance shot warily to his eyes. They were gunmetal gray and squinted against the sun. Did the guy think he was Clint Eastwood or something?

"You need not be rude," she managed, forcing herself to say something and not to gaze too deeply into those eyes.

He looked her over, from head to toe, with a scrutinizing gaze that made her feel very uncomfortable. For all his tight-lipped machismo and the fact that he was toting a very lethal-looking weapon, he just didn't look like a killer. *Well, neither had Ted Bundy.* She fumbled in her alligator bag where she was sure she'd put the paper with her directions, even though she knew this was the right place.

"Lady, are you lost or something?" He tossed his head so the waving black curls framing his face fell over his ears.

"Of course not," she said. Oh, no, she thought, where was her Aunt Helena? Had the man done something to the kind, elderly woman? "I never get lost."

"You look pretty lost to me," he said, trying not to stare into the messy innards of her pocketbook.

"If you'll just give me a minute, I'm looking for my..." she began. She gave up on finding her directions. "Could you at least lower the gun?" she muttered.

He didn't budge.

"What *can* I do for you?" he repeated, trying to fight his exasperation. If there was one thing he didn't want anywhere near him, especially during his afternoon target practice, it was a city woman. And she had city written all over her in big block letters.

"First, you can start off by not shooting me," she said, finally steadying her voice. She put as much of a tough Brooklyn accent into it as she could, even though he hardly looked the type to be intimidated.

"Sorry, ma'am, but I don't generally shoot women." He smiled a sharklike smile that he hoped would send her packing. "Just an occasional child." He tried not to notice that the bluest eyes he'd ever seen were watching him anxiously.

"Right," she said. "I'd noticed there weren't many kids in the neighborhood." *Not many adults, either,* she thought, trying not to glance at the mountainous landscape. She meant to keep her gaze fixed on that gun.

"Anyway," he continued, "I don't want to be picky, but would you mind telling me why all your worldly possessions happen to be on my front porch?"

"Your—your porch?" Her jaw dropped. Conceivably, in other circumstances, she could be wrong, but there really were no other houses, not one. She swallowed, taking in his strong, powerful-looking body again. Maybe this was Helena's handyman.

"Lady," Bronson said, "are we going to stand here all day playing Mexican standoff—" He suddenly gave her what in another situation could have sufficed as a grin, exposing a wide mouth full of strong, white, perfectly aligned teeth. "Well," he continued, "I guess we can't really have a good old regular-style Mexican standoff, seeing as I'm the only one with a gun." *Even if he knew darn well the safety was on.*

"I was looking for my great-aunt," Peachy said, still doing her best Brooklynese. "Helena Lofton. This is her place?"

Bronson laughed. He'd known there was something familiar about that pale, freckled skin and shock of red-rooster hair. She was sophisticated and pretty, all right, but she still looked exactly like that old fool, Kyle Lofton. "So you're a Lofton," he said dryly. "I guess if you're only half as crazy as Kyle, that's some small improvement for the neighborhood."

*Crazy!* "Look," she said in a voice she reserved for the subway at rush hour but knew would work just as well in the country, "I don't have a crazy bone in my entire body. It seems perfectly reasonable to ask what you're doing here. And if you could kindly—if you can manage to do anything kindly—direct me to my great-aunt. She's expecting me." Even in New York, she thought, she never saw attitudes this bad.

Now that she'd dropped the Brooklynese, Bronson noticed the woman's accent sounded exactly like his deceased wife's. Inadvertently, he lowered the barrel of the rifle while his gaze dropped to her long, bare, slender legs. He had no intention of thinking about the bones in her body, crazy or not, but he hadn't been with a woman in a long time. And just looking at this one made his body ache.

"Sorry," he said abruptly, "but it's just not every day that a girl—"

"Look here," said Peachy, sidestepping the lowering gun. "I'm no girl. I'm thirty—"

"Oh, pardon me," he said.

"I'm just not the stodgy old crusty type," she continued. "Okay?" She had half a mind to add *threatening* and *gun-toting* but didn't. She glared at him.

"I'm hardly stodgy, sweetheart," he managed. What *she* was, was attractive, he thought. Like some exotic bird, with that feather boa around her neck, ruffling in the breeze beneath her red hair.

"Stodgy or not—"

"Not," he said.

She swallowed, having to at least admit the truth in that. The man was extraordinarily handsome. "Well, anyway, I have just asked a simple question," she said. "Why are you so—"

"Difficult?" He shrugged. "Helping damsels in distress has never been my strong suit." His lips twisted into what might have been a teasing smile.

"I'm hardly distressed and I'm certainly not a damsel, so would you please just give me a straight—"

"Sorry," he said. Watching her small pink lips pucker and turn kissable, he knew it was definitely time he sent her to Helena's and out of his sight. "My name's—"

"I don't care what your name is," she said flatly, realizing that her need for self-protection was taking a back seat to her anger. "And I don't know where in the world you come from, either—"

"Where *I* come from?" Bronson interrupted. It was becoming difficult to concentrate on what she was saying since the longer he stared at her, the more he was aware of his total and very traitorous response to her. "I've got something to tell you," he finally managed.

"It's about time," she put in.

He grimaced. "Well, you're not going to like it. Are you ready to listen—"

"No," she corrected him. "You listen to me. I simply won't stand for this kind of treatment." She paused, wondering how this man had managed to get so far under her skin. How was she going to get the peace and quiet she deserved with this character around?

"Now, I expect you to put down that weapon," she continued. "And if you don't think I can handle you, you've got another think coming. I've seen more guns bought, sold and shot on the streets of Manhattan—''

"Manhattan," he interjected. "I knew it. I just knew—"

"Manhattan," she continued, "where I've seen more silly old guns than could be found in this whole, entire state—" She cut herself off abruptly and set her face more firmly in a fixed, rigid and very serious expression. "And so you really better quit trying to intimidate me—"

Briefly she realized that his good looks were intimidating her far more than the gun, and that if he weren't thirty or thirty-five she wouldn't be rambling like an idiot. "And just tell me where my great-aunt is," she continued. "And, also..."

Bronson half listened to her ongoing tirade. If she'd just close her trap for half a minute, he could straighten her out and send her on up to Helena's. But city woman that she was, and in the riled-up state she was in, she just might try to wrestle the rifle from him. In the process, she would certainly kill them both.

Suddenly he decided there was just one way to stop her. He lowered the rifle, leaned it against the doorjamb, and took a quick step forward. He told himself it was simple self-defense. It was calculated to give her a bad impression of him. It was guaranteed not only to get her off his porch, but also to get her out of his life forever.

The fact that he was more attracted to her than he had ever been to anyone on first sight had zilch to do with it. And, he argued, even if he hadn't been with a woman for six long years, which he had not, this silly little move would not affect him in the least. He just wanted her to shut up and listen to reason.

So he stepped closer, lowered his mouth, and kissed her.

# Chapter Two

She was as stiff and unyielding as a washboard. But then Bronson hadn't expected her to still be standing here at all. No, he'd expected her to bolt like a wild animal. That was why he was kissing her...to make her run. Wasn't it? And he'd just meant to give her one of those silly little old hunt-and-peck kisses. The kind of kiss he would give his grandmother. Instead his lips were drinking in all the warmth of her mouth and savoring all her taste. It was pure honey-salt, mixed with peppermint, as if she'd been eating candy. He stepped even closer, thinking that maybe having her around the neighborhood wouldn't be so bad after all.

Peachy drew in a deep, quick breath as he closed the inches of space left between them. She knew she was in serious trouble. Instead of backing away, which is what she'd intended, she leaned forward, letting her tongue meet his halfway. Against her will, her lips were warming to the pressure of this stranger's mouth.

His tongue licked at her bottom lip lightly and then at her top lip, and then plunged inward again, deep inside. No one had ever kissed her so playfully or with such growing assurance. The man had seemed so tough and testy, but if his way of kissing was any indication, that rough exterior only hid a more teasing nature.

In her mind's far reaches, she knew that this was very wrong. But the scent of him was as earthy and compelling and heady as the fresh country air. From the first moment she'd laid eyes on him, she'd felt a spark of attraction, the kind to which all reason took a back seat. She snaked her arm around his waist.

How could this strange, thoroughly inappropriate kiss seem so right? So almost fated? It seemed like a kiss of remembrance, as if it had happened before, but it hadn't. Well, she thought vaguely, while her mind whirled with the assault to her senses, maybe it *had* happened . . . in her dreams.

He sent his tongue deep between her lips again and she felt a response so immediate that all her passion threatened to surge forth. His body seemed to meet hers at every point and white heat suddenly coursed through her veins, tunneling downward to her stomach. It was as if she already knew each inch of him . . . as if she had always known him. It was like déjà vu. Like magic. Like . . .

She'd gone mad!

She wrenched herself from his arms. Had the interchange taken split seconds? Minutes? Longer? She stared levelly at him, hoping to communicate that what had just happened had not happened at all.

His lips were reddened and swollen-looking, and now they curved into a teasing half smile. "Well," he said. "Whoever you are, you're sure some kisser."

"You assaulted me," she burst out, trying not to recall how willingly she had responded. It took everything she had to keep the flush from rising to her cheeks. The last thing she'd meant to do on this trip was start kissing a man other than her fiancé. What had gone wrong?

He arched one of his dark brows. "Assaulted? Felt pretty mutual to me, sugar," he said lightly, the teasing smile not leaving his lips. His gray eyes dared her to differ.

She wished she could hightail it to a powder room to regain her equilibrium, but there was no chance of that under these circumstances.

"So, do you always kiss women who have the misfortune of running into you?" she finally asked, striving to maintain his light, teasing tone. He sounded as though he kissed women with that kind of expertise all the time. And it had sure *felt* as though he'd had a lot of practice, she thought.

He looked her up and down slowly. "No," he finally said, the testy tone creeping back into his voice. "I only kiss the ones I find attractive." His gaze settled on her eyes. "I pride myself on being selective."

"You don't even know me!" It was bad enough that she could still feel the heat of his mouth against hers and that her heart was still pounding, but the man was acting as if what had just happened was the most natural thing in the world.

"I might not know you," he said softly, with the faintest hint of a chuckle, "but I'm beginning to think I want to."

"On the basis of kissing me?" she asked. She tossed her head, hoping she didn't look the least bit affected by what they'd just done. "In my book," she continued haughtily, "people want to get to know one other on the basis of their *personalities*." She drew in a quick breath. She knew she was beginning to sound mean, but she simply couldn't help it. It was better to sound mean than deeply interested, which is how she actually felt.

His sexy lips pursed in a bow shape and it was clear he was trying not to laugh. "Well," he said after a moment, "so far, on the basis of your personality..."

His voice trailed off, as if her personality left something to be desired. "Oh," she managed. "I assume other women—*strangers*—step right into your arms without so much as a complaint, mister." It was hard to tell whether she was making him mad or amusing him. His lips lifted in response to her words, and she had to admit that she liked his smile. Even under the circumstances, it was hard not to smile back at him when he looked at her that way.

His smile became a Cheshire-cat grin. "Well, you sure did," he finally said. He squinted at her. "I mean, if you were complaining, I sure didn't hear it." His gray eyes narrowed even more and sparkled.

"Well, I'm complaining now," she said flatly. Even though she *had* stepped right into his arms. Had she really kissed a stranger with more passion than she had ever felt with her fiancé?

He stared at her for a long moment. "Have it your way," he said.

She braced herself for what was coming. Clearly, from his change in tone, he had some other card up his sleeve. Apparently, they were back to a game of one-upmanship. And somehow, she had a sneaking suspicion he was going to win. But how had he expected her to respond to the way he'd kissed her? Did he really expect her to melt right into his arms at first sight?

He was pointing up the hill. "I hate to tell you this, sweetheart, but that's your aunt's house."

Her gaze followed the sinewy length of his muscular arm, stopped for a moment on his wide, unseasonably suntanned hand, then continued to the tip of his index finger. It was pointed at the ramshackle outbuildings in the distance. The buildings that were her phoenix from the ashes. The ones she was to torch and destroy, so she could decide how to conduct her life after her marriage to Wellington Vanderlynden.

Bronson watched her lips, which he now knew were very kissable. She pulled them into a pout, the kind that said he was personally responsible for yet another beautiful woman's unhappiness. He felt so guilty, he almost offered to put in a modern toilet for her. Then he came to his senses. Hadn't turning her off been the whole point of turning her on?

The way she'd kissed had changed his mind about that, of course, but it hadn't seemed to change hers. Still, as much as she wanted to hide her feelings, she couldn't. Her eyes were bright and her skin was flushed and she still hadn't quite regained her breath. He watched her small mouth snap shut. Her eyes gained a steely expression.

*Never let them see you sweat, Lofton,* she coached herself. She pressed her hand to her heart, as if she'd missed a very close call. Which, since she was still feeling the taste of his lips on hers, she knew she had. With one touch of his mouth, the man came seriously close to threatening her whole future.

"Thank heavens," she said. It took everything she had to continue, but he was not going to threaten her future, not if they were going to be neighbors for the next millennium, which they were not.

"You know, I looked at this place and was... well...somewhat upset, as you can imagine. To come all the way from New York to visit, only to find—" She smiled as sweetly as she could. "Well, this was a great disappointment."

She glanced at her aunt's miserable excuse for a house again, then looked at him, still fighting the incredible jolt of awareness his kiss had sent through her. "I really didn't think that the place on the top of the hill could be hers...and when I saw...well, I thought I was going to have to turn around and head back to the city. But now it looks like things are working out just fine."

Bronson realized his eyes were still fixed on her mouth. He glanced away immediately, only to find he was again staring into the deepest, most beautiful set of clear blue eyes he'd ever seen. He could still read desire in them, too. Loud and clear.

"It looks like we'll be neighbors," she continued, extending her hand. "At least during my visit. Not that we'll be seeing each other. I've come to the country on a personal retreat."

Bronson had to fight not to roll his eyes. Not knowing what else to do, he shook her hand, which was pretty darn strange since he'd just kissed her, and admirably well, in fact. Her palm was sweating. And well it should be, he thought. What a little liar! Helena's place was a disaster area.

"Peachy Lofton," she said brightly.

*"Peachy?"* he queried. He tried but was unable to match her confident self-satisfied tone. He dropped her hand. What kind of name was "Peachy"? Even though he had half a mind to call her bluff, he smiled. Two could play at this game. If she was choosing to ignore what, for him, had been an amazing first kiss, and if she could muster that overdone Brooklynese, he could certainly put on his best sugar-coated country twang.

"Well, sweetie," he said, letting his voice drip with irony, "I sure wouldn't want to offend your fine city sensibility any longer by keeping you on such a wretched, tumble-down little ole porch. I've always loved the old Lofton *estate* myself—" At least, he thought, it was true that he wanted to buy it. He mustered a sad expression. "But you know what they say, the grass is always greener on the other side."

Peachy stared back up the hill. The grass—where there *was* grass—had grown wild with weeds in the April rain. The false smile she'd plastered on her face was beginning to hurt a little. "Well, that's the thing about clichés. They get to be clichés because there's so much real truth in them."

"I see you've got a philosophical bent," Bronson managed. "Your new place ought to be just the thing to help you find yourself during your—" he drew his mouth into the wryest smile he could "—uh . . . retreat."

"Well, it was certainly nice to meet you," she said. She realized he hadn't told her his name, but decided that was just as well. She had no intention of seeing him again. He

might be better than good-looking, but the last thing she
needed right now was an involvement. And, anyway, she
was fairly sure his kiss was calculated to get rid of her. No
man came on to a woman so immediately if he really was
interested. No, it was crystal-clear he wasn't looking for any
friends. Somehow she would force herself to forget the soft
feel of his lips.

"Yeah," he finally said. "So nice to meet you, too." He
suddenly smiled that quirky, teasing smile of his again.
"Since we've already kissed, do you still expect me to bake
the customary welcome-to-the-neighborhood apple pie?"

"Of course not," she said as sweetly as she could. "I
think you've done quite enough already, thank you."

He couldn't help but chuckle. "Well, if there's anything
*more* I can do, just let me know."

She stared levelly into his eyes and couldn't help but
wonder if bedroom eyes could be gray. Usually they were
blue, after all. But these bedroom grays were saying she had
an open invitation that had nothing to do with apple pie.
"Like I said, you've done quite enough," she managed.

She turned abruptly, ready for a grand exit, the kind that
would put him in his place, but in their interchange, knowledge of her whereabouts had vanished. She wasn't in Manhattan!

No grand exit was available. She was stuck—trunk, hat-
boxes, and all. There were no taxis, subways or limos. She
gazed again into his eyes, beginning to panic. "I'll send for
my things," she said stiffly, hoping her great-aunt had a car.
Judging from the state of her property, she might not.

Turning away, a genuine smile broke through her false
one. Bright yellow glinted through the willow tree. The
man's odd combination of drop-dead good looks and lousy
attitude, not to mention that kiss, had flustered her so
completely that she'd forgotten all about Bernie.

It was a real stroke of luck, even if it was the *only* stroke
of luck she'd managed to have all day. She turned and fixed

her bright blue eyes on her neighbor's gray ones again, then nestled her fingers and thumb under her tongue.

*Don't fail me now,* she thought when a sputtering spit sound threatened to emerge from between her lips. Heaven knew, her mouth was still kissing wet at the moment and just right for a perfect whistle. Oh, why did the man's eyes have to be so darkly gray, so squinty and so expressive? She blew again. Nothing. He cocked his head and looked at her as if she were out of her mind.

*The third time's the charm.* She blew with all her might. And it was a great whistle, the kind that would have made her father proud.

"I do believe I'll take a taxi," she said with all the nonchalance she could. She turned daintily, tossing one end of the boa over her shoulder. She let her heels fall on the porch steps with resounding, definite clicks.

Bronson watched her walk toward the footbridge. Her feather boa blew in the breeze and her hips swished. He hadn't seen a skirt that short since 1967. He'd been twelve. Looking at her perfect, slender legs, his mouth went dry. Somehow the only consolation was the fact that her heels were sinking into the grass, and she looked pretty undignified when she had to tug them out of the soft earth. He could see her well-formed, nice-looking feet threaten to slip out of the shoes altogether with every step. Kissing her was one thing, and now, looking at her body was something else. He felt another surge of longing.

"Oh, brother," he whispered. He couldn't let her walk to Helena's in high heels. It would be easy enough to drive her umpteen bags over in his Blazer. Hell, if he didn't, Helena would give him a big piece of her mind. The crazy niece was walking over the bridge now, waving and whistling to nothing but thin air.

"Who's the babe?" Tommy asked, coming up behind Bronson.

Bronson took in his sixteen-year-old's heavy-metal band T-shirt and the black leather jacket that he wore, even in warm weather and even in the house. He sure hoped his son hadn't witnessed that kiss. "Helena Lofton's niece."

Tommy laughed and shook a head of long black curls identical to his father's. "It's hard to imagine that class act having Lofton blood. She musta been brought by that stork you used to tell me about . . . the very kind stork with great taste in legs. You gonna take her out, Dad? She's definitely a better catch than Virginia Hall."

"Now, Tommy, Virginia's nice," Bronson said.

"Yeah," said Tommy. "But not *that* nice." .

"Well, I'm not taking anybody out," said Bronson gruffly as he rummaged through his pockets for his car keys. All the women in the neighborhood speculated about his intimate life, and Bronson hardly wanted his son to start, too.

Yet another whistle cut through the air. Did she really think she was going to get a taxi? Didn't she even realize that she was in the middle of nowhere? "And you should concentrate on your schoolwork, Tommy, not my dating practices," Bronson added after a moment.

"What dating practices?" Tommy asked with feigned innocence.

Bronson continued to watch Helena's niece. That was what too many years in New York did to a person, Bronson thought with conviction. He had lived there himself for eight years. He had gone to college there and interned at the New York Animal Hospital. Money-obsessed people, noise, fast pace and crime were certainly things he could live without. Besides, New York was no place to raise a son.

"Good luck, lady," he muttered, jingling his keys.

"If you don't lighten up, Dad, you're gonna become—"

"Stodgy?" Bronson asked, arching his brow. After all, that was what she'd called him.

"Stodgy's a pretty good description," said Tommy.

Her voice cut through the air. It was even louder than her whistle. "Taxi," she yelled. "Taxi."

Bronson did a double-take. A yellow Checker cab was puttering down Smith Creek Road. Soon, it was so close that he could see the smart black jets pushing from its exhaust. "Some people sure have all the luck," he said. He turned and went toward the kitchen. The cabbie could get her luggage. *He* had a dinner to prepare.

In the kitchen, Bronson donned an apron. It was an old, tattered, ruffly affair with a sheer pink sash that had belonged to his wife. It was one of the few things of Andrea's that remained, he realized now. Damn, why did citified Peachy Lofton have to show up like some kind of old history book?

The good thing about country women, he thought, bending down to peer into the lower regions of his refrigerator, was that they took good care of simple country widowers like himself. They didn't expect him to put on airs and become something he wasn't, either. The evidence was right here. There was leftover ham, courtesy of Ellen Logan, and leftover beef roast, courtesy of Virginia Hall.

All Bronson had to do was heat some biscuits and boil a vegetable. Rummaging in the refrigerator, the minty taste of Peachy's mouth came back to him. He grabbed the tin of biscuits with more force than was necessary, trying not to recall Peachy's startled look when she'd seen his gun. It was just his luck that she'd interrupted his afternoon target practice.

Yeah, he thought wryly, some alpha man he was. He reached behind himself and tightened the pink sash over his jeans. If only Peachy Lofton could see him now....

PEACHY KNOCKED on the wood frame of the screen door, still trying to forget how her great-aunt's neighbor had simply stepped right up and pressed his mouth to hers. It was the kind of crazy, unrealistic thing that happened in

movies…not in real life. Had he been so attracted to her l
just couldn't help himself? She certainly wanted to flatt
herself with that idea, but then it seemed just as likely he
meant to push her away. And if that was the case, she real
was in trouble, since she wasn't likely to get that kiss out
her mind anytime soon.

She knocked again. When no one answered, she let he
self into the house. Wasn't anyone in wild, wonderful We
Virginia normal? Spanking clean as the room was—by we
come contrast to the rough exterior—it hardly offered th
country ambience she had imagined. Glancing around, sh
wondered if her uncle really had hidden his money. Wel
whatever he had done with it, he certainly had not investe
in decent home furnishings.

"Hello, there," boomed a loud, drill-sergeant-like voice

It had to be her aunt. She was small in stature, with a ver
erect posture, and long gray hair that was done up in a bu
and bound with strips of brightly colored cloth. Blue eye
peered at Peachy through bifocals. The next thing she knew
Helena had her in an embrace that threatened to squeeze th
life out of her.

"You have to be Peachy! You're the spitting image o
your uncle Kyle." Helena released her. She pointed throug
a window. "Who's that?"

"Bernie," Peachy said. "My taxi driver." She started t
ask Helena about her neighbor, but forced herself not to
She'd come here to think about her upcoming new life. Sh
reminded herself that the man at the bottom of the hill wa
not on her agenda. All she needed was a bubble bath. Pe
riod.

Outside, Bernie had abandoned his cab to circle an an
cient tank of a convertible. The rusty car had more than
few dents and seemingly no roof.

"That vehicle hasn't gone anywhere in years," Helena
said now. "Wish it did, but it doesn't. Bronson won't fix it
since he thinks I'm too old to drive."

Peachy vaguely wondered who Bronson was. She had hardly expected her great-aunt to have much company and hoped he did not visit regularly. They watched as Bernie opened the car door and pulled the hood release.

"He's handy!" Helena exclaimed, tugging Peachy's arm. "Think he likes roast?"

"You can't invite a cabdriver—" Peachy stared at her aunt, aghast. Hadn't Helena ever heard of robberies and muggings?

"I'm old," Helena said, pulling her toward the door. "Humor me. Just introduce me to your friend."

"He's not my friend," Peachy managed. "He's my damn taxi driver."

"Glad to see I've got a niece who curses," Helena said. "I was afraid you'd be overly proper, like your mother. Not that I don't like Petulia, mind you, but she'd hardly make it in a place with no indoor toilet."

"No indoor toilet?" Peachy felt the breath leave her body.

"There's a shower," Helena said, forcing her out of the door. "Just no toilet."

"No tub?" How was she to relax without baths? In an outhouse? And how was she to relax after having been kissed in a way she had never been before?

Outside, once the introductions were made, Helena gave Bernie what seemed to be her best, beaming smile.

Bernie lifted his baseball cap graciously from his head and smoothed his few gray hairs into place.

"Your niece said you were beautiful in photographs...."

Peachy's mouth dropped. That was a complete lie. It was exactly the kind of sweet, social lie her mother always gave.

Helena laughed. "Something tells me you're making up stories."

"Maybe so, ma'am," said Bernie. He winked at Helena.

Far down the hill, Peachy could see her neighbor's quaint white house gleam in the rosy light of the oncoming dusk.

If she had any sense at all, she would turn right around and head back to the city. In New York, she'd be dressed to the nines and en route to some cozy new overpriced bistro with Wellington. All right, she suddenly fumed inwardly, perhaps she could still be stirred by soft caressing kisses from another man....

Now, if she was going to keep up with the Joneses, a toilet was going to have to be the first order of business. She could hardly even begin to *think* about relaxing without a toilet. A toilet. She flashed Bernie a smile every bit as bright as Helena's. Just how handy *was* he?

"I really need to unpack," she said, thinking she could leave Helena to the dirty work of enticing Bernie to play fix-it man around the farm.

She realized that neither Bernie nor Helena had heard. They were gazing deeply into one another's eyes.

BRONSON'S MIND had been unusually preoccupied and dinner hadn't been one of his best. The biscuits were a little more burned than he generally liked them and his green beans were raw, even though he was sure he'd boiled them enough. In the six years since Andrea's death, he still had not perfected the art of bachelor cooking. Only Virginia's roast turned out all right.

He'd found himself staring at his teenage son throughout dinner, wondering whether or not his own lack of culinary talent was having irreversible effects on Tommy's growth. It was just the kind of dinner that made him think maybe he did need to get himself a woman, after all.

Bronson realized he'd been staring out the window for some time. It was a moonlit night. The sky was clear, filled with stars, with no hint of the heavy fog they'd had lately. He rinsed the last dinner dish and plunked it into the drainer. As much as he kept trying to ignore it, a voice kept running in his head, saying, "Peachy Lofton, Peachy Lofton, Peachy Lofton..."

"Did you say something?" he yelled over his shoulder.

"Why *won't* you buy me a car?" Tommy yelled.

"Why *should* I buy you a car?" Bronson wiped his ruuny-looking hands on a dish towel and then headed upairs. "Aren't you tired of this topic? You could work and ive some money yourself, you know," Bronson continued, coming to stand in the doorway of his son's room. ommy's hair was still wet from his shower, but true to orm, he'd put his leather jacket on over his pajama botoms.

"No, I can't. Not without your help. Larry's dad is gonna elp him. We live in the middle of nowhere. Without a car, can't get a job. How am I supposed to get to work? The chool bus? I went to that special driving school because you aid we could talk about me having a car when I finished. nd I got an *A* +, too. You just don't want me to have a car ecause—" Tommy cut himself off.

"Because your mother..." Bronson said. "That's just not rue."

Tommy smiled. "That's okay, Dad."

Bronson leaned in the triangle of the half-open doorway. ndrea's wreck had everything to do with why he didn't vant Tommy to drive. He always denied it, but both he and ommy knew it was true.

Another look at his son reminded him of why he had to tay away from relationships. Even if Peachy Lofton had the icest legs he'd seen in a micro-mini for a very long time, nd even if she had the kind of feisty, spirited way about her hat something—everything—at the core of him responded o, he liked his life with his son.

Bronson conjured up an image of sexless womanhood to rase Peachy Lofton's legs from his mind. Large, buxom Mrs. Brown, his third-grade teacher provided the perfect mage. With her tightly bound, prematurely gray bun and ray suits, she could squelch any fiery notions caused by the ew addition to the neighborhood.

"'Night, Dad," Tommy was saying.

"'Night, buddy," Bronson said.

Bronson sauntered down the long, wide hallway. Mittens, the family cat, appeared and followed him. In his own bedroom, Bronson kicked off his shoes, slowly unbuttoned and shed his denim shirt, stretched and then laid in the middle of his huge, king-size bed. There was no denying the fact that Peachy Lofton's kiss made the bed seem twice as big as usual. He flexed his muscles as the orange tabby jumped on his stomach. The white paws that had been responsible for her name stretched for his chest.

Bronson lifted Mittens and purred, imitating the sound of the cat perfectly. "Mittens," he whispered in a teasing tone, "you must keep me from wanton New York women...or you get no tuna fish."

"TAKE A BIG SWIG, dear," Helena said. "You're going to need it!"

Peachy groaned. Already, she was regretting her necessary upcoming trip to the outhouse. Had night really passed? Between dreams about her neighbor, and Bernie and Helena's night-long chatter, Peachy felt she hadn't slept at all. Apparently both Bernie and Kyle had been in the military; they'd traveled to many of the same places. And Bernie wanted to fix the car, install a toilet, and look for Kyle's gold with his metal detector. All he wanted in return was free meals and mending. Since both Bernie and Helena were hard of hearing, they'd shared this information at the top of their lungs. Sometime near sunup, Peachy had finally dozed.

Now Peachy detached her water-filled, pink strap-on sleeping mask and opened her eyes just in time to see Helena plunk a mug of strong-smelling coffee by the bedside.

he vaguely registered the fact that Helena was all dressed
p and ready to go somewhere.

"Awake now, dear?" Helena tightened her grasp on the
avy handle of her old-fashioned pocketbook. She had the
mpatient attitude of someone who'd been waiting a long
ime.

"No, no, no," Peachy grumbled. She fumbled for her
merald-green quilted robe, made her way around Helena,
ind headed for the living room. It was her first day, and
he'd meant to sleep at least until noon!

She realized Helena was watching her expectantly, and
ooked out the window. Apparently Helena was even worse
han her mother when it came to planning other people's
ives.

"Don't you want to hear the news?" Helena asked.

"May I please wake up?" Seeing a scurry of activity at the
pottom of the hill, Peachy picked up the field glasses on the
windowsill. Her neighbor was cleaning the interior of his
Blazer. He was shirtless, even though the April morning was
undoubtedly a little chilly. He was leaning in the passenger
door, and she could see the muscles of his broad back rip-
pling in the early-morning sun. The skin of his back looked
smooth and shiny, and his shoulders were rounded and
powerful-looking. Watching him, Peachy felt her mouth go
dry.

A teenager, who could only be his son, ran out the door.
The kid said something, then ran back inside. Her mouth
dropped. Was the man married? And to think of the way
he'd kissed her!

She glanced at Helena, who gave her a censuring look. "I
gathered from the bird-watching magazines lying around
that you like to watch birds," Peachy managed, still wondering if the man was married. Impossible, she thought.
Divorced, she decided.

"Not really," Helena said shortly. "There are robins jays, an occasional blackbird. You can watch *that* bird mos evenings. He works eight to three, four days a week an most Saturdays. Now, do you want to hear my news o not?"

For the first time Peachy smelled the bread and bacon Helena had cooked her breakfast. Feeling guilty, she said "Sure, I really do." She managed an interested if sleep smile.

Helena drew up her shoulders, until she was standing ramrod straight. "Bernie and I are getting married."

Peachy could only stare. For the briefest moment al speculation about the man at the bottom of the hill flew from her mind. There wasn't enough coffee in the world to prepare her for this.

"Now the date's not set in stone," Helena continued. "Tonight, Bernie bowls. I'm making a pie tomorrow and I want you to mulch my garden. Then we have to get a toilet. So, it'll probably be next Tuesday, if you're not busy. You're my bridesmaid and it'll be good practice for your own wedding. Bronson West is best man—I called him bright and early this morning. Not everyone sleeps as late as you do, you know—so the wedding will have to be late afternoon, when he's not working. It's a shame we have to use Bronson, but so many of Bernie's friends have passed."

Peachy was still staring at Helena in horror. "Passed?" she finally managed to echo. She blinked and sipped her coffee.

"Passed on," explained Helena. The elderly woman peered searchingly into Peachy's face after a long moment had elapsed. "Honey," she finally said, "'passed on' is a way of saying they're dead."

"You can't do this!" Peachy leaned against the back of a chair for support. For a fleeting instant, having com-

letely forgotten her own situation, she wondered why any-
ne would ever want to get married.

"Do what, for heaven's sake?"

"Marry Bernie! I mean, I'm sure he's nice—"

"Oh, he *is* nice! I haven't met anybody quite so nice since
yle died, and certainly no one who likes to garden the way
do. And we'll save on taxes." Helena suddenly stared at
eachy, open-mouthed. "Why, you think I'm too old, don't
ou?"

"Of course not," Peachy said swiftly, shaking her head
ack and forth in quick denial, even if that was exactly what
he thought.

"Well," said Helena, gripping her pocketbook handles,
I am and I know it."

"Well, you're a little—"

"And that's exactly the point," Helena finished. "Just
hink, if I'd met Bernie in two more years . . . think how old
'd be then! You only go around once and there's just not
much left of *my* once. And he's going to find where Kyle put
ur money and then we're going to Florida and get a
ondo!"

"Now, Helena, did Kyle really hide money?" Peachy was
waking up fast.

"Yes, he did," said Helena. "Probably in the caves be-
eath the house."

"Caves?" Peachy sipped her coffee again. It was so
trong that her nostrils flared.

"Dear, this is limestone country. You can't go ten feet
without stumbling in a cave." Helena placed her pocket-
ook on an end table. "I have to say that I am somewhat
urprised by your attitude."

"Attitude?"

"Well, given the fact that you're engaged, too, I'm
ounting on your help. By Tuesday, we need invitations and

flowers. As soon as you dress, you have to take me to ge
bridal magazines.''

Couldn't she manage to get away from weddings for on
single, blessed day? "Then there's always the dress," Peach
muttered, trying to keep the irony from her voice.

"Oh, no!" Helena exclaimed. "That's all taken care o
Bernie helped me with my old trunk late last night."

For the first time, Peachy noticed the old, open steame
trunk in the far corner of the room. On top was an ancien
Merry Widow, risqué even by contemporary standards. Sh
managed to blow out a shaky sigh while Helena skipped t
the trunk like a spry schoolgirl.

When Peachy saw the dress, she shut her eyes. She opene
them again, hoping against hope that it had somehow dis
appeared. But no, Helena was holding it up against her flo
ral-print shirtwaist. It was satin, lacked extra frills, and it
straight bodice sparkled with sequins.

"Oh, I know it's yellowed a bit," said Helena. "But yel
low *is* the appropriate color for a second wedding. And i
does still fit."

"Oh, my God," Peachy whispered.

It was all true. During the night, her great-aunt had be
come engaged to her taxi driver. They were going to b
married, and the date, if one could call it a date, was Tues
day. Not only that, but her great-aunt was going to wear a
dress that had yellowed with age. It was a flapper wedding
gown; an original, one from the twenties.

Peachy moved toward her great-aunt, hoping to talk som
sense into her. Helena rushed forward, wedding dress i
hand, and enclosed Peachy in one of her effusive bear hugs

"Since you're engaged, I knew you'd be happy for me
We're going to live right here and be happy as peas in
pod."

"Happiness does not even begin to cover what I feel," Peachy managed.

How had she escaped her own wedding, only to prepare for someone else's? She could handle it, of course. The only thing she couldn't handle was seeing her neighbor again. That one kiss had lingered on her lips all through the night... and in a way, that still threatened her future.

No, things would be fine, even if she *had* fled one aisle— however temporarily—only to march right down another with some old codger named Bronson West.

# WEEK TWO

*All dressed in white...*

# Chapter Three

"Now you go stand by Bronson," a very nervous Helena said. She had already introduced Peachy to Minister Jackson, who was to perform the ceremony, and now she was pushing Peachy toward the church door.

"Sure, Helena," Peachy said as she smoothed the front of her blue linen suit skirt. Of course, Helena hadn't bothered to tell her exactly who Bronson was, and when she turned around to ask, Helena was gone.

Peachy's eyes rested on an elderly gentleman in a black suit. He sported a dapper striped red-and-black tie and wore a matching handkerchief in his breast pocket, so that just the corner showed. He was leaning heavily on a silver cane, and he was the only man by the church door. He had to be Bronson.

Peachy smiled brightly at the man and made her way toward him, thinking it was a beautiful spring afternoon, just the right kind of day for a wedding.

"Bronson?" she asked as she reached the man.

"Eh?" He leaned forward, smiled agreeably, and touched his hearing aid.

"Bronson?" Peachy asked, raising her voice. "Bronson West?"

A strong, muscular arm slipped beneath Peachy's elbow. Then a wide hand lightly touched the sleeve of her blue spring suit in what was almost a caress. She started to turn but she couldn't since the man's lips were right by her ear. At just the touch, she felt her heart flutter. When she felt his breath, she tried to swallow but couldn't.

A sexy, teasing voice said, "You only wish I was ninety, sugar."

Peachy turned and found herself staring right into a freshly pressed white shirt. Her nose was so close she could smell a woodsy pine scent and starch. She glanced up, only to find she was staring right into that set of sparkling, deep gray eyes. They were the very same set of eyes—not to mention lips—she'd been trying to forget all week. Her mouth dropped. "Now, why would I wish you were ninety?" she finally managed, matching his playful tone.

"You'd be a lot safer that way," he said.

Watching his lips curve farther upward, into that wry, tantalizing smile she was beginning to feel she knew intimately, she smiled back. As soon as she did, she felt her inner tug-of-war set in motion again. She really shouldn't be flirting with the man, not after the way he'd kissed her. "Do you mean to say I'm in danger?" she finally asked archly.

"Absolutely." When he squinted, his eyes seemed to sparkle even more. And they left no question as to what exact kind of danger they were talking about.

Peachy felt a telltale flush rise to her cheeks. Clearly nothing had changed. The man's sheer presence was ungrounding her, just the way it had a week before. Just the way it had during the week, too, she thought guiltily. After all, she had done her share of spying from the window. "Well, don't hurt me," she said lightly.

"I wouldn't hurt a flea," he said. He glanced around easily as people began to flow inside the church, dressed in their wedding best. His gaze returned to her eyes.

"Well, I'm fortunately not a flea, so I guess I still might not be safe." She looked him over slowly. His well-tailored gray suit jacket hung perfectly on his broad shoulders and he wore a string-style country tie that somehow made him look a little rakish . . . and more than attractive.

"You might not be a flea," he said slowly, lowering his voice to a near whisper. "But you do have a sort of bite."

She half expected him to relinquish his hold on her arm, but he didn't. "So *you* better watch it," she said.

He looked into her eyes for a long moment, then let his gaze travel downward to her throat and chest. It seemed forever before his eyes made their slow trek back up and looked into hers again. "Believe me," he said, his deep, almost bass voice still teasing her with its singsong sound, "I am."

She squinted at him and smiled. The man was clearly an unconscionable flirt. "Am what?"

His eyes traveled downward yet again, seeming to linger on her throat. "Watching it," he said.

Unable to think of an appropriate comeback, she said, "Well, looks are for free." She glanced toward the church door and realized that Bronson West was gone. She'd have to find him soon.

"Anything other than looking would *undoubtedly* cost me," Helena's neighbor was saying.

Peachy looked at him for a long moment, wondering how any man could look so good in a color as dull as gray. But the gray of his suit matched the gray of his eyes and made his tousled strands of longish hair look even blacker. "And just what price do you think I'd exact?" she finally teased.

His arm still twined with hers, he now lifted it and brought her hand to his chest. He laughed. "Why, my heart, sugar," he said.

Every time he said "sugar," it sounded like *shu-ga,* and she thought it sounded sweet. *Too sweet.* Beneath the fabric of his shirt, she could feel his heart beating in a slow, steady rhythm. He brought her hand back down to waist level.

"I'm hardly a heartbreaker," she managed.

He looked at her in mock surprise. His mouth fell ope and his tongue grazed his top teeth. "Now, you mean to te me you haven't even broken one little heart?" he asked in Southern-sounding drawl.

She laughed. "Maybe one or two," she conceded.

He clucked his tongue in a way that sounded less lik clucks and more like kisses. "See, I knew you were a dan gerous woman."

Now her lips parted in mock surprise. "I've never an swered *my* door with a double-barreled shotgun in hand."

"Single barrel," he countered lightly. "Rifle."

She realized they were still standing arm in arm. Not tha she'd exactly forgotten, but the touch had certainly become comfortable. "Well, either way, I don't threaten animals o children," she responded.

"Or women?" He laughed. "I don't threaten animals anyway. I'm a vet."

"Yeah?" She cocked her head and continued looking up at him. It was just her luck to run into a country vet, she thought illogically. *Country vets are romantic. There was one in the movie* Baby Boom. She shook her head, as if to clear it of confusion.

"Yeah," he was saying. "I run my own clinic."

"Sounds fun," she commented.

He nodded.

It was just too easy to be with this man, Peachy though when he fell silent. For a full week she'd tried to erase him from her thoughts, only to be drawn right into a conversa tion with him again. And what was worse was that this conversation was more amicable than the last. She sighed and disengaged her arm. "It was good to see you again," she said as lightly as she could. "But I've got to go—" she flashed him a smile "—and hook up with my best man."

He looked down and shot her another one of his quirky, irresistible smiles. Then he leaned forward, right by her ear, and whispered, "I *am* your best man."

She drew back. "I'm afraid to ask," she said lightly. "But my best man for what?"

"Your best man for just about..." He paused, his eyes lingering on her lips. "Everything," he finished.

She felt a flush rise to her cheeks. "We'll see about that," she said, still meeting his teasing tone.

He chuckled again. Even the man's chuckles had that teasing, wry sound, she thought. They were half throaty and half a deep bass, sexy hum.

"I certainly hope so," he said.

Even though her arm was no longer twined through his, they were standing very close, so close she could swear she felt the tiny movements of his arm muscles as his breath rose and fell.

"Meantime," she said, "I've got to find Bron—"

"I *am* Bronson West," he said. He drew his head to one side and arched a brow. Then he wiggled both brows up and down.

She smirked playfully and rolled her eyes. "You wish."

He laughed. "Now why would I wish something like that?"

"Because then you'd have the extreme pleasure of escorting me down the aisle," she said.

"You mean you want to marry this Bronson character?" he asked playfully, looking shocked. "A man you don't even know?"

She laughed in response. "I'm the bridesmaid," she explained. "And I really need to—"

At that moment Minister Jackson ran up to them. "Bronson, you're not actually giving Helena away," he said. "You and Peachy march in together and then Bernie and Helena. That's the way Helena wants it."

Peachy's mouth dropped and she felt Bronson's arm snake back through hers again. He gripped her arm more tightly this time. A little possessively, she thought. Or was that just her wishful imagination? She was so surprised, she barely listened while Bronson squared away the last details with the minister.

"Why didn't you tell me?" she asked when the minister was gone. During every single interchange with this man, she felt as though the ground was moving beneath her feet. She'd like to throw *him* for a loop. Just once.

He cocked his head and smiled down at her in what was hardly an apology. It was clear he liked having the upper hand. "I tried, sugar."

"Not very hard," she countered.

He only laughed and began escorting her toward the door. While they'd been talking, the wedding-goers had taken their places in the pews. "Ready?" he whispered as a preliminary organ song wound down.

"As ready as I'll ever be," she said. She was ready to march down the fool aisle, yes. But hardly ready to spend the next hour just four feet away from Bronson. She had the most horrible suspicion that an involvement was inevitable... and in a month, she was getting married. She felt a tiny burst of temper.

"Why do you always seem to have some wild card up your sleeve?" she whispered when they'd reached their marching position.

He edged closer and said, "Sorry, sugar, I can't hear you."

She knew he could hear her just fine. The sparkle in his eyes made it very clear that that was an intentional excuse to decrease the space between them. "You heard me," she teased, calling his bluff.

He sent her a chagrined smirk. "What wild card?"

"Like not telling me which was Helena's house, or that you were Bronson West, for instance," she whispered just as the wedding song sounded.

"I like to keep 'em guessing," he whispered back, his breath ruffling the hair by her ear.

"Them who?"

"Them you," he whispered.

BRONSON TRIED to concentrate on Minister Jackson, but kept thinking of the almost electrical shocks he'd felt each time he'd linked arms with Peachy. It had taken everything he had not to haul her into his arms while they marched down the white runner in the aisle at the small country wedding. He glanced past Bernie and Helena now, at Peachy. She was staring—a little meanly, he thought—into the bright, beautiful bouquet of wildflowers that had been shoved into her hands at the last minute. The flowers were strewn with blue and silver streamers.

The woman was definitely moody. Just as they'd begun marching, her mouth had shut into that thin, prim little line. And her blue eyes now looked far more like ice than the proverbial poetic twin pools.

"Do you, Helena, take Bernie, to be your lawful..." the minister was saying.

Peachy grimaced into her handful of daffodils and violets. She couldn't really see, but certainly felt, Bronson West's gaze. Why wouldn't he just quit staring at her? And why in the world would any man make her feel inept? She was smart, well-educated, rich, attractive and desirable, as her engagement proved.

"I do," Peachy heard Helena say, after all the have-and-hold business was thankfully over and done with.

Heaven only knew what Bronson thought of this overly hasty marriage between the senior citizens, she thought now, fighting the embarrassed flush that threatened to creep into her cheeks. Fortunately, Helena had decided to wear a gleaming white shawl over the wedding dress. Even Peachy had to admit that she looked pretty, her face glowing as a bride's should.

"Do you, Bernie, take Helena, to be your lawful..."

Peachy realized she had been staring unabashedly at Bronson's mouth. It was wide, even when he wasn't smil-

ing, with full lips. She averted her gaze, but accidently me
Bronson's gray eyes. They seemed more intense than ever i
the dimming afternoon light of the small, intimate church.

She stared back into her flowers, but not before she had
noted, yet again, how truly good he looked in a suit. She
never would have expected him to own such a suit. It molded
itself over his broad shoulders in such a way that she could
barely keep her eyes off him. He had a narrow waist and fla
stomach, too. The suit was classic without looking stuffy
and every bit as warm, summery gray as his eyes.

Yes, she thought, trying to tune out the next set of to-have
and to-holds, she had become a little obsessed over the past
week. In fact, she was experiencing something resembling a
girlhood crush. And that was ridiculous. They were from
two very different worlds and she was getting married in a
month. Nevertheless, every time she so much as looked at
him, she got two oversize left feet.

She released a sigh when Bernie finally said, "I do."

Bronson knew full well she was trying to look everywhere but at him. After all, they were supposed to be directly facing each other at an altar, on either side of Bernie
and Helena.

He'd figured she was as poor as Helena, but now he decided the Loftons must have tucked some money away
somewhere. Her blue spring suit was of fine linen and exactly matched the blue of her eyes. The yellow daffodils she
was nervously clutching seemed to glimmer against the suit.

Had he really kissed her? Somehow, he felt as though he
wanted to do it again, just to make sure. Oh, yes, he did
want to kiss her. Bad. He looked away, telling himself he
*liked* being alone. Or at least he'd become very accustomed
to it.

Fortunately, the minister seemed to be reaching his closing remarks. As far as Bronson was concerned, there was
nothing worse than having to wear a suit and tie. But he
knew that really wasn't the problem. The problem was that

he'd much rather spend the afternoon flirting with Peachy, even if he had no intention of any serious involvement.

He felt a vague twinge of guilt, since he was considering the pros and cons of a casual love affair while he was standing in a church. And right at the altar, too, when he was best man at a wedding. And weddings were about lasting love and commitment. Well, he knew firsthand how that went. No, he was having none of it, he told himself now. Minister Jackson, he realized, was looking at him pointedly.

"The final prayer," the minister said under his breath.

Bronson fumbled with his prayer book. When he glanced up, Peachy was smirking at him, clearly amused that he'd been caught not paying attention. To cover his embarrassment, he winked at her, knowing they were acting as silly as school kids. Then he bowed his head and prayed.

What was that sexy little wink for? Peachy wondered, suddenly too distraught to bother with the prayer. He'd had that look on his face again, as if he were about to tell her some secret.

Perhaps she really should ask him out for dinner or coffee, just to make friends, of course. Besides, she could even think of it as her own private bachelorette party, couldn't she? All women needed to experience a last final attraction before settling down. Actually, it was traditional. Wasn't it? She shook her head as if to clear it of confusion for what felt like the umpteenth time that day.

When the church organist began pounding out the traditional wedding song, she knew she had never been so glad in her entire life. She had hardly asked to be here, across from her neighbor, who made her feel about as coordinated as a five-year-old, especially not when just a week before she'd fled all this hoopla about dresses, bouquets and music. The more she'd admitted her attraction to Bronson during the ceremony, the more she realized she had to stay away from him.

And now, she thought, if she could just manage the approximate hundred feet of white-draped aisleway gracefully, she would be home free. She absolutely could not entertain the idea of asking him on a date. Peachy turned toward Bronson and smiled guardedly.

He smiled back and offered her his arm. "Ready?"

To cover the fact that his nearness sent awareness right through her, she hooked her arm through his with far more force than was necessary. She only made herself stumble. He caught and righted her.

"Well, don't kill me," he whispered, bringing his crooked elbow and thus Peachy even closer.

She bumped lightly against his side. "I'm not trying to kill you," she managed. She'd only meant to communicate that any touching between them would have to remain pure business.

He gave her a lazy, impertinent smile, as if they had all the time in the world. "Could have fooled me," he said.

"The whole congregation is staring at us," she said under her breath. And they were. It felt as if she and Bronson had been standing there for an eternity.

"Yes," he said, his slow smile turning into an amused grin. "The natives do look a little anxious."

"So, are we going?"

"Well," he said, unable not to tease her, "I don't mind being the center of—"

"Attention?" She tugged him forward. Thankfully, he didn't offer further argument, even if Peachy had to concentrate with all her might on every single step. His arm beneath her hand felt solid and strong. He was exactly what was making her nervous and what steadied her, all at the same time. How was she ever going to deal with the aisle at Saint Patrick's? It had to be ten times as long, and this aisle seemed to go on into infinity. As soon as they reached the open double doors, she mumbled a "Thank you so much, Mr. West," and fled.

Mr. West? Bronson stared after her while the wedding-goers began to mingle around him. Some, he realized, were already heading toward the reception building. Peachy Lofton, he decided, once he'd watched her blue-suited hips sashay out of sight, was definitely the moodiest woman he had ever met. She had either stared directly at him or tried to avoid staring directly at him throughout the whole wretched ceremony. He could swear those heavy-lidded eyes were full of desire. And not just for anybody. For him. Why in the world had she just called him "Mr. West" in that distanced tone?

He felt a hand clasp his shoulder and turned. "You didn't really wear that jacket to a wedding, did you?" Bronson groaned.

"Chill out, Dad," Tommy said. "Trust me, Mrs. Lofton—er, Smith, now, I guess—looked weirder than me."

"You're not supposed to say the bride looks weird," Bronson said. "We're at her wedding."

Tommy grinned. "Yeah, but what about that Peachy? Hubba-hubba, Daddy-o."

"Daddy-o?" Bronson said with irony. "Tommy, I'm your father. That's not the way a son talks to his fa—"

"Why, I thought you two looked so cute together." Tommy reached up, lightly pinched Bronson's cheek, and burst out laughing.

"Sometimes I think I liked you better when you were younger, nonverbal and in diapers," Bronson quipped.

"Oh, dream on," said Tommy. "You know I was never in diapers."

Bronson laughed. "I changed enough of them to know."

"Well," Tommy continued, "I'll only quit teasing you, lover boy, if you'll buy me a car."

*Lover boy?*

Before Bronson could respond, Tommy was headed off toward the reception. He and Peachy Lofton looking "cute" together! Ha! She wasn't even cute just by herself. All right, she really was damn pretty, but on his porch she had acted tough, even bossy, like a woman who was well used to getting her own way. And even though the Loftons seemed poor, she'd managed to deck herself out in that exceedingly tasteful suit. Yes, she was sophisticated, too, but probably without one blessed drop of down-home country humanity in her soul. Still, in spite of that, not one hour had gone by without him thinking of her kissable mouth.

He put his hands in his suit pockets and began to walk toward the reception. Apparently Helena hadn't wanted Bronson near her legs, so she had handed him a garter earlier. Now he could feel it, resting in his pocket. That was a relief. If it was in his pocket, rest assured he wasn't going to catch it.

He rounded a corner and, glancing up, realized he'd run right into Peachy. She was all flustered and her leg was raised high off the ground and crooked strangely in the air. It really was raised in a very unladylike fashion, even if he could only feel grateful for the eyeful of thigh, which was quite nice.

"Got a problem, sweetheart?" Bronson realized they were facing each other over a trash can.

"No, I'm fine," she said quickly. "Just fine."

Now he realized that the wedding bouquet was on top of the trash and that her awkward pose was due to the fact that she was stomping it down, amid old church flyers and soup cans. In fact, one of her very dainty and expensive-looking high heels had stabbed right through a daffodil petal.

He watched her half hop in an attempt to disengage the petal, then right herself to a more appropriate pose. But the daffodil still clung. It was vaguely embarrassing, he thought, as if someone had just exited a public rest room with a square of tissue stuck to the shoe. He had to fight not to laugh.

"Here," he said.

Peachy watched with horror as Bronson stepped forward, swiftly knelt like some knight in armor, and lifted her shoe. She had no choice but to lean forward, with both of her hands planted firmly on his broad shoulders for support. Given the rusty edge of the trash can, she told herself that his shoulders were the lesser of two evils, even if, feeling them beneath her palms now, she was sincerely beginning to doubt it. She was also fairly sure her face had turned as red as her hair.

"Just pull it off, for heaven's sake," she managed. "It's just a flower petal. They don't bite." The man was still merely holding her foot up, with his hand beneath the heel of her blue pump.

He glanced up. "Oh, I don't know," he said. "I kind of like you this way."

"What way?" she snapped.

He grinned. "At my mercy."

He smiled at her for a long moment, until she found herself smiling back, then he finally pulled off the flower petal and tossed it in the trash. When he stood, he was just inches away from her.

"I know this looks kind of strange..." she began, trying not to sound defensive. She wondered if she should lie, saying that she'd found bugs in the fresh-picked flowers or something. Oh, why had she pulled such an impulsively childish stunt?

"Do you always display such a bad attitude at weddings?" he finally teased. Her face was beet red and, somehow, the white seam of her stocking had twisted around to the front of her ankle. "Or is it just this particular wedding?"

"There's nothing wrong with my attitude," she said weakly as she smoothed the front of her skirt. Seeing his glance, she tried to daintily lift her foot again without falling. She righted her stocking seam. *Why does this man keep catching me off guard?*

He cocked his head and then pointedly glanced down at what was left of the bouquet. A cigarette butt clung to a blue streamer, as if for dear life.

"I—I guess I don't like weddings much," she said when his gray-eyed gaze meshed with hers.

He edged a little closer.

"Oh, no, you don't!" She leapt back.

He leaned downward, tilting his shoulders at an angle. "Now, did you really think I was going to kiss you?" He couldn't help but feel pleased. So his kiss had affected her, after all.

"Of course not!"

He placed his hand over his heart. "Well, don't act like it was the plague or something."

It kind of was, she thought. And worse, she kind of wanted to do it again. No, she definitely wanted to do it again. "I—I mean, not that..."

He bit his lower lip, and then cleared his throat in mock seriousness. "Now, I admit, it was a little forward of me, sugar," he said.

"Very forward!" She could feel her face turning even redder. "You and I seem to have gotten off on the wrong foot," she continued quickly, hardly trusting the direction he might choose for their conversation. "I'd meant to discuss it with you."

"Discuss?" He stared at her, feeling very curious about where she was headed. This was certainly a city woman's way of approaching things.

"Yes," she continued. "I thought maybe we could call a sort of truce. I don't mean best friends, just amicable neighbors while I'm in town."

"Truce?" He smiled. "I didn't know we were fighting. And I sure don't see why we can't be friendly."

"I said friends, not friendly," Peachy managed. She shook her head, feeling more confused than ever. Half of her wanted to get rid of him and half of her wanted to ask him out.

He leaned even closer, hoping she wouldn't back away from him this time. And she didn't. "So, Peachy, what's the diff—"

"There's a very big difference between *friends* and *friendly*," she said.

He said nothing, only looked into her face. He was making her nervous, all right. The woman was clearly attracted to him.

"Maybe we could just get together for a cup of coffee or something," she said. She swallowed when he didn't respond. "I mean, we sort of keep running into each other...."

It was just too tempting not to tease her a little more. "Well, sugar," he said slowly, as if considering, "I really don't date much and—"

"Neither do I!" she exclaimed. "I'm engaged!" Her mouth dropped. No man had ever turned her down. She'd just said coffee. It wasn't as though she'd asked him to marry her or something.

He stared into the trash can again for a long moment. Women who were engaged did not treat bridal bouquets the way she did. Not to mention the fact that she didn't kiss like an engaged woman. Her body had bent against his like a reed in a strong, wild wind. Of course, he *had* wondered all week about that rock on her ring finger, but it had seemed impossible.

"Tell me you're kidding," he said.

"About what?" she asked, wishing she could get the defensiveness to leave her voice. She stared right back at him.

"You're engaged?"

She put her hands on her hips. "Does it seem so strange that a man might want to marry me or what?"

He laughed. "Not at all," he said. "I just figured from the way you kissed—"

"I'm engaged," she practically shouted. She realized where her hands were and took them off her hips and clasped them in front of her, hoping that made her look at least a little more dignified.

But she simply couldn't be, he thought. A woman in love, in deep, until-death-do-us-part kind of love, would be incapable of responding to him the way she had.

"And also," she continued, "I thought you might be married, to tell you the truth." She swallowed. "Your wife was to be included in the invitation, of course." She tried to mask her features, but rejection didn't come easily to her. And now he undoubtedly thought she was some kind of two-timer.

It was the worst timing in history. Tommy's voice cut through the air. "Dad! Larry has an old Nova I could fix—"

Bronson glanced over his shoulder. "Be right there," he yelled. He turned back to Peachy. Her face had gone from beet red to dead white. "I may have a kid—" he began.

"No," she said weakly. "You clearly *do* have a kid. No 'may' about it."

"I do have a kid," he continued. "But I'm not married. I mean, I was once but..."

Although Peachy hardly wanted to ponder the why of it, she felt a rush of relief. Bronson West wasn't married, after all. "Well, that's...I mean, it's good to have been married when you have children...." Why was he making her say such ridiculous things?

Looking at her now, he felt half-jealous, even if that was ludicrous under the circumstances. Still, he'd thought of nothing but her all week, only to find that she had some fiancé. Once she'd plied him a little more, he'd had every intention of giving in to her invitation.

But engaged women, he thought now, required a little more consideration. "Like I said, I just don't date, uh, have coffee much." Why hadn't he guessed that she was engaged? He glanced at the flowers again. "And I'm not much for weddings, myself."

"Well," she said, "at least we seem to have that in common."

He looked into her eyes. Why did she have to be so damnably attractive? "So, congratulations on your wedding," he said. "I mean, I'm sure you'll feel better..."

"Oh, I feel fine," she managed. "Better already. And I am hungry, too, and the reception's started..." She gestured vaguely toward the reception building. "Well, goodbye."

"Good to talk to you," he said. Even though it was the usual social line, it sounded incredibly awkward in this situation.

"Well, goodbye," she repeated. Then she turned and made a beeline for the reception. Oh, what kind of fool had she just made of herself? She never had difficulty talking to men. Somehow this one seemed to defy every past experience. So what if his accent was a little twangier than the average New Yorker's? So what if he looked better in a suit than most guys on Fifth Avenue? And so what if he made her kiss in a way she'd never known she could? The man had turned her down! *Down.*

Her walk was turning into more of a stomping march. He really was kind of interesting! And it was hard to imagine a man such as that raising a son alone. Had he left his wife? Or had she left him? And why did he end up with custody?

Finally, she wondered if she was really attracted to him at all. It just had to be the fact that he wasn't attracted to her that was drawing her in. After all, he had turned her down flat. She flung open the door to the reception building. *Just forget it.*

Bronson toyed with the garter in his pocket long after she'd made her great escape. Watching her storm away, with all her strange, paradoxical qualities, and in the form-fitting blue suit that clung to her every curve, he wondered why she'd asked him out.

If she was truly engaged, and if she'd thought he might be married, and if she was asking for a date, then that meant she was suggesting something that might lead to a last fling. Still, she somehow didn't seem the type—she blushed too easily and he clearly made her nervous. And even if she was, he wasn't sure he was interested in a casual affair... if they went out, if it worked out. If...if...if....

"Dad...? Dad...? *Da-ad?*"

Bronson was so lost in his thoughts about Peachy that he only half registered the fact that his son was speaking to him about yet another car.

He rummaged in his pocket, found the garter, and thoughtfully tossed it into the trash on top of the flowers. Somehow, given their joint confusion, the bouquet and garter seemed to belong together.

She simply couldn't be engaged. No, he thought, staring into the trashed bouquet and shaking his head, there was one lady that no man was going to shanghai into a wedding dress.

"I DON'T SEE WHY *I* have to wear it!"

"S-shu-ssh," Petulia Lofton hissed in Christine's ear. "You're Peachy's exact same size and this is a very small favor."

"Where is she, anyway?" Christine said. "I don't like lying all the time!"

"Sh—" Petulia turned away, her stylishly roomy trousers and wasp-waisted Donna Karan jacket turning gracefully with her, and bestowed a beaming smile on Jean-Paul Latouse, who had designed her daughter's wedding gown.

Petulia eyed the gown for the umpteenth time, attempting to ignore the fact that Christine, rather than Peachy, was modeling it. Its portrait neckline and fitted basque bodice fell naturally to the full skirt of white organza and shimmered in the soft light. The cuffs of the illusion lace sleeves were dotted with tiny Italian crystals and the bodice back was held tightly by crystal buttons. An elegant strand of pearls trimmed the hip and would match the seven-tier pearl choker that was to grace Peachy's neck.

"This is only a fitting to measure the hem, of course," Jean-Paul said. The trim, fit, balding man knelt at Christine's feet. "And I'm finally meeting the bride! My assistant said you were a charmer." He lifted and dropped the bottom of the skirt. "I went all the way to Venice for the crystals," he continued conversationally.

"Lovely," Petulia said. "Just the way I've always imagined it." It would look so beautiful, she thought, in the white aisle of Saint Patrick's. Peachy's bouquet would be of rich textures, too, and of different-size blooms from lilies, pink-and-wine sweet peas, and roses. The flowers would gleam with metallic accents; gilded leaf clusters of dull, heavy gold would be strewn through them.

"So they call you Peachy?" Jean-Paul cocked his head, still considering the hem. "Your mother said you were named Petulia, after her, and that Peachy's a nickname."

Christine glanced at Petulia in frustration. Petulia stared back pointedly. "Yes," Christine said, stretching her lips into what was more a grimace than a smile.

"Well, you're a lucky lady," Jean-Paul said, moving to another section of the gown. "Wellington Vanderlynden's quite a catch."

"Yes he is," Christine agreed. "I don't see how Pe—I mean, how any woman—could ignore..." Christine interrupted herself and coughed delicately.

Petulia's mouth dropped. Could Christine be developing feelings for Wellington? *Impossible.* They were congenial, but that was only because Petulia had insisted Christine placate the poor man in Peachy's absence.

"Well, it's a good thing you like Mr. Vanderlynden so much," Jean-Paul said, laughing.

"Oh, I do," Christine said. "He's so funny, really amusing company. Ambitious, smart and—" She cut herself off.

"Good," Jean-Paul said, smiling. "After all, you're going to marry him."

Petulia sighed. She was going to have to get back on the phone again. She had called everyone she could think of in an approximate ten-country radius, except for Julia Von Furstenburg, who wasn't available. Charles, who had not seen Peachy for a week now, was beginning to voice suspicions.

At least, Petulia thought, looking at Christine, she did have one compliant daughter. Even if Christine was not being entirely polite, she was willing to play the part of bride. That had saved quite a lot of embarrassment. Christine was younger, but she and Peachy looked enough alike to fool such people as Jean-Paul Latouse. It did seem that Christine was going overboard, though, when she raved about Wellington in that overblown manner....

Petulia sighed and asked herself the magic question yet another time. *Where, oh, where, was Peachy?*

## Chapter Four

Benny Goodman songs blared from the old hi-fi in the living room, making Peachy wish she were dancing—the way Bernie and Helena were dancing now—twirling under soft lights. She didn't have the heart to check her finances; she was fairly sure that whatever money was at the bottom of her pocketbook was all she had left.

She didn't mind staying in her bedroom, but it was after eleven and her stomach was rumbling in response to the sweet, enticing scents of bread and meats. Well, certainly Helena and Bernie meant to feed her, she thought. She had long since changed into jeans and a sweatshirt, and now she glanced in the mirror, finger-combing her hair into place.

As she did so, she thought again of Bronson West. Why had he hedged on something so innocent as a simple coffee? And how could he have turned her down! She reminded herself that if she was even so much as thinking about dating another man, she would have to call off her engagement first. Wouldn't she? She turned and plopped down on her bed.

Unfortunately, Peachy wasn't sure that dating exactly described what she most wanted to do with Bronson. She could still almost feel the sweet, soft pressure of his lips on hers. When they'd kissed, the muscles of his thighs had begun to strain against hers and his tongue had warmed until it had felt searingly hot, like a flame flickering inside her mouth. Or like a dozen tiny flames all flickering at once.

Even though she'd managed to wrench herself away, she'd hardly done so before she'd felt the strongest, deepest, almost undeniable jolt of need. . . . It hadn't helped that he'd looked so damnably good in a suit, either. And she liked men in suits. Not that she hadn't wondered all day what it would be like to help him out of it. She groaned aloud. There was no use denying the fact that the man brought out a more aggressive side to her personality. And he seemed to have such a teasing, irascible nature that she didn't even want to fight her response to him at all.

She sucked in a breath, reminding herself that she had seen him shirtless. When she'd watched him through the field glasses, cleaning his truck, she could barely believe all the tiny muscles evident on his back and how very smooth his skin looked. Somehow, it seemed as though he was just begging to be touched. She'd wished he would turn around, but he hadn't.

Still, she could imagine his chest. She expected it to be just as strong-looking as his back . . . and she hoped the curling dark hairs that were bound to be there weren't too thick, but just enough that a woman could run her fingers through them. And not just any woman. Just her.

"Peachy," she said aloud, "you've gone truly crazy." But she simply could not get the man out of her head. Not his teasing, which excited her. And certainly not his body. She leaped from her bed and headed for the living room, determined not to moon like some fool fourteen-year-old.

A table had been placed in the room's center and covered with a lace cloth. It was set with silver and adorned with a candelabra. All six candles blazed. Loose violets floated in small crystal bowls, their purple petals shimmering in the candle glow. Peachy looked over the scene and couldn't help but feel a deep twinge of romantic longing.

The food had been carried in and was heaped on the small table. There was a basket of waxy, shining fruits, a basket of woven breads, and two platters of meat. For all its modesty, it looked like a wedding feast for kings.

Peachy leaned in the doorway and coughed delicately. Helena and Bernie, who were still in their wedding attire, were dancing. Swiftly for a man of his age, Bernie spun Helena around and dipped. Then he planted a solid kiss on her cheek and righted her to a standing posture, all in one movement.

"Peachy!" Helena exclaimed. She flushed. "I had no idea you were here. What was I thinking!" Helena ran from the room, returned with an extra plate and silverware, and hauled another chair to the table. She shoved Peachy into the chair. After that, Bernie seated Helena and then himself, and then the two stared into each other's eyes.

In New York, her mother had been driving her nuts, but at least she had not felt alienated. And she sure felt alienated now. It was disturbing to see that the oldsters had conjured more romance this evening than she had managed to experience in her whole lifetime.

She realized her plate was of the regular dime-store variety. Over and against the other two empty, waiting plates, which were of fine china, hers did not exactly grace the table. Also, Helena and Bernie's places were set with silver. For her, Helena had grabbed mismatched flatware. As latecomer, Peachy's chair was shoved at the corner of the table. She had to put her knees indelicately on either side of the protruding table leg.

Feeling embarrassed, she stared into the flickering candles. This was their night for love, not hers. And somehow, Wellington couldn't give her such a night. What she wanted was for her own eyes to light up, the way Helena's did when she looked at Bernie. She wanted her face to flush in just that way and her eyes to gleam. And the only man she'd found who made her heart really race and her limbs go

akimbo in that crazy chemical way had turned her down fo
a fool coffee date!

"Getting in some pointers for your wedding?" Bernie fi
nally asked as he served Helena's potatoes.

Hardly. She was thinking about Bronson West. "I hop
you didn't think I meant to crash your wedding dinner?"

"But what are you going to eat, dear?" Helena asked.

That was a good question. "I told Bronson I'd visit,"
Peachy lied. Bronson was the only local she knew. At thi
point, hungry or not, she had no intention of crashing
honeymoon.

"Bronson's such a wonderful fellow," Helena said, no
sounding at all sorry to have Peachy go. "Well, you'd bet
ter run along, dear."

Peachy deposited the extra dish and flatware in th
kitchen on her way outside, and grabbed a handful o
crackers. As soon as she'd lied to Helena, she wondere
whether or not to swallow her wounded pride and really visi
Bronson. The wedding feast would be an acceptable ex
cuse. Unfortunately, his house lights were out. The onl
light visible at all in the wooded countryside was the flood
light on his front lawn.

She suddenly shivered. Where was she going? That wa
her problem, in general, she fumed. She'd never had an
very clear idea of where exactly she was going and why. Sh
thought of blacksnakes, rattlesnakes, gophers, foxes and
wildcats.

Glancing back toward Helena's, she could see Helena and
Bernie in the window. They moved slowly, in small, tight
oh-so-romantic dancing circles. *Oh, how I want a night lik
that.* The thought came unbidden. *Just one single time.* Bu
here she was, standing alone in the darkness.

And then a light came on.

It was an upstairs light, and when Bronson moved into the
space of the window, and looked out, Peachy jumped be
hind a tree. *He can't see you,* she thought. Nonetheless, sh

tayed put. As much spying as she had done lately, and as many covert glances as she'd sent him during the wedding eremony, she was beginning to feel like Agent 007.

She leaned against the tree and stared at him. She watched s he tugged the ends of his white dress shirt from the vaistband of his slacks, and then began to slowly unbutton he shirt, starting from the bottom. How she wished he radn't turned her down! But on the other hand, she was well aware that it was for the best. She was spoiled rotten and ased to getting what she wanted even when it wasn't good or her. And what she wanted right now was Bronson. *But ou can't have him.*

"My, oh, my," she whispered, feeling the color come into ner face. She was starting to feel truly guilty. But not so guilty that she wasn't going to watch. He leaned his head back and rolled it from side to side, then shrugged out of the hirt. It fell gracefully over his broad, very round shoulders and dropped to the floor. He was wearing a tank-style un-dershirt, which he now tugged out of his slacks.

In one swift motion, he pulled it off. Then he tossed his read and ran a hand through his thick, black, tousled curls. His chest was every bit as enticing as his back, she thought. And then she started to walk toward the house, like a moth drawn to flame.

WHEN BRONSON HAD FOUND her in the middle of the night, curled so sweetly on his porch swing, his mouth had gone dry. In sleep, her expression was vulnerable and the lines in ner face vanished. It was absolutely impossible to imagine ner wrestling verbally with him or to imagine her trashing a bridal bouquet.

Now, in the soft morning light, she looked just as beau-tiful. He'd tucked a down comforter tightly around her, and she was sleeping as peacefully as a child, her face nestled against the cool, soft fabric. He reminded himself not to compare her to a child. Children and animals were his absolute weak point.

Nonetheless, he still wondered if she really was engaged. Not that he really gave a damn. He'd thought about it ever since he'd caught her tossing away those daffodils, and he'd finally decided that pursuing her was his best option. If he didn't, he'd go straight out of his mind just thinking about her. And engaged hardly meant married, after all.

He gently shook her. "Mornin', sweetheart," he whispered. Beneath the down, he could feel the round curve of her delicate shoulder. "Peaches," he said in a singsong voice. "Peaches and cream."

Her eyelids fluttered. She squinted at him, then glanced around. She looked back into his face. There it was again...that teasing little smile of his.

"No, honey," he said. "Now I know you think you're dreaming, but it's really me."

She blinked. "You?" Where was she?

He grinned. "In the flesh."

She stared at him, suddenly remembering how she'd watched him undress the previous night. She gulped.

"I brought you some coffee and breakfast," he said.

She slowly sat up, pulling the covers around her, even though the spring morning was warm. "Oh," she managed, taking her food and coffee. "That's very sweet of you." As soon as she spoke, she realized she was vulnerable. In the morning, it took her defense mechanisms forever to get fully in gear. And she had trouble guarding herself against Bronson even when she'd been awake for hours.

She often felt contrary in the morning, but sometimes she woke with a goofy feeling, a slap-happy, punch-drunk sort of feeling, and now she couldn't help but smile lazily. Her gaze roved over his denim shirt. The man, she thought, would definitely look better without it. "The honeymooners were keeping me up last night," she offered groggily.

He chuckled and leaned casually against the porch rail, stretching out his long legs and crossing his cowboy boots, one over the other. "Honeymooners have a way of doing that," he said.

She arched a brow. "Even if they're in their seventies?"

He cocked his head and sent her a long, assessing gaze. "True love never dies," he drawled. Then he pursed his lips playfully. "You looked so comfortable when I found you last night that I didn't bother to wake you. I just figured I'd let you sleep."

"See," she teased between sips of coffee, "I told you I was in no danger around you."

"Don't think waking you didn't cross my mind," he said with a wicked grin. In fact, he thought, she'd come pretty close to being ravished. "But I figured if I made one false move, I might well have made every move in the book."

She laughed. Then she looked down at the comforter, as if seeing it for the first time. The thought of him covering her and looking at her without her knowledge made her feel a little exposed. She hoped her mouth hadn't been open in some nighttime drool posture. "Well, thanks for keeping me safe," she managed. The way he was flirting with her, she had half a mind to ask him if he was the same man who'd turned her down for coffee just the day before, but she didn't. *It's best this way.*

Staring down at the plate, she was as surprised as she had been at the smart cut of his wedding suit. The plate contained a bagel and cream cheese, sliced kiwi and mango, and a hunk of Brie. The coffee was twice as strong as usual. It was a real New York breakfast. What had she expected? Grits, fried onions, gravy, and okra—or some such concoction—she admitted to herself. She wondered vaguely if she wasn't a bit of a snob.

"You made this yourself?" The image of the gun-toting Bronson just didn't gibe with the way he arranged a plate. Her own culinary skills were next to nil, even with things one

just had to slice. She tried not to look overly impressed.
"Everything looks so...*perfect*. What's inside your house?
A restaurant?"

*A bedroom,* he thought. That was what was inside his
house. He started to tell her that the plate was a combination effort—via Ellen Logan, Virginia Hall and even Janice
Cummings—but he decided the admission wasn't necessarily in his best interest. He shrugged. "Nothing to it."

She started to say that she herself was a lousy cook, but
then changed her mind. He was a country fellow, she
thought, and probably liked women who knew how to cook.
"Yeah," she said. "I like to cook myself." She flushed. It
was one thing to want to impress him, but another to outright lie. What was happening to her?

"You like to cook?"

She realized, with a sinking heart, that he looked incredibly pleased. "Love to," she managed.

He grinned. "Feel free to cook for me anytime, then."

"A woman's place is in the kitchen and all that," she said
lightly.

"A woman's place is wherever she wants to be," he
countered.

She smiled at that. And her place, she'd decided, was going to be in the work force. "Do you like working?"

Not nearly as much as he liked watching her suck at her
juicy slice of mango, he thought. If she really had been
suggesting they get together, in a man-woman kind of way,
watching her eat was certainly further warming him to the
idea.

"I love working," he said, though it was an odd question. He thought yet again that he had never met a woman
quite like her.

"I've got to look for a job today," she said. The idea had
slowly been forming and now, she thought, it was time.
Some temporary employment might help her decide what
she'd like to do after her marriage.

"Oh?" He had hardly expected her to work. Did she plan on staying? He tried to look away from her lips, which now sucked at another mango slice. Her lips were wide and wet, and their color was naturally red. "What kind of work?"

She shrugged. "I studied business at Harvard, so I guess something businessy," she said slowly.

"Pretty impressive," he said, running his hand over the soft wood of the porch rail. But what was a young, Harvard-educated, engaged businesswoman doing in his neck of the woods? She'd claimed she was visiting, but now she wanted to look for a job, even though she was supposedly getting married. The woman was about as unpredictable as they came. And he couldn't wait to see what she'd do next.

He watched her polish off her plate. "About that coffee," he said.

"Don't worry about it," she said quickly. She swallowed the last sip from her mug and looked into his eyes. "I suppose we're having it now. And maybe it's better that we don't..."

He chuckled and leaned toward her. "But maybe I've changed my mind."

"But maybe I've changed *my* mind," she countered. She knew that a date was exactly what she wanted, but she also knew it was a mistake she might come to regret. "Maybe sometime next week or something," she added vaguely.

"So you haven't *entirely* changed your mind?" He was smiling, but the smile didn't quite reach his eyes. Their gray depths were probing her features, and he didn't look as if he intended to take no for an answer.

"I definitely want to get to know you better," she said.

Now his eyes sparkled. "Yes, but how much better?"

She sent him a playful smirk and then stretched in the porch swing, smiling into the first rays of May sunshine. And then into Bronson's face. "I'll have to think about that," she finally said. "But right now, I've got to run."

He watched as she stood and folded the comforter. She was petite, but not without curves. She had just the kind of body he liked. She handed him her plate and mug. "Where're you headed?" he asked.

"To find a job," she said. With her looks, education and travel experience, a job was the least of her worries. Wasn't it?

She said goodbye and headed down his porch stairs, half wishing she'd made a firm commitment for a date and still telling herself it was best that she didn't.

"Hey, honey," he yelled.

She turned. He was standing on the porch, still holding her dishes, with one booted leg raised and resting on the porch rail. His longish black curly hair was blowing in the breeze. How could anyone manage to look so good in the morning?

"Yeah?"

"See you soon," he said.

"If you're lucky," she returned.

PEACHY PULLED UP to a curb and slammed Helena's old convertible into park. Bernie had got the car running again, even if trying to maneuver it was another matter entirely. Peachy glanced in the rearview mirror. She looked great. She was perfectly coiffed. She had applied her makeup exactly the way her mother's consultants had instructed her. And she was wearing a beautiful tailor-made spring suit of pastel blue.

Blue was, by far, her best color, she fumed inwardly. Any blue looked twice as blue against her bright red hair. Blue brought out the blue, almost violet, of her eyes. She looked so good that she wished she had run into Bronson. She bet *he'd* appreciate how well turned-out she was.

Well, looks, travel experience and fancy educations did not count on this particular job search. She had spent hours running between an agency and various job sites.

She had explained her situation—that she wanted to try a job, to see if she liked working. At first, she'd been honest about her personal income, but admitted she was between checks.

"Yes, but what's your experience?" the woman had asked.

Finally the woman had sent her on interviews: as a maid, a clothing salesclerk and as a temporary telemarketing operator.

"If you have a six-figure income, why in the world do you want to be a maid?" the interviewer for the maid job had asked. She had stared at Peachy as if she were an alien.

After that, Peachy decided to tell the salesclerk interviewer that she desperately needed money. But the woman looked her up and down, taking in her suit and jewelry. "Are you in the middle of a divorce or something?"

"No," Peachy had quickly said. "I'm engaged."

The woman had shaken her head. "Engaged women don't stay long. Especially not if he's the kind to buy outfits like that!"

At that point, Peachy had hoped her engaged status might be a plus with the telemarketing people, since they *wanted* somebody temporary. But the telemarketing interview had been even worse.

"What have you been doing with yourself? Do you have a husband? Children? Job experience of any kind? Oh, no," the interviewer had finally said. "We definitely want someone more responsible."

Peachy stared through the windshield and down the two-lane highway. The world was her oyster? Ha! The only good thing that had happened so far today was seeing Bronson. Thinking of oysters made her stomach rumble. After a long lunch, she would start with the classifieds. Maybe she'd treat herself to a really nice steak filet and some asparagus.

Peachy rummaged in her Anne Klein business bag. What? she thought with horror. She knew she hadn't been watch-

ing her money, but could she really only have $1.17? She
recounted the change. Yes, it came to seventeen cents.
Thank heavens, Helena's tank was full!

She *had* to find a job now. She sighed, closed the bag, and
shoved the gear into drive. If she ever got out of this mess,
she was never, ever, going to act impulsively again, she
promised herself.

She pulled away from the curb. The one thing in her favor was that she owned Fancy Foods, or at least had stock
in every store. She might have to live on hamburgers, but she
wouldn't starve. She'd gotten free meals from Fancy's everywhere from New York to Rome.

She headed toward a shopping mall in the distance. Sure
enough, there was Fancy's. She could see it from here.

BRONSON OPENED the small refrigerator in his private office, rifled past his assistants' bag lunches, pulled out a cola
and cracked the tab. At the sound, Watchdog's eyes slowly
opened. The rangy old bulldog mutt lifted his head and
glared at Bronson.

Bronson shot the dog a smile. "Sorry to wake you,
buddy," he said. "But some of us have to work." He unbuttoned the lab coat he'd thrown over his denim shirt,
sauntered to his desk, and sat in the swivel chair. Then he
raised his long legs and crossed his boots on a corner of the
desk.

"Ungrateful mutt," he teased when Watchdog lumbered
over and sat at his feet. Bronson rubbed the dog behind the
ears. It had been a pleasantly uneventful morning, the
greatest crisis of which was a Pomeranian's rabies shot.
Bronson's assistants, Jilly and Thomas, were now checking
the farm animals in the barn next door. "Remember when
you were a lost, little old stray dog?" Bronson asked the
mutt.

Watchdog hung his head and then lay by Bronson's chair. He'd found the dog the year before, and had tried to take him home, but Watchdog had been so happy to find a place of residence at the clinic that wild horses couldn't have dragged him out of Clean and Preen. So, Watchdog had become an office dog.

"So what do you think this fiancé looks like, Watchdog?" Bronson asked conversationally. "Blue suit, red and blue tie, with some kind of spiffy-style oxford shoes? No passion in his lousy soul? Now what would a looker like Peachy Lofton want with a fellow like that?"

Watchdog gave a sleepy moan and rolled on his back with his feet in the air. "I know you don't want to hear all this," Bronson continued, leaning down and rubbing the dog's stomach. "But don't forget, you owe me. Wish she already had a job, Watchdog. 'Cause if she did, we could go give her a little visit, now couldn't we?"

Bronson chuckled. Watchdog was staring at him with round, earnest brown eyes. "I'm telling you," Bronson said, "she's got that look in her baby blues." Watchdog stared back, as if to say, "What look?"

"That look like she just can't live without me," Bronson drawled. "But then, she's hard to read," he continued. "For all I know, she'll change her mind and pack up and leave before we can even blink. She's just that kind of a woman. And you know what? I kind of like that quality in a woman. Keeps me on edge."

Bronson chuckled again. "Now, if I was just a dog like you, all this business would be over and done with. I'd just trot right on over to her house, tell her I like her brand of perfume, and that would be the end of it. So maybe I just oughtta make like a wild dog before she bolts . . . trot over and bare my teeth and demand my pleasures. Now where do you think she'll end up working—if she ends up working— huh, Watchdog?"

"WHAT DO YOU MEAN—invalid?" Peachy nearly shrieked. She was standing in the manager's office, in the back of Fancy Foods.

"Your ID cards aren't picture IDs," the manager said. He was slight of build and still had pimples. The name tag pinned to his polyester uniform read Darrell, and he looked as though he couldn't be more than sixteen.

"If you're really Peachy Lofton, I don't see why you won't let me call the New York office to confirm that fact...and no matter who you are, you can't just walk in, order food, and then start to eat it, without paying for it and without offering some sort of explanation."

"Please don't call New York," she managed. If he did that, everyone would know where she was. She sighed and said, "Maybe you want me to wash dishes for my food?"

Darrell relaxed some in the chair behind the manager's desk. "We do have a position open," he said. "But it comes with more responsibility than that. You'd be working the register and cleaning the dining area, as well." He gave her a thorough once-over. "Think you could handle it?"

She stared at him in shock. A maid, a salesclerk, a tele-marketing operator—yes. But she was worth six figures a year, even if she was cash poor, and she simply couldn't imagine fast-food employment in her own restaurant. Her stomach rumbled, breaking through her denial. "How much does it pay?" she managed. How indeed, did she get herself into these situations?

"Minimum wage to start," he said. "But you'll find we reward good work. You'll have a salary review in six months, at which time, you'll receive a four percent raise, if you're worthy." He paused. "Now, what size uniform do you take?"

Was she really going to work in her own fast-food chain? And for minimum wage? Minimum *rage* was more like it, she thought. That measly sum was hardly going to keep her in the style to which she was accustomed. But then, had she really expected to find a great job when she had no work experience? *Wake up to the real world.* She sighed, hoping against hope that she could view this as an adventure.

"Look," said Darrell, "I'm trying to do you a big favor. Usually, under these circumstances, what I'm supposed to do is call the cops. Now, what size are you?"

Cops? Peachy felt her heart drop to her feet. "Most of my clothes are tailor-made," she quickly said. "I just don't buy off-the-rack, and you know how sizing varies between designers...."

Darrell heaved a heavy sigh.

"Eight," Peachy said. "I guess I take about a size eight."

"Eight," Darrell repeated. He rifled through packages of cellophane-wrapped bright orange uniforms behind his desk. "Welcome to Fancy Foods," he said, handing her a packaged uniform. "Time clock's in the back."

"NOT HAMBURGERS AGAIN!" Tommy exclaimed. He was still complaining when Bronson shoved him through the smudgy glass double doors of Fancy Foods.

"I have to go back to the clinic tonight and I don't feel like cooking."

Tommy shoved his hands into the pockets of his black leather jacket. "Cooking? You never cook. Do you call boiling a vegetable cooking?" He got in line beside his father. "Besides, I hate this place. It's dirty and gross and they just have regular hamburgers, with no extras. Plus, everything in here is orange. It's disgusting."

Tommy sighed. "Besides," he continued in a cantankerous tone, "you still didn't tell me if you'll help me buy that Nova from Larry. I could get a job to help. I'd take that car even though there's a truck I really want. Dad? Dad, are you even listening to me?"

Bronson hadn't heard a word. He moved up in the line, still staring at the woman's back. It had to be Peachy. He had never seen short hair that color of red on anyone else, not in his entire life. God, he thought, did that orange uniform clash with her hair! Still, the color aside, the woman could sure do wonders for clothes. She could even make a fast-food uniform look good. The polyester top was well-fitted and showed off her breasts and waist. He couldn't see the pants, but he wished he could.

But she had gone to Harvard! Or, he thought, had she lied about that? Still, even if it weren't true, he was sure this wasn't the kind of job she'd been looking for. And she was well-spoken, well-dressed, classy and clearly smart. Not to mention the fact that she was a good ten years older than all the other employees. He watched Peachy bag an order of fries as he stepped up to the register.

"Now, c'mon, Peachy," said a teenager whose name tag read Jane. "This time, we want you to go ahead and give it a try. It's not nearly as hard as it looks."

Peachy smiled, but wondered how she'd get through the day. Her feet ached from standing so long and her face felt soiled from working under the hot heater lights that kept the fries warm. Well, her best clay mask with a double astringent would probably help. The important thing was that she was working.

She turned around... only to find herself staring at Bronson. She glanced downward, taking in his loose denim shirt and snug-fitting jeans, with one quick breath. "Bronson," she managed.

He smiled. "Hey there, sugar," he said.

"I'm Tommy," Tommy said. "I saw you at the wedding."

Peachy said, "Hi." Beside her, she couldn't see but felt Jane crossing her arms over her chest.

"Darrell gets mad if we fraternize with guys," Jane said.

Bronson chuckled. "At the risk of fraternizing—I guess Harvard degrees aren't what they used to be," he said.

Peachy laughed. "I didn't have much job experience." She tried to tell herself there was no reason to be embar-

rassed. So what if she was bagging fries in a polyester outfit? So what if she was wearing bright orange—the no-no
color for redheads? She undoubtedly looked her very worst.

"You went to Harvard?" Tommy stared at her incredulously.

Peachy glanced around and then shook her head. "It's a
long story," she said.

"One I'd sure like to hear," Bronson said, lowering his
voice. He leaned forward and tugged the sleeve of her uniform playfully.

Peachy smiled. "In all its sordid details?"

"Especially its sordid details," Bronson returned.
"You're just about the most unpredictable woman I've ever
met."

"Unfortunately, you've caught me at a bad time," Peachy
said lightly. She glanced at Jane, then shifted tones, still
smiling at Bronson. "Today, we're offering free fries if you
order a Fancy's Fattest—that's a half-pound burger, with a
choice of two cheeses, Cheddar or..."

"Provolone," Jane supplied. "Don't worry," she continued, addressing Peachy, "after a while, you'll remember
the specials with no problem. They repeat."

Peachy knew it was provolone, but looking at Bronson
again had seemed to short circuit her memory cells. She
managed a nod.

"A Fancy's Fattest with Cheddar," Bronson said.

"Same," said Tommy, still watching her quizzically.

Somehow, Peachy managed to complete the order without a hitch. The whole time she was ringing up the pur-
chases, she could feel Bronson's eyes roving over her. She
blew out a long breath of relief when Bronson and Tommy
had carried their trays to the dining area and seated themselves.

"A lot of people have left," Jane said, not a moment
later. "Now Darrell wants you to clear trays and mop the

dining area. After that, you need to wipe down all the stainless."

Peachy had never mopped a floor in her life, but after a brief demonstration, she found there wasn't much to it. She started at the very farthest end of the room from Bronson, deciding that fraternizing might get her in trouble on her first day on the job. Still, she soon found herself gingerly mopping the floor around Bronson's feet. He had on pointy-toed cowboy boots.

"Did you really go to Harvard?" Tommy asked, popping the last of his fries into his mouth.

Bronson had not been able to keep his eyes off her bent mopping figure. Her uniform bottoms were a tad tight and her backside was just about the most luscious thing he'd ever seen. Now he lifted his boots, trying to help her out.

"Yes, I really did," she said, dunking the mop into the bucket with a loud plunk. She tried to avoid Bronson's bemused gaze.

"But are you really engaged?" This time it was Bronson's soft, low, lazy voice that met her ear.

Peachy strained the extra water from the mop and then slapped the mop against the floor again. "Yes," she said. *But I'm not in love.*

He smiled, unable to take his eyes from her face. "Congratulations again, then," he said, wishing Tommy weren't there. It would be bad enough for his son to see him come on to a woman. But an engaged woman?

"Thanks," she said, wishing she had the nerve to protest. She was engaged, all right, but her meditative retreat had clarified the fact that she had a two-timing heart. And every time she looked at Bronson, it beat and pounded and thudded until she thought she'd pass out like some Southern belle.

And now, she thought, if she did decide to call off her wedding, she certainly would not have the nerve. Not if a career for her meant mopping the floors of Fancy's every day for the rest of her life. She couldn't see, but knew a wan expression had suddenly crossed her features.

When she glanced up, Bronson was giving her a kind smile. "It'll all work out," he said, as if he could read her mind.

Maybe things really would turn out for the best...somehow. Still, if the choice was between marrying a man she didn't truly love and being a cashier, she did not know how.

"Things always happen the way they're fated to," Bronson said reassuringly.

Meeting his friendly gaze, Peachy suddenly believed him. Against all logic and reason, things just might work out fine.

She smiled. "Thanks for the vote of confidence."

"Any time," he said.

She awkwardly stared down at her bucket, then turned away and began mopping the floor again. For what seemed an eternity, she could feel Bronson's penetrating gaze on her back. It felt as though he was burning holes right through her.

# Chapter Five

Petulia coiled the phone cord around her manicured nail. "No, no," she said to Peachy's maid of honor, Julia Von Furstenburg, "nothing is wrong, my dear. It's just that my daughter told me she was leaving town for two short days, and I simply cannot recall where she said she would be. Is she in Milan, by any chance?"

"No, and I can't imagine that Peachy would come here just for two days. I mean, the flight itself takes nearly two days. Maybe she took her skis to Moire's."

Petulia sighed. "Moire who?"

"Matico. She's in Alaska. I'll give you the number."

Petulia withdrew a small gold Steuben's pen from its velvet holder and carefully wrote the number on what she was now secretly referring to as the search-for-Peachy pad. "And by the way, dear, how is your gown?"

She half listened while Julia talked about her dress. Like the other bridesmaids, Julia's dress was of organdy, with a square Venice lace bodice and full skirt. All would wear opera-length gloves and floral caps of fresh white roses with silk leaves. Where Julia's gown was a pastel blush, the others were deep cream.

Petulia already knew that Julia's dress was nearly completed. She had called Julia's seamstress herself. Unfortunately, now that she had finally reached Julia, she had also established that Peachy was not visiting any of her brides-maids.

"There seems to be quite a lot of static," Petulia said, cutting Julia off.

"My end's crystal clear," Julia said.

So was Petulia's. "Sorry, my dear," Petulia said. "I simply cannot hear one single word." Petulia rolled her eyes and replaced the receiver. If she had known that motherhood would entail tasks such as searching the world for a wayward bride, she never would have become a mother at all, she thought now.

Where was Peachy? Petulia had made neat, cross-referenced lists, with categories for countries, school organizations and activities associations. She had even called ex-boyfriends. That had certainly taken every ounce of her courage.

What could Peachy be doing with herself? Petulia knew full well that wherever she was, she was low on funds. If she had any forte at all, it was organization. She knew more about the management of her daughters' money than they did. Peachy's last dividend check had surely been spent by now.

While she dialed, she suddenly felt more than a little fearful. If Peachy had no money, who was feeding her? Peachy could neither cook nor earn money. She had never even attempted those things! At the thought of her frivolous daughter holding a job, Petulia laughed aloud.

No, if Peachy was not at Moire Matico's, then she was...where?

PEACHY COLLAPSED in the front seat of the old convertible. Her shift was finally over, it was fully dark now, and she had never been so relieved or tired. Were people absolutely insane? How did they manage to work for a living—day in and day out—without killing themselves in the process?

And for what? She did the necessary mental calcula-
tions. For approximately twenty-five dollars, after taxes.
Twenty-five measly greenbacks! Her legs felt numb from the
knees down, her neck ached, and no amount of soap had
seemed to take the grease from her skin. She hadn't even
had the strength to change back into her glamorous blue
suit. And her uniform was not heavy enough for the now
chilly night air.

She blew out a long breath and swore to herself that she
would, from here to eternity, be kinder to waitresses, sales
clerks and anyone else who had the stamina and poise to
endure a service position. She thought back, with distaste,
on the people she had sent hip-hopping about—to fetch
more sour cream, to bring a rarer steak.... Well, she would
never act that way again.

She shoved the gear into drive and hoped her right foot
could find the energy to depress the gas pedal. Not only was
it dark and chilly, but fog was rolling in. That didn't portend well for her drive home.

A voice called to her from across the parking lot. "Night,
Peachy. You did a great job. Thanks!"

She turned in surprise and couldn't quite believe that tears
sprang to her eyes. She fought them and her fatigue, but realized that the small reward of voiced thanks could go a long
way after a strenuous day of work. It was the first time
anybody had ever told her that she had done a good job. She
savored those words.

"Thanks, Darrell," she yelled. She waved and pulled out
of the lot, thinking that Darrell really was nice. She stared
ahead now, into the thin wisps of fog.

Not only did she like Darrell, but she had been surprised
at the competency level of her other co-workers. Some were
ten years younger than she and yet they supported children—how, she couldn't fathom—on their wages from
Fancy Foods. Jane, as well as two others, Melissa and Joy,
had real difficulty paying baby-sitters. Darrell was eigh-

teen, married, and his wife worked. He had the same problem; so did workers she had not met yet.

Driving up the two-lane highway, Peachy wondered if Darrell might help her set up a day care. It wasn't such a strange idea. Not to mention that some other changes might help. Other fast-food establishments at the mall were doing far better business.

Everyone complained about the food. The uniforms, in Melissa's words, "sucked eggs"; there was no health-food bar, no salads or fruit, and the orange decor made everything look unappetizing. A jolt of anger shot through her. It was no wonder that her business—her father's business, she quickly amended—was sliding toward the red.

She pulled off the highway onto a narrower road, shivering against the cold. She concentrated on her driving for a moment, to make sure she made the correct turns. Unfortunately the fog was getting worse. Suddenly a smile made its way across her face. Granted, she was tired to the bone right now, but what if she made the changes Fancy's needed?

If she could make the West Virginia Fancy's profit margin increase, then a Happy's Hot Dog and Fancy Food's merger would no longer be so necessary. In that case, she could call off her wedding—if she wanted to, of course—and perhaps appease her family. And, if she could show an increase, or even the promise of one, that might help her get a better job in New York.

Her spirits plummeted just as quickly. She could hardly manage such a thing in three weeks. Rome wasn't built in a day. But this wasn't Rome, she thought, it was just Fancy's, and she could at least give it a shot.

She drove beneath an overpass and onto the small, curvy road that led to Helena's. She had overdriven a stop sign. She peered through the fog. It had really thickened and the empty road seemed suddenly eerie. She wished the convertible had a roof. Above her, on the crest of a hill, she thought she saw headlights. That comforted her. Another car was making its way toward her through the dark night. She continued driving, thinking of Bronson and of when she might see him again. His one kiss had just felt so absolutely fated and right. . . .

Without any warning at all, something moved in front of the convertible. Peachy swerved toward the road's shoulder, but not without first hearing a hard, dull thud.

Then everything happened in split seconds. She bolted from the car. Lying on the pavement, in the headlights, was a deer. It wasn't moving. She had hurt it badly. Its eyes were flung back and she could only see the whites, but she could feel its breath when she lowered her hand to its nostrils.

Why wasn't she watching? Was she ever going to change into a more responsible human being? She had hit this deer because she had been thinking of Bronson. Fortunately, the headlights she had seen earlier still advanced.

"Stop!" Peachy yelled when a truck reached her. She waved her arms and let out one of her ear-piercing, taxi-getting whistles. Dusty air floated in the wide, round beams of her headlights. In that light, the hair of the deer's wounded hindquarters looked almost black.

A man got out of the truck. He was bearded and friendly-looking, and wore a flannel shirt. "Hit a deer?" the man asked. "You okay?"

For the first time she realized this probably was not an uncommon event in the mountains. Nonetheless, this was her deer. She had hit it. And all because she'd been thinking about Bronson. "Yeah," she said, pulling an old blanket out of the back seat. "Would you help me get it in the back?"

"Sure," he said. He took the blanket from Peachy, made a stretcher of it, and helped her lift the deer into the back seat of the convertible.

"Be careful!" he called through the window, once he was back in his truck. "She just looks stunned and might move on you."

Peachy made a U-turn and followed him back out. They parted ways at the overpass. Then Peachy pulled into the first convenience store she found. She jumped from the car, ran to a pay phone and began scanning the Yellow Pages. How could such a small town have so many vets? She thought of Bronson first, but realized she was now in yet another of those caught-off-guard situations. Besides, she couldn't find any West Clinic in the book.

Glancing from the Yellow Pages to the car, she saw that the deer was still stationary. That, at least, was good. But a car full of teenagers stopped in the road and began blasting their horn.

"Hey, lady, you look like a real deer to me," one kid called out.

Someone yelled a sick joke about Peachy's *deer-iere*.

"Shut up," she finally shouted. She had not felt quite this upset since she'd left the hubbub of the city. She whispered aloud, "Johnson's Pets, The Boarding Palace..." Talking made her feel calmer, but her pulse still beat in her throat.

What had the man said? That the deer was just stunned? She blew out a breath. That the deer might "move on her" was not exactly encouraging information. And staring at all the ads was confusing.

She wanted to scream that she'd grown up in Manhattan, which was a logical place. There was no wacky Aunt Helena, no overly quick marriages, no hidden gold, no scary caves, and finally and most of all, no men like Bronson West to excite her. There was simply an Uptown, a Downtown, an East Side, a West Side. And that covered it, unless you were some bohemian who lived in the Village, which she definitely was not.

"Clean And Preen!" she suddenly exclaimed. The place was on the only street she recognized. It was near Helena's florist.

She ripped out the ad, ran over, and shoved it in the front seat of the convertible. She fastened her ancient, rusty seat belt and turned from the convenience lot to the pavement.

"Oh, no," she whispered, looking in the rearview mirror. She could see the deer rocking itself, attempting to throw its front legs forward.

"It's okay, sweetheart," Peachy said in as encouraging a tone as she could. Unfortunately, her voice only further excited the deer. It let out a long whinney. Peachy realized that she'd never been in such close proximity to a wild animal, not unless petting zoos somehow counted. "Sh—We're going to a vet. He'll fix you right up." She felt the hard thud of a kick. It felt as if a hoof was coming right through the back of the seat.

And everything looked so unfamiliar. Grant, Lincoln, Jones Street . . . Where was Eleventh? Behind her, the deer let out another whinny that moved her nearly as much as it frightened her. "Please," she whispered, though no one was there, "help me find Eleventh."

By the time she found the street, the deer was wide awake. Its two back legs, which were apparently quite healthy, thrashed wildly in the air. She had to duck, peeking up at intervals to look over the high, mammoth dashboard. "Please quit kicking me," she whispered. The deer, she realized, was far more heartbreaking when it was stationary. Now, both she and the deer were terrified.

BRONSON HAD BEEN GOING through his accounts in his office. Somehow he hoped to shuffle his funds so that he could make Helena an even more generous offer for her land. With even just a few acres of her property, he could move his clinic next door to his house. If he needed to, he could still maintain the barn behind his current office building. Moving his clinic had long been a dream of his.

Thinking of the property made him think again of Helena's niece. Each and every time he met her, he generated more questions about her that he wanted answered. So many things about her didn't add up now that he had to know what she was really like. And he certainly never figured he'd still be lusting after her when she was wearing a polyester uniform that clashed with her hair. But polyester, he'd found, had nothing on blousy cotton. The fabric had stretched and curved right over her figure as if molded to her.

Even now, Bronson could taste that warming salty flavor of her lips. He could still feel the way her body had melded to his, completely pliable, soft and yet demanding and full of need. He had never felt anything like it. And she hadn't seen his kiss coming, either. He wondered how it would feel to have her openly wanting him . . . waiting for him.

Whoever her fiancé was, he was obviously crazy. After all, the man could presumably have her near anytime he wanted. And Peachy was just the kind of woman no sane man would want to part with. How could the guy let her run off like that?

Bronson still didn't doubt it might be a mistake. He had always been the committing kind. It was all or nothing for him, and that's why he didn't date casually, because he did not do anything casually. He never had. He did not have any intention of getting married again, and so that seemed to preclude serious dating.

And yet, Peachy was very, very sexy. And she was only visiting, not destined to stay around long. But why wasn't the fool woman planning her wedding? Spending time with her fiancé? Why did she act so high and mighty when she clearly needed money? And why was she working at Fancy Foods?

He sighed. It was inevitable. If he *were* to ever have a casual affair, she was perfect. Whatever the specifics, she was engaged, after all. And their one kiss had felt as if it was sealing their fate. Chemistry certainly was not everything, and yet, when it was right, it counted for quite a lot. When it came to casual affairs, it was absolutely the most important prerequisite. And even if he couldn't get her into bed, he at least intended to have just one more taste of her lips.

"Watchdog," he drawled, glancing toward the corner of the room, "I just feel like I'll die if I don't."

Bronson stared through a window of the low-slung, brick clinic building. It was so dark and foggy outside and so bright inside that everything beyond the window seemed to be in shadow. Still, he thought he could make out some tank of a car meandering in the middle of the street.

He rose, with half a notion to go yank the driver from the car. Where, in fact, *was* the driver? For a moment there seemed to be no one at all, as if the car were driving itself. A head bobbed up, then back down again. Was the driver looking for something on the floor? Was the driver loaded? Didn't the fool know these roads were dangerous?

He watched the car pick up speed. In split seconds, he realized that it was Helena's car. It was headed over the curb, through the parking lot, and straight for him.

Inside the car, Peachy froze. She was afraid to sit since one of the deer's powerful legs might catch her. She had felt the sinewy strength of those legs through the back of the seat more than once now. The sharp, stony-looking hooves felt solid and hard. Still hunkered down, she careered toward the clinic doors. Then she quickly slammed the gear into park.

No sooner had she done so than she felt a well-muscled arm pull her free of the car. She rolled onto the pavement, but her cheek hit the man's jeans-clad thigh. The denim was so snug, she could feel his muscles move beneath it, and the fabric was worn to a texture so soft it felt like silk. He was crouched down beside her.

"What the hell do you think you're doing?"

His voice was so close to her ear that she could feel the warmth of his breath on her neck. And there was something oddly familiar about the voice. She tried to turn her head, but she had rolled from the car at an odd angle, and now her eyes could only move from one of the solidly built legs to his lower body. Staring at him in that manner, right into the apex of his thighs, she could hardly find her tongue. No matter how hard she tried.

She let herself be pulled farther from the car and then found that the man had the gall to fling her over his shoulder and carry her toward the clinic. She stared between his two wide shoulders. The movements of his muscles were barely concealed beneath the tight lab coat. As shocked as she was at being manhandled, she couldn't help but take in his spicy, earthy, masculine smell.

"I was looking for a vet, not an animal," she finally managed to mutter. "Please put me down."

He was clearly angry. In fact, he sounded more than angry. He sounded furious. And that tone, coupled with his body type, surely didn't bring her any comfort. "*A,*" he was saying, "don't you know you could get killed? *B,* you should never drive in this fog. And *C,* you should never, *ever,* drive with a wild animal in your back seat."

She started to explain herself, but then decided his macho act did not deserve an explanation. "A lot of people would have just left that animal," she argued. She suddenly squirmed in his arms, wishing he had the decency to put her down. "Here's a little something I just learned," she said. "It's my best deer imitation."

Bronson said nothing, only tightened his very strong grip on the backs of her thighs. He wished she would quit moving every which way in his arms. With every twist, he could feel the hard, well-toned muscles of her legs against his shoulder and chest. The more she moved, the more he wanted to haul her right down into his arms and kiss her.

He was so close he could smell the sweet floral scent of her shampoo and beyond that the scent of her skin. He knew good and well he didn't have to carry her inside. It was just an excuse so that he could feel her wrapped tightly against him again.

With his free arm, he pulled open the clinic door. "You really could have killed yourself," he said.

Once inside, he leaned forward, bending at the waist to deposit her in an empty waiting-room chair. It took him far more than the average effort to raise his head, which was pointed down at her lap. He slowly raised it, though, and allowed his eyes to travel over her stomach, her breasts and then her face. God, but she was beautiful, he thought.

Peachy's jaw dropped. Whatever night chill she had felt in the car completely vanished. She felt purely flushed. Clean And Preen, she thought. As in Bronson West's clinic. Sure enough, Bronson was staring at her again with that even, probing and very penetrating gray-eyed gaze.

In spite of the fact that she was overtired and had just had a close call, she felt a rush of pure desire. She wanted so badly to change, to become practical and responsible and to do the right things, but she had to admit that the pull she felt toward this man was immediate, complete and undeniable. It was simply akin to magic. Couldn't she do something a little naughty, just one more time?

She felt her pent-up emotions rise. "Oh, dear," she said, unable to wipe the hysterical grin from her face.

"I didn't know we'd reached the stage of exchanging endearments," he said in his trademark teasing tone.

And everything in his tone implied that they had reached some stage and that he was willing to move on. She shifted uncomfortably in the hard chair, as if to escape his eyes. She was not absolutely positive, but she was fairly sure that if passion was what she wanted—a last fling before her marriage—then the most interesting man was wholly within reach. He was only inches away. He was still squatting, right in front of her. All she had to do was twine her fingers through that mass of soft, curling black hair and pull him to her.

He smiled wickedly. "You know, sugar," he said, "you don't really need to come up with such odd excuses to see me."

She arched a brow. "Like I really, intentionally, hit a deer, just to see you."

He shook his head in mock confusion. "Well, some women do go to any lengths..."

"I see," she said in a wry, playful voice. "Women just won't leave you alone. They chase you a lot, huh?"

He suddenly burst out laughing. "No," he said. "Mostly they bake for me." His grin settled into another irascible smile. "You're the only one who chases."

She tossed her head lightly. "Keep dreaming."

"Oh, sugar," he said. "I will. We'll certainly have to exchange more small talk later, but for the moment I've got a wounded body to contend with. And you're one woman who should never be behind the wheel of a car."

With that, he turned and vanished into another room. She watched as moments later he reappeared and ambled to Helena's car with a foot-long syringe. He pulled a gurney behind him with his free arm. The thing looked as though it weighed a ton.

"Mind giving me a hand?" Bronson asked a moment later. His heart was still racing from the feel of her in his arms. But he couldn't think of her now; he had to take care of the deer. Unfortunately, his understudies, Jilly and Thomas, were still hard at work. Jilly was neutering and Thomas was cleaning the place. He glanced down at the gurney, which was stuck in the double doorway.

What was he going to do with the deer? And, he wondered, staring at the now anesthetized animal, what was he going to do with Peachy Lofton? She was completely unpredictable and he had to admit that was setting him on fire.

In fact, looking at her now, across from him, on the othe side of the gurney, he knew his attraction had already take a back seat to his anger over her lack of caution when driving.

"Just tell me exactly what you want me to do," she sai now, glancing nervously at the deer. "I'll do whatever yo want."

The deer, Bronson knew, wasn't going anywhere, at leas not for a while. And he couldn't help but tease her. "What ever?"

She glanced up. He was smiling at her with that slow, lazy smile and when he wiggled his brows, it became crystal clea that they were in the realm of double entendre. "With th deer," she qualified, smiling. Although she wanted him t like her, she was just as worried that he actually would. An it was pretty clear he did.

Bronson's smile vanished, and in its place came a very businesslike expression. Inside, he felt a pure rush of joy. H hadn't had such fun with a woman in years. "Come along then," he said.

"No," she said.

"And why not?"

"Because you have that look again," she said.

He glanced over the deer and tried to look as innocent a possible. "What look?"

"That wild card look," she said.

"And I bet you're just dying to know what's up my sleeve." He leaned forward, placing his elbows on the gurney.

She stared at him for a long moment and tried not to laugh. "So what is it?" she said.

"Nothin' but my arms, sugar," he drawled.

He said it in such a way that it was clear he wanted to wrap those arms around her. Or was that just her imagination?

She smiled. "So what do we do with the deer?"

"Like I said," he said in a mock crisp tone, watching tiny spots of color form on her cheeks, "just follow me."

"Certainly," she replied with the same formality. She sent him a quizzical glance.

Together, they wheeled the deer into an examination room. She shuddered and tried not to crinkle her nose. She detested antiseptic smells.

Once the deer was situated, Bronson turned to her. "Scalpel," he said.

She walked toward him, hoping he didn't really expect her to do anything genuinely medical, anything involving blood, for instance. She could work with French fries—she had resigned herself to that—but she drew the line at blood. "Why do you need a sca—"

"Exploratory surgery," he said gruffly. At the shocked expression on her face, he burst out laughing. "For all your city street savvy, you can sure be gullible." He ran a hand through his curls, pushing the hair off his forehead.

She blew out a sigh. "Why are you always so difficult?"

Bronson glanced at the motionless deer and then at Peachy. She sounded genuinely concerned. He hoped he hadn't hurt her feelings. That was the absolute opposite of the effect he had been after. But if the very far reaches of his memory served correctly, some women just did not like to be teased. Still, he was fairly sure she wasn't one of them. "Does it bother you?"

She shook her head. "Actually, no. But people do generally take to me with more of a shine."

It was just as he'd thought. She was a woman used to getting exactly what she wanted. "And you think I don't?"

"Do you?" she asked.

He grinned. "Do I have to tell you all my secrets?"

When her mouth dropped open to protest, he said, "What I really need for you to do is let me know if this animal's eyelids begin to flutter."

For the next few unbearably silent moments, she tried to keep her eyes glued on the deer's face and attuned to even the slightest of movements. The soft probing of Bronson's hands on the deer calmed her. He seemed very steady and sure of himself. She knew the deer would be just fine under his care. His hands moved slowly and smoothly, with complete confidence.

It was clear he felt a kinship with animals. His touch was as delicate as it was sure. Probably anything would be fine under his care, she suddenly thought. And unbidden, came the thought that his was a love touch. How would he touch a woman? He seemed extremely patient and gentle, but she'd felt his body grow taut and strain against hers when he'd kissed her. Would the depth of his need and passion overwhelm his more gentle side? She did her best not to pursue that line of thought further.

Instead she told Bronson how she had hit the animal and when she finished, asked, "Is he going to be okay?"

Bronson glanced at her and chuckled. "So are you really that unpracticed when it comes to anatomy?" he asked.

"She," Peachy quickly corrected.

"You didn't answer my question," he teased.

"I'm engaged," she said lightly. "How could I be unpracticed?" But looking into his face she knew she was...or that she would be with a man like Bronson.

He only smiled. Glancing at her face, Bronson had to admit that he was moved by how seriously she treated the animal. She was genuinely troubled. And she was right about the fact that many people would have just left the critter in the road.

"Sure," he said after a moment. "I think she'll be fine." He glanced at her hands. They were pale and seemingly delicate, and yet they were strong. She kept both of them planted softly between the deer's ears. If there was one thing he loved, it was the animals he treated. They never demanded anything and, somehow, it seemed they never left the way people did, even though that really wasn't true.

He felt he could watch the calm, serious expression of Peachy's face forever. "Would you like to go to the ramp festival with me next week?" he asked, trying to keep the tone of his voice casual. "It's right down at the church."

The words had come almost unbidden and now he couldn't believe how anxious he felt. Would she say yes? If there was one test of how a city woman took to the country, it was a ramp festival. Not that it really mattered to him whether she liked country life-styles or not, he reminded himself. She was engaged and he was merely pursuing simple companionable pleasure.

Was Bronson really asking her out? Or was this another one of his jokes? *Ramp festival.* She racked her brain. She wasn't necessarily a genius, but she thought she had a fair vocabulary. Still, "ramp" didn't ring any bells. And unwilling to admit that—not that she really cared whether or not he thought she was smart, of course—she decided to act as if ramp was her middle name. "I just love ramp festivals," she said brightly.

Bronson bit back his smile. He was fairly sure she had no clue where he was taking her. He lightly slapped the deer's flank. "Good," he said. "Next Sunday night."

"Unless I have to work," Peachy suddenly said.

Bronson nodded just as his assistant, Jilly, peeked in the doorway. The young woman waved an instrument in the air. "Mrs. Hoover's poodle is less than man now," she said.

Bronson introduced the two women, then turned to Jilly. "Think Thomas'll help you move this deer into the back pen, for observation tonight? Tomorrow, I think we'll be able to drive her out and let her go."

"Sure," said Jilly, "I'll get Thomas." She disappeared.

"C'mon," said Bronson. "I'll give you a lift home."

"Thanks, but I've got my car," Peachy said. She needed some time alone to process the fact that she and Bronson

now seemed to have a real date. Ever since she had first see
him, she had not been able to hold on to her common sense
Was she so flighty that her own engagement meant nothing
to her? She pushed that thought aside. Anyway, she
thought, she was more than anxious to get to *Webster's* to
look up "ramp."

Bronson had let some time elapse, as if to gather his
forces. He was turning on her again. It was no more Mr
Nice Guy. "There's no way I'm letting you drive in this
fog," he said in an overly argumentative tone. "I've seen the
way you drive."

She thought of being cramped in the Blazer with Bron
son, in the dark. Alone. In the fog. "I'll make it just fine,"
she said.

"That's right," he said. "Because you're coming with
me."

# Chapter Six

If there was one thing Peachy detested, it was being ordered around. Bronson was acting like her mother or Helena. In the parking lot, Peachy tugged her uniform top tightly around her upper body, against the chill of the cool night air, and fumed inwardly. For the first time she wondered if her own actions might have something to do with the fact that so many people in her life seemed controlling.

"See," she argued. "The fog's not that bad. Besides, Helena might need her car in the morning."

"Cold?" Bronson asked, ignoring her reference to the fog. There was no way he was going to let a woman, particularly a city woman, drive in this weather and on these roads, he thought. Granted, it was nice to have yet another excuse to be in close quarters with her, but he was also concerned for her safety.

He pushed her gently but forcibly toward his Blazer, shrugging out of his lab coat as he walked. He put it around her shoulders. "It's lightweight," he said. "But it's all I've got."

"It's fine," Peachy said as he opened the Blazer door for her. At least the Blazer would be warmer than the roofless convertible, she thought, even if she did hate being spoken to in that tone. Who did he think he was? Mr. Commando?

Undoubtedly, Bronson would soon be ordering her around at a ramp festival, too, whatever that was.

The lab coat's collar nestled near her face. It smelled of ammonia, cleaning agents, soap and Bronson. She realized she had already come to recognize the way he smelled. The same smell had clung to the comforter he had wrapped around her. "Well, I'd still prefer to drive my own car," she said as he got in and slammed his door. "The fog really has lifted, Bronson. I don't understand why you're insisting that I can't drive."

Why couldn't she just quietly and graciously accept his offer of a ride? he wondered. He knew she had good manners if she just chose to use them. Most women would be happy to have him give them a lift. Ellen Logan and Virginia Hall would be pleased, for instance. So would Janice Cummings, for that matter.

"You're coming with me," he repeated with a tone of finality, even though it was a moot point. He had already turned the key in the ignition.

He pulled out of the lot and drove toward the overpass. "And that's that, sugar," he continued. He noted with satisfaction that the fog really was thickening. He wasn't being unreasonable. He knew he wasn't.

"Sugar?" Peachy glanced at Bronson, who was concentrating on the road. He looked tired from the long day's work and, for the first time, she noticed the tiny lines etched by his very beautiful eyes. Suddenly the Blazer hardly seemed big enough for the both of them, even though there was a stretch of empty seat between them. "You said 'sugar' a little sarcastically."

"I tend to use endearments when I'm mad," he said.

"You use them when you're not, too," she said.

Her high-and-mighty tone had returned. "Does that bother you?"

"No." She'd nearly snapped the word.

Bronson wondered if he owed it to Peachy to at least tell er that someone close to him had died in a wreck on these oads. "Sorry," he added suddenly. "When I use 'sugar' ke that, I do mean it sarcastically. I know it's a bad habit."

"Well," she said, "it is." No New York men she knew alked that way, even if she did kind of like it. Yes, she and 3ronson really were from two very different worlds. A reembrance of his kiss crept into her consciousness, as if to rove that there were some places where the two worlds met.

He negotiated the overpass. "I said I was sorry." He lanced across the car seat at her. He wasn't sure whether his rotective attitude had to do with her specifically, or vhether he would have felt the same way about anyone who vas inexperienced at driving mountainous roads.

"Just what did I do wrong, anyway, besides wanting to lrive my own car?" Perhaps her own personality really was esponsible for how much other people seemed to walk all ver her. If so, she would have to change. And now was as ;ood a time as any to begin taking up for herself. "Well, not ny car, Helena's car," she amended. "But I don't see why uch a simple thing would be so upsetting."

She stared through the windshield. They were on the nountain road now and there were no streetlights. Everyhing looked dark and eerie. She had to admit, if not to 3ronson but to herself, that the fog was getting thicker and he was now glad she wasn't driving. "I am a decent driver," he finally continued defensively.

"Sorry," Bronson said. "But these roads are curvy and dangerous, even when there's no fog. And you might crash."

"I wouldn't crash."

"You might *well* crash."

"What's it to you if I *do* crash?" she asked, no longer able to hold back her temper. "I think you just like to be in control of things." She wanted to take the words back immediately. But he did remind her of her mother. Would she

ever have her own life—one that she herself was maste
over? She began to fume inwardly about how little time sh
had had for the meditative retreat she'd planned. She des
perately needed to think about just this issue.

She was so deep in thought that she only vaguely regis
tered the fact that Bronson had brought the Blazer to a fu
stop at the side of the road. She glanced at him. He wa
turned almost fully toward her. Soft shadows fell across hi
face, adding darkness to the hint of beard where he hadn'
shaved since morning.

She could fault her mother for always getting her way, bu
she also knew that she herself had many of the same flaws
Besides, if Petulia Lofton was controlling, it was hardl
Bronson's fault. "Sorry," she said. "My mother's a bi
controlling and I sometimes overreact. I just don't take wel
to being told what to do, and—"

"Look," he said, cutting her off, "I don't know any good
way of putting this, but I do have my reasons for wanting to
see you safely home. My wife died out here. She crashed on
night in bad weather." He could even show her the exac
spot. Not that he would, but he certainly had each detai
etched into his memory. He turned back around in the sea
abruptly, threw the gear into drive, and headed on down the
road.

Peachy stared at him in shocked silence. How could she
have been so insensitive? Why hadn't she picked up on the
fact that something more was going on with Bronson? No
one acted the way he did without reasons. She leaned over
and put a hand on his shoulder. "I—I'm so sorry," she said.
"I just didn't know." She swallowed. "And my mother is
really controlling. She's completely taken over the planning
of my wedding, my activities every day, and even what she
thinks I should do in the future. So, like I said, I overreact."

When he said nothing, she continued. "Especially now...I feel like I'm thirty and still under my mother's wing."

She flushed with embarrassment at her own rambling, but still, the silence that would follow if she quit speaking seemed worse. "I'm really afraid I'll be one of those people who never really leaves home. In part, my marriage, for me, was meant to—"

She started to remove her hand, which she'd placed on his shoulder impulsively, but Bronson's hand suddenly covered hers. His palms were a little calloused, but when her hand curled, twining into his, she could feel the softness of his fingers.

"To get you out of the house?"

She was glad he had spoken. Only his words had stopped the rambling flow of her too revealing speech. Still, hearing her thoughts spoken aloud by someone else made them sound odd to her, as if she was hearing them, somehow, for the first time. Marrying to get out of the house was something eighteen-year-olds did. "In a way, yes," she finally admitted. "It just felt like it was time to get married. And my fiancé seemed like the perfect choice."

He squeezed and she could feel his strength and the pulse of his fingers warming her skin. "It's okay to be mad at me," he said, thankfully changing the subject. When he released her hand, she fought a strong urge to grasp his again. "Tommy accuses me of being overprotective all the time. He's probably right. I can be unreasonable."

Peachy righted herself in her seat and stared through the windshield again, still feeling her fingers tingle from his touch. His skin was so soft and warm and dry and she was sure she wanted nothing more than to run her hands over it...over the hills of his chest and the valley of his stomach.

Outside, the night air was heavy and moist. Now, she could barely see the end of the hood. Bronson slowed the

Blazer. She watched him lean carefully into the hazardou
curves, his broad, enticing shoulders curving toward th
wheel. They went up and then down a hill. The only sound
were the steady hum of the engine and the whirring turn o
the tires. And their own soft, rhythmic breathing.

Peachy didn't know what to say. She wondered if he'
fantasized about her the way she'd fantasized about him
The tension in the car felt so thick she thought she could cu
it with a knife. But maybe it was only felt on her side. She
hoped not.

"It's really kind of strange out here at night," she man
aged after some time. Her voice was almost a whisper. The
fog had cast an unearthly gray blue light over the moun
tains.

"Yeah," he said, in the same soft tone. "It's like yo
think you should be hearing owls." He glanced at her and
gave her a slow half smile. "Sometimes you do, you know.'
His glance lingered on her face before he turned his eyes
back to the road.

"What?" she asked after a moment.

His eyes sparkled in the dark. "Hmm?"

"You looked like you were going to say something," she
said. She wondered if he really had or whether she was
seeking weak excuses to hear the deep bass sound of his
voice.

"I don't think so," he said. But he'd almost told her just
how beautiful he thought she was. He wanted to tell her that
she amused him and aroused him…and above all, made him
wonder what she'd do next.

"I never heard an owl before," she said. She stared again
into the fog. If it had not been for Bronson's solid presence, the thickness and strangely ethereal look of it would
have frightened her. She had never seen anything like it before. Fog in New York meant you couldn't see the top of the
Chrysler building, not that everyone and everything com-

pletely vanished. She scooted just a little closer to him in the seat, glanced at him, then stared into the emptiness.

The fog was a moist, warm gray, like Bronson's eyes. And looking into it, she felt just as lost as she did when she gazed at him deeply. "I'm really glad you're driving," she said softly. "It's so dark . . ."

"I better slow down some." He was barely touching the gas pedal. In spite of the danger, he loved the fog for precisely that reason. It was so dark, shadowy, smoky and mysterious. Somehow, it moved him and made him feel that he was deep in the heart of the country. It made him want to pull over and snuggle Peachy next to him . . . and forget about everything else in the world. He drove forward at a crawl.

"It's really hypnotic almost," she whispered.

"Yeah." He nodded. Somehow, he was glad he had told her about Andrea. He wanted her to know. Still, he felt a little bad about the way he had told her and about the fact that he had not disclosed the whole story. She now knew what everybody in Smith Creek thought they knew . . . that he and Andrea had a fine marriage and that he was simply a grieving widower. "Sure you're warm enough? If you want, help yourself to the heating controls."

"Thanks, but I'm fine," she said. "How can you see?" She peered out into the night, into the nothingness. The headlights gleamed for only a few feet and then disappeared. Soft floating mist spiraled upward in the wake of the lights. The particles seemed both random and purposeful at the same time and she could hardly keep her eyes from them. She blinked as if to dispel their magical hold on her attention.

"I see by feel, I guess," Bronson said. "I've lived here all my life, or most of it, anyway. I lived in New York for a while. I went to school there."

"How long were you there?" she asked, thinking that his stay in New York explained some things about him. He was

definitely a city dresser when he wanted to be. She though
again about how good he had looked at Helena's wedding.
There had been nothing of the gun-toting country bumpkir
about him at all.

"Eight years," he said.

"You're nearly a native. Miss it?"

"No offense," Bronson said. "But no."

Peachy smiled. She thought of her own upbringing in the
city, of how different Bronson's childhood must have been.
"Must have been great to grow up here," she said. "No
crime, no city-mean streets, just trees and mountains. Did
you grow up in the house where you live now?"

"Yeah. It was great," he said, trying not to think of the
many rooms in the house that were empty now. Rooms that
were studies and junk rooms and dens, since he hadn't ever
had the large family he'd meant to have.

"I've got five brothers. They're spread out, all over the
country. I was the only one who wanted to stay." And he
had wanted to stay because he'd wanted the life his parents
had had, with a house full of kids. "My parents are in Arizona. Retired."

Peachy smiled again. She was seeing a quieter side to
Bronson, one she hadn't suspected was there, and she liked
it. "Great place to raise a son? Here, I mean, not Arizona."

"Yeah." He nodded and glanced her way. In the dark, her
soft-looking short red hair looked almost auburn and the
shadows played lightly over her skin. "But Arizona's probably good, too. You? Guess you're ready to start a family."
He looked away quickly and concentrated on maneuvering
through the fog again. The woman didn't really intend to go
through with her fool wedding. Did she?

She sighed. "I guess." She looked across at him, taking
in the way his tall body nestled against the seat. She'd never
thought of herself as a back and shoulder girl. But looking
at Bronson, she knew she was now. "I really want to work

on my career." She smiled. "Doing something other than working at Fancy's. I mean, I keep thinking that marriage might not really be enough to...sustain my life."

He stared straight forward. Perhaps she was Andrea all over again, he thought, remembering how his wife had missed her career connections in the city, not to mention her family who lived there. Still, there was something different about Peachy. Undoubtedly, she'd focus her ambitions, but she was soft, too, in a very womanly way. He guessed she would make a good mother as well. "That's good," he finally said.

She couldn't help but note that his words had a hollow ring. "What's wrong with pursuing career goals?" she asked.

"Nothing." He glanced at her again and their eyes met and held for a moment. "I just think that people are more important than jobs. Families..."

She sighed. "My marriage is different," she said with utmost candor.

Bronson felt his temper rising a little. On the one hand, he was interested. On the other, her marriage was the last thing he wanted to be thinking about. He would rather think about dropping her off, walking her to the door and kissing her good-night. He figured the topic of fiancés was a step in the wrong direction. "Different?" he finally said. "How so?"

She shrugged. "Somehow, the engagement latched itself on to a business deal between my father and my fiancé's father. I suppose I resent it, but the fact is that the marriage will be financially beneficial to my family."

He nearly stopped the car again. "You're marrying for money?" He tried to keep his voice level. He could not imagine such a thing, not for this woman. She might be from a city that he thought had a knack for breeding cynicism and self-centeredness in some, but she was not the gold-digging type.

She glanced into her lap. "It's not exactly like that." She felt a flush rise in her cheeks. Every time Bronson voiced her own concerns, it was as if they were thrown into relief. Seeing her life through his eyes made everything seem different. Her mother would never be upset if money were a deciding factor in a marriage, not even if it was admitted outright.

Yet, when Bronson said such a thing, it really sounded vile. Now, as on the day when he had caught her tossing the bouquet into the trash, she felt herself experiencing her actions through his eyes. And Bronson's eyes saw with honesty. His character was as upright and straight as a ruler. She didn't know what to say in her own defense. She looked out into the night, feeling as confused as if she had long been wrapped in a fog as heavy and thick as that which they drove through now.

He tried not to feel sorry for her situation. Undoubtedly, she was not going to be very happy, not if she didn't wise up and follow her own heart. He didn't know what to say, either. He sighed, thinking all he could try to do was kiss some sense into her.

It was the owls that saved them from silence. Suddenly, he leaned forward, squinting through the gray windshield. "Hear that?" he whispered. He rolled down his window with his free arm. They coasted slowly along a short straight stretch of road.

Peachy pulled the lab coat more tightly around herself against the rush of cool air. She leaned toward his open window. Her chin nearly rested on Bronson's shoulder. "What?"

When he turned, his lips were so close that she could feel his breath. "Listen," he whispered.

And then she heard it, the low hooting coo of an owl. "That's an owl?" She glanced up at Bronson.

"Sure is, sugar," he said. He glanced down and one of his very gray eyes seemed to twinkle, as if he had winked at her.

She realized that if he felt judgmental about her reasons for marrying, he was going to thankfully keep it to himself. She stared into his eyes for a long moment, until after he'd looked back at the road.

Aware of their close proximity, she leaned back in her seat, though she had closed the gap between them. She cocked her head, still hearing the soft, low, receding sound of the owl. "It's almost scary sounding," she said. "They sound sort of like pigeons." She half smiled and shrugged her shoulders. "That's about as close to nature as we get on Eighty-fifth Street."

Bronson smiled sympathetically and moved to roll up the window, thinking she might get cold.

"Don't," she said, nestling back deeply in her seat. "Not unless you're cold. I'm chilly, but sometimes I like the way the wind feels."

"I know what you mean," he said. "I don't mind it myself." He leaned over the wheel. It was becoming nearly impossible to see. He was glad Peachy didn't mind the cold because pretty soon she was going to have to get out and direct traffic. The fog, once thin, smoky wisps of gray, had become a thick sheet and settled far down onto the road, as if it were a blanket, putting the mountains to sleep.

"You must have really loved your wife," she said, her voice low. She watched his face, which was intent on the road, and then looked back through the windshield into the blanketing gray. She realized that she did not really expect a response.

For some reason, Bronson didn't mind that she'd said that. Perhaps it was because of the fog, he thought. It was so dark and all-encompassing that it changed his mood, softening him. And the night was so quiet and they were so alone that it felt as if they were the only living beings anywhere. It was a time for telling secrets. Somehow the thick fog made it seem like a night for magic. Besides, she had divulged quite a lot about herself, both with words and wha he could read between the words.

"There was a time when I loved her more than anything else in the world," Bronson finally said, feeling compelled to be as honest with her as she had been with him. He stared into the dreamy, hypnotic fog, and slowly took a curve "But the fact is that she was going to leave me before she died. We no longer loved each other and she didn't like living here. She romanticized the idea of living in the country It was different when she actually did it."

Unbidden, Peachy wondered if she had ever loved Wellington more than anything else in the world. And she had to admit that the answer was no. But perhaps that was why a companionable marriage was a better bet than a passionate one. A man like Bronson would only be capable of giving all his heart, she knew. And hearts got broken. Still, she couldn't imagine really fighting with Bronson. What would it be like to have a man like him around all the time? She imagined a life of teasing, flirting, laughing . . . and a lot of passion.

"Andrea, my wife," Bronson suddenly continued, "wanted us all to move back to New York." He paused. "I didn't want to go. I wouldn't go."

"I don't blame you," Peachy said quietly. "It's beautiful here."

She realized that Bronson had brought the Blazer to a full stop again. They had been driving at such a slow pace that the stop was barely noticeable.

"Sorry, sugar, but you're going to have to get out, just a few feet in front of the car and direct me," he said now. "We'll go to Helena's and I'll walk up in the morning and get my car. Okay?"

"Sure." Peachy stepped out into the chilly air and slammed the door. She wanted nothing more than to get back inside, in the warmth, next to Bronson, and wait out the weather. She walked through the weak headlights and hen turned to face the Blazer, standing in the murky light of the beams. "Just don't hit me," she yelled.

"Don't even say that," he called.

"Oh, God, I'm sorry," she returned, realizing what she had said. "You're a little close to the road's shoulder on the left side," she continued. She tried not to shiver against the cold, but she could feel the bumps rise on her arms and her nipples bead against her uniform.

He thought he heard her voice waver. She couldn't possibly be frightened, could she? Not Peachy Lofton, trasher of wedding bouquets. She was definitely not the type to scare on a dark night. He could just barely make out the outline of his white lab coat in the gray air. It was far too large for her and hung down to her knees. The shoulder seams, he could tell, were well off her shoulders and the sleeves hung half-empty.

"How am I doin', sugar?" he called.

"Keep coming."

"You look like a ghost who's been let loose in a hospital ward," he called.

For the first time since they'd been at his clinic, she heard he teasing singsong sound come back into his voice. She smiled. "Thanks a lot," she responded.

Bronson thought her voice sounded weak, at least by comparison to the bite of the remark.

"Veer right," she called, her voice stronger. The dark chilly night made her uncomfortable. She was used to traffic, subway trains, sirens and people, but absolutely no one was here. She could not really see through the fog, but felt he looming shadows of the mountainous hills rising on either side of the road.

"Like that?" he called. "Did I veer far enough right?"

Even the truck was only a vague outline in the fog. She suddenly thought of magic cars that drove themselves, of *Chitty, Chitty, Bang, Bang* and Stephen King's evil ghost car, *Christine*. She could only make out the teensiest hint of

Bronson on the other side of the windshield. "Keep com
ing," she said.

"What?" he called through the rolled-down window. "
can't hear you."

His voice was soft, but it carried. It was a voice, she sud
denly thought, that must have both perturbed and seduce
a number of women. It was that kind of voice, but it wa
also—seductive or not—making her feel very safe. "Kee
talking to me, Bron," she suddenly called.

"Bron?" he yelled back. "Is that as in b-r-a-w-n?" H
expected that to make her laugh, but she didn't. "What d
you want me to talk about?" From the tremor in her voice
he was fairly sure that the indomitable Peachy really was
little frightened.

"Veer left a little," she said. "And talk about any
thing."

"Darlin', your eyes are like twin crystal lakes," he called
He was relieved when he heard her laughter bubble forth i
response. "Your lips are like blushing rose petals. Nothing
is more red than your lips. And nothing is more white tha
your bare skin, not even the pale, waxing moon itself."

"How poetic," she called with irony. She listened to hi
soft, sexy, wonderful voice, and smiled. Blushing rose pet
als, indeed! Nonetheless, she was aware that the word
sounded good, and Bronson's saying them made them
sound even better.

"You okay?" he called.

"If you turn right, you're in Helena's driveway," she said
now. She felt a rush of relief at that. Soon, she would be
safely inside. She was really cold and her teeth had begun to
chatter.

"Do you get scared out here?" he asked as he turned the
wheel.

Peachy stared again into the weak headlights. This night,
though magical enough when inside the Blazer with Bron
son, did seem scary now. "A little," she admitted. "I'm

ised to so much noise. At home, walking down the sidewalk, I've got a constant whir of activity and conversaional static to keep me company.''

"True," he said, laughing. "It was for just that reason hat I left." He could barely see her now. She was standing n the beams of the headlights and for a moment she seemed :o waver in the light like a real ghost. It sent a chill right lown his spine. "Peachy?"

"I'm fine," she called.

He threw the Blazer into park. He had meant to drive all the way up to Helena's door, but now he told himself that Peachy wasn't used to standing out in the fog this way. She wasn't Tommy, after all, he chided himself. Getting out and going toward her, he realized that she was shivering, too. Her spikey hair had fallen, loosening into waves in the moist night air. Without actually touching her, he knew how the soft dampness of it would feel in his hands.

"I'm fine, really," Peachy repeated. "I'm just not used to being outside at night like this."

He put his arm around her shoulders tightly. "You just snuggle up to me and get warm," he said.

Peachy relaxed against Bronson's arm. His body was larger than hers and he seemed to wrap all around her, like a blanket. "Thanks for walking me to the door," she said, nodding toward the magical outline of Helena's house.

"Now, did you really think I'd desert you in the fog?" He tightened his arm around her, liking the way she felt crushed against his side and chest. "What kind of man do you think I am?"

She glanced up, smiling. "I'm not sure." She had felt very alone, standing in the fog, but now with Bronson's real, solid presence pressing against her, she felt her nerves settling down. A warm tug of arousal seemed to pull her even closer to him. "But I think I'd like to find out."

Bronson's gaze met hers. The corners of his wide lip curled into smile. "You already know all my darkest se crets."

"Oh, I do?" She was still smiling.

"Most people don't know that Andrea and I were havin, difficulties before she died."

He was holding her so tightly that one of her arms wa pinned to her side. She wiggled, releasing it, and snaked i around his waist. "Your secret's safe with me," she said.

The fog did strange, magical things to his eyes. The looked blue gray now and almost damp with moisture. She glanced away, realizing that she had been staring deeply inte them.

"A lot of things about you reminded me of my wife," he said. "I mean, they're superficial similarities . . . I'm sorry was so rude when we first met."

She realized that they had fallen into the same exact step with one another. There was no bumping or knocking or awkwardness when they walked side by side. She laughed "What was so rude, anyway? I mean, all you did was kiss a complete stranger."

They drew up to a stop at Helena's porch. She only real ized in retrospect that she had become used to the kind, re assuring feel of his arm around her shoulder. When he removed it, she realized that it had been there for some time and that something had happened between them on the drive home.

Everything was different now. The odd magical quality of the fog had seemed to make the whole character of the way they related to each other change. She wasn't at all sure if she wanted it to happen. She wasn't sure if it *should* happen. But it had happened.

He was standing in front of her and studying her face. "Well," he finally said, "the way I kissed you was a little rude."

When he had first met her, her skin had seemed too pale, her eyes too brightly blue, her hair and mouth too red. Looking at her now, he could see small lines beginning to form around her deep blue eyes. They gave her face substance and character that he had not noticed before. Peachy Lofton was going to age into the kind of woman one called handsome.

"It wasn't all that rude," she said. "I mean, it was at first . . ." She glanced toward the door. In spite of her move to go, she remained rooted to the spot. She watched as he merely cocked his head, slowly moving it to the side in that sexy way he had.

"Guess I better go." Her mouth had suddenly gone so dry that her words came out in a croak. She managed a weak smile and turned to go inside. She glanced over her shoulder at him. "I'm looking forward to the, uh, ramp festival."

He smiled. And it was one of his more teasing, naughty smiles. "Me, too."

He leaned forward suddenly, caught her hand, and turned her around. "Don't you want to know how I kiss when I'm not in a bad mood?"

She took a step forward, closer to him. She was cold again, now that she'd left the circle of his arms, and she knew the tight uniform did nothing to conceal how the cold was affecting her body. "Are you a better kisser when you're in a good mood?" she managed lightly.

"If you come here," he said, "you'll find out." Holding her at arm's length, his gaze moved over her face, and then dropped, looking at her body. His eyes rested on her chest. Seeing her nipples against the fabric of her top, a warm, liquid shot of arousal coursed straight to his groin. He looked back at her face. She'd known how and where he was looking at her, but for the first time she hadn't bothered with a blush. She was looking at him with pure, undisguised want.

He watched as she took another step into his arms. As she neared, he pulled her arms around his waist. He hadn't even kissed her and he could feel the tightening of his jeans. If she came any closer, she was bound to feel it, too. He slowly ran his hands over her sides and around her shoulders.

"That feels so good," she murmured, pulling him closer. She brought her body against his, length to length.

He gazed down into her blue eyes, then licked his lips lightly, and smiled. He rested both his hands at the back of her neck, lifted her face and lightly licked her lower lip. He licked her top lip, then, wanting to tease and excite her. Very, very lightly, he bit her lower lip and then the top one.

And when she took a sharp breath, he rested his mouth over hers, as if to capture it. Unable to tease her any more, he sent his tongue deep between her lips and felt her dueling back, while her arms pulled him even closer. He could feel her hardened nipples press into his chest. He lifted his mouth from hers for a moment. "Oh, sweetheart," he said.

"You do kiss better when you're in a good mood," she said in a husky voice before he leaned down to claim her lips again. She drew her hands over his back, exploring the curves of his muscles, rubbing him, hoping she was arousing him, and clung to him tightly. She had never felt so excited by a man in her life. She lifted her arms and ran her hands through his hair, letting her fingers twine into the soft strands.

He was licking her lips again, teasing her, driving her to distraction. She arched against him and suddenly swallowed hard, feeling his arousal pressed against her. She realized things had gone farther faster than she had imagined possible. She leaned back, broke the kiss, and smiled. He nuzzled his head against her hands.

She let out a shaky breath. "I think I had better go in," she whispered.

He chuckled. "Escaping while you still can?" he teased.

She laughed. "Exactly."

He drew her quickly to him again and kissed her lightly. Before he ambled down the porch steps, he ran his hands over her arms as if to further warm her. And then she watched him go.

"Sleep tight, sugar," he called over his shoulder. As an afterthought, he added, "And dream about me."

From the doorway, Peachy watched the fog slowly swallow him up. This was one night, she knew, when she definitely would not sleep tight. She remembered Bronson's soft voice, his sparkling gray eyes, the feeling of his arms wrapped around her and his kisses. Now she pulled his lab coat more tightly around her. No, tonight she would be very lucky if she managed to sleep at all.

"RASH," Peachy said. "As in rash behavior." She flipped backward a few pages in the *Webster's* on the table and squinted down into the columns of words. While she read, she tied the tie of her Fancy's uniform into a bow. She would definitely have to talk to Darrell today about new uniforms.

That the day could be sunny and clear amazed her. There was no evidence of the previous night's fog. In fact, by the time she'd awakened, Bronson's Blazer was gone and Helena's convertible had been returned. It was as if the strange night hadn't happened. Had she really hit a deer? Had Bronson driven her home? Had he really kissed her in a way that had made her feel as if she might not stop?

Outside, Helena stopped her trek toward the house briefly, to give Bernie a kiss on the cheek, then Bernie continued walking down a garden row with his metal detector. He'd been going carefully and methodically over the property, looking for the supposedly hidden gold.

Peachy turned back to *Webster's*. "Rash. Raspy... randy..." Why did every word have to have a vaguely sexy connotation? She glanced up when Helena came in, the handle of a basket slung over her arm. Leafy dew-damp tops jutted out of the basket.

"Ramp," Peachy suddenly exclaimed. She read definition number one. "'A graded plane...'" Was Bronson taking her to some kind of sporting event?

"Ramp is right," Helena said with a heaving breath.

"Oh," Peachy said. "Do you know what a ramp is?"

Helena plunked her basket on the table beside the dictionary. "Here," she said. "Go ahead and help yourself. They're stronger than ever this year."

"Wild onions?" Peachy managed. She stared quizzically into the basket with a slow sense of dawning horror. Bronson West was taking her to a wild onion festival!

# WEEK THREE

*Lovely to see...*

## Chapter Seven

"They look fantastic together!" Angelica Vanderlynden exclaimed. "I can't believe my contacts disappeared!"

Petulia cringed inwardly. For some time, Angelica had been under the impression that Christine, who was dancing with Wellington at the pre-wedding bash, was Peachy.

"I really should try those new throwaway contacts," Angelica continued. She flicked her wrist downward as if to illustrate that glasses would just not do her evening gown justice.

"You look lovely," Petulia remarked, taking in the other woman's cream taffeta gown. Wellington's mother had his same perfect blond, blue-eyed features; a suntan seemed to have been coded in the family's genes.

"As do they!" Angelica nodded toward her son and Christine.

Petulia realized with horror that the couple in question were now headed their way.

"Oh, Christine! It's you," Angelica said when Wellington had escorted Christine to the future mothers-in-law. "What a gorgeous gown."

"She looks fabulous. Doesn't she?" Wellington asked.

His mother nodded while Christine spun in a full circle, modeling the strapless teal dress. Her cheeks were still flushed from dancing.

"Wellington was just telling me about a new idea for a hot dog," Christine said breathlessly. "What do you think of a foot-long hot dog with a honey-mustard sauce? After all, we use honey-mustard on steaks. The bun would have to be—"

"Sourdough, maybe," Wellington said. "But let's forget about hot dogs and just dance again. Okay?"

Seeing the lights gleaming in Wellington's eyes, Petulia wondered if she should have let Christine wear Peachy's new gown, but Christine had begged and had then threatened to tell Wellington that Peachy had disappeared.

"By the way," Wellington asked now, "how's Peachy?"

Petulia shook her head. It was easy enough, under the circumstances, to look genuinely distressed. "As I said, it's a twenty-four-hour flu."

"She's ill?" Angelica turned to Petulia.

Why did everything Angelica Vanderlynden say seem to have ten exclamation points behind it? "She'll be fine," Petulia reassured.

"Perhaps I should look in on—" Wellington began.

Petulia shook her head no. "Thank you, dear, but Charles just took her some of Alva's hot soup. We hardly want the groom to get sick, too. Now, do we?"

"So Daddy just checked on Peachy?" Christine asked.

"Indeed he did," Petulia said flatly. She saw her husband approaching. "Now, please, why don't the three of you relax in the other room? Angelica was just saying she needs to sit . . ."

"I didn't say—" Angelica began, but before any protest was completed, Petulia maneuvered Christine, Wellington and Angelica next door, just in time to prevent her husband from mingling.

"Are you sure the doctor said the bug is highly contagious?"

"Absolutely certain, dear," Petulia said, kissing her husband's cheek. As much as she wanted his support in this matter, Petulia would rather bear it out alone than see him hurt.

"Wellington checked on her, anyway," Petulia lied.

"Well, dear," he said, his expression softening. "Would you care to dance, then?"

Petulia's smile was without artifice. "I thought you'd never ask."

Moments later, leaning on her husband's shoulder, Petulia half hoped Peachy was having a good time. But that was impossible, she knew. What could be more romantic and wonderful than dancing cheek to cheek with a special man at a formal dance?

A RAMP FESTIVAL! She stared at the dresses strewn across her bed. She had tried everything from full formal to jeans before leaving her room to ask Helena what she should wear.

"I'm wearing my best dress," Helena had offered.

She had carefully surveyed her great-aunt. The best dress was apparently yet another floral-print shirtwaist.

Now she was not any clearer about the dress code than she had been an hour before. Only her short, springy, olive sundress seemed perfect, but it was in her closet in New York. Tonight she felt as if she had actually underpacked for the first time in her life.

At least work was going well, even if she had doubts about the choice of dress. She had convinced Darrell that she was Peachy Lofton and he had agreed to help her make some changes at Fancy's. She'd borrowed from Helena and could use her own paycheck. And Helena had offered her sewing skills. Soon employees would have attractive uniforms in teal and bright blue, and they hoped to have the space downstairs painted for a day-care center. Already employees were taking turns baby-sitting on select days.

How could she think about work when she had to be dressed in less than an hour? She shut her eyes, waved her

hand haphazardly over the bed and picked a dress. It was a
sexy, black, spaghetti-strap number, with a slit. She realized it was probably what she would have worn anyway.

She reminded herself that she was engaged; she had no
business wearing her very sexiest, raciest dress. And the
previous night, she well knew, there had been a party for her
and Wellington. A wave of guilt washed over her. It was so
overpowering that she sank onto the bed.

Could she help it if she wanted Bronson to see her in this
dress? Just one more time, she thought, she wanted to see
his eyes light up with male appreciation. Besides, she told
herself, this was not really a date. They were just neighbors
getting together for a little local event, right next door at the
church.

Still, her guilt had rendered her completely immobile. She
did not want to marry. She knew that now. And she would
never have to work, not if she attended to the proper management of her finances. Not that she didn't like working.
She did, more than anything she had ever done. Even if it
*was* mopping floors, it was rewarding.

Slowly it dawned on her that she would have called off her
wedding by this time if it weren't for the fact of the merger
agreement. Unfortunately, her engagement, which she had
embarked upon honestly enough, believing she was as in
love as she ever could be, had come to mean quite a great
deal to her family.

She could, and would, happily take the blame and carry
the burden for her own mistake, but could she really make
the members of her immediate family suffer, too? She
schooled herself not to blame her mother, but it was difficult. After all, it was Petulia who had first seen what a
family gain this marriage would be....

She could almost see the crushed, hurt expression on her
father's face and the slow, weary drooping of his shoulders. She could almost see the exact defeated way he would
look if she did not show for the wedding. Bronson may have

felt judgmental concerning the fact that she was marrying for money, but he himself had said that families were of utmost importance. Certainly he would understand.

Helena's head bobbed in the crack of the door. "You better get dressed!" she exclaimed.

Peachy glanced down at the sexy black dress in her hand. She had already showered, washing with a special scented soap. She had taken extra care with her makeup, applying just enough that her best features were accentuated, but not so much that it was truly noticeable. She had styled her hair in a wavier, looser fashion.

She could hardly make a final decision about her marriage right now. Helena was right. She needed to get ready. And, she told herself firmly, nothing would improve her own mood more than feeling beautiful and well turned-out for Bronson.

"Thanks, Helena," she said. She stood and began rifling through drawers. She found a lacy strapless bra and, when she checked, found that her good black wide-brimmed straw hat had thankfully not been crushed in its hatbox. She sniffed at three different perfumes before choosing a musky scent with a hint of flowers. Then she began to dress with a vengeance.

"KISSING LOTTO! Numbers a quarter! Get your number now," a woman called, making her way down the long line of people who waited, paper plates in hand, to reach the buffet. "Bronson!" the woman exclaimed when she reached him.

"Virginia," he said. He nodded and introduced Peachy. Bronson fished in his pocket, found change and handed the coins to Virginia. She gave him two tickets, one of which he promptly handed to Peachy, his touch lingering on her palm in a soft caress.

Peachy felt the woman give her a thorough twice-over before moving on. Her gaze was clearly appreciative, if a little jealous. But Virginia herself was tall and slim and very pretty. Still, Peachy felt self-conscious about her dress. Floral-print shirtwaists seemed to be not only Helena's, but *everybody's* best dress. Even Virginia's.

"Your competition, sugar," Bronson said, following her gaze.

She laughed. "One of many?"

He chuckled. "Maybe," he said. "But you're definitely the belle of the ball."

"Thanks," she said, gazing into his eyes. When he'd picked her up, he'd kissed her lightly and playfully, and the sweet, naturalness of it had left her with a warmth she still felt.

"So what do you think of our ramp festival?" Bronson asked, staring down at her. It was impossible for him to take his eyes off her. As inappropriately dressed as she was, she looked like a knockout. So much so that his mouth kept going dry. He swallowed. "What you expected?" His lips stretched into a teasing smile. "I mean, with your love of ramp festivals and all."

The festival, she had to admit, was much the way she had thought it would be, with its lively, loud crowd and long line of tables laden with brightly colored cloths. But she hadn't expected Bronson to look even better in dressy country attire than he did in a conservative suit.

"The food actually doesn't look half-bad," she finally managed. She wasn't looking so much at the heaping spoonfuls of potatoes and ramps that were now being ladled onto her plate, but at Bronson's starchy-white, Western-style shirt with its string tie. The shirt was tucked very neatly into his snug-fitting, well-worn, soft-looking jeans.

"You'll love the food," he said, holding out his own plate for a helping of ham, ramps and green peppers. Because he was taller than she and because she now held her head at a tilt, he was seeing her face through the patterned swirls of the black straw hat. He wanted to tell her that she looked

even better than Greta Garbo—that was what he was thinking—but he didn't.

He swallowed again, taking in the veil-like shawl that
covered her bare shoulders and the thin straps of her dress.
"Surprised at how good it all looks?"

Peachy laughed. "Yes, but I still promise not to breathe
on you."

His eyes narrowed into squinty, laughing slits. "Oh," he
said. "But that's the whole point, Peaches."

*Peaches, not Peachy.* She felt suddenly, uncomfortably
weak-kneed. Why had she tried to fool herself hours earlier? This was a date. And as such, it meant more kisses
from Bronson were right around the corner.

She smiled at him and then glanced away. Doing so, she
realized that she was the talk of the town. Why hadn't Helena offered her a little friendly advice? Why hadn't she told
Peachy to wear something else? The warmth of Bronson's
desirous gaze was everything she'd wanted, but she wasn't
sure it was worth enduring the envious glances from the female quarter.

When their plates were full, Bronson led Peachy to a table and pulled out her chair, seating her with his hand lightly
caressing her back, in the best of country fashion. "Breathe
on me all you want," he said, grinning, picking up their
earlier conversation. "Onions or no onions."

His own breath was so close to her face that she could feel
the heat of it. His lips were nearly touching hers. He
swooped toward her and smooched her lips lightly, loudly,
and very publicly. She was fairly sure that other women were
now sending her full-fledged hate daggers with their eyes.

"You see," he began in a teasing tone, "years ago, come
mid-May, everyone was eating ramps, but on different days.
Then some wise soul got the great idea that everyone should
just eat them at the same time. Thus," he concluded, drawing his brows up in a sage, scholarly glance, as if anything
having to do with wild onions could carry the weight of ac-

ademic logic, "the great solution to onion breath within the close-knit community was born."

"Thank you for the historical background, Professor West," Peachy teased, lifting her fork. "Here goes," she said. "My first real contribution to the community."

Bronson watched her swallow her first bite, still taking in the splashy black ensemble. He was well aware that all eyes were on them and he felt proud to be squiring her around. At first, he had felt a rush of male response. Then he'd felt guilt, thinking he should have told her what to wear. Finally, he felt relieved. She could never fit in a community like this. Now, he realized that she wore the dress so casually that many didn't even notice it any longer. And, paradoxically, he was now glad she seemed to fit in. He sighed. She was confusing the hell out of him.

It was surprising to her, but each dish did taste even better than the last. The wild onions were stronger than most, but once cooked, they were definitely less lethal. In fact, they tasted almost sweet.

And Bronson was apparently more than respected in the community, a fact made clear when people stopped to say hello and to thank him for fixing up some well-loved pet or another.

Peachy joked and made small talk in the middle of the whirlwind of activity. She found that women who had initially seemed standoffish now warmed to her. Between visitors, Bronson informed her that her deer was fine. He had driven it back to the woods in a horse trailer and had set it free. Somehow, that fact made her feel free, as well. Or maybe it was just the fun, lively people at the festival.

People got such a kick out of how Peachy had driven through strange neighborhoods with the deer that Peachy found herself telling and retelling the story countless times at Bronson's insistence.

"So you really went to Harvard?" Tommy asked just as Peachy was finishing her last bite.

Peachy turned from Bronson and a young married couple to whom he had just introduced her. "I sure did," she said to Tommy.

Tommy shoveled another bite of ham and ramps into his mouth, then took a healthy gulp of water. "So why are you working at Fancy's?"

"I want to make some money," Peachy said honestly, deciding she rather liked Bronson's son. He had a wry smile and a quirky sense of humor that had made her chuckle throughout the meal. She could already plainly see that he was going to be a looker just like his father.

"I want to make some money, too," he said. "Dad says I've got to buy my own car if I want one. But there's no way I can get a job unless I have a car first."

"Couldn't he buy the car and then let you pay him back?" Peachy asked, frowning. She didn't wait for a response, but fished in her pocketbook for a pen. "Exactly how much money do you need?"

"Well," said Tommy, "the truck I really want is fifteen hundred." He added proudly, "It needs a lot of work, but I'm a whiz with mechanics. It'd be no trouble for me to fix it up, and I just found out that Bernie knows even more about cars than I do. He said he'd be happy to help." Tommy's face fell. "If I ever get a car, that is."

"Fifteen hundred," Peachy murmured, jotting figures on an unused napkin with the speed of light. "We need a greeter at Fancy's. You would just have to stand at the door, welcome the customers, and tell them about our specials.

"It's a new position the manager is letting me institute. It pays minimum wage, but if you did it twenty hours a week during school terms—when do you get out of school?"

"June first," said Tommy.

"A good day for you and a bad one for me," she muttered. "Well, in that case, if you work twenty hours until then and forty this summer, you could pay him back before fall, and with ten percent interest." She passed the napkin to Tommy. "My manager, Darrell, would have to approve you, of course."

"Of course," Tommy said. "But my dad..."

Peachy realized that Bronson was watching her. She had been so immersed in her rows of figures that, for just the briefest of moments, she had forgotten him. Now he smiled.

Bronson couldn't help but notice the way Peachy's face changed when she was deep in thought. Her mouth pursed and looked more kissable than ever, like a cupid's bow-shaped mouth. What in the world was this woman doing to him? Suddenly he felt like a heel for not helping Tommy buy his fool car. Before he knew what was happening, he found himself saying, "Do you mind if I see that napkin?"

Bronson surveyed the tiny, neat-looking rows of figures. Peachy sure wrote numbers in a way that meant business. In fact, he could probably use someone like her to go over his own accounts, he thought wryly. He looked into her bright blue eyes. "Well," he finally said, "it looks like you've got my interests at heart. What's ten percent of fifteen hundred?"

Peachy tried her best not to wince. Apparently, numbers weren't Bronson's forte. The thought came to her that his strong point was in making her feel like an incredibly desirable woman. His eyes had been roving over her dress throughout the evening. "One hundred and fifty," she said.

"Well, Tommy," Bronson said, "if you get the job at Fancy's, we'll shop for a car."

"Could I get the truck instead of a car?" Tommy asked.

"I don't see why not," Bronson said.

Peachy winked at Tommy. "See, I didn't go to Harvard for nothing." Tommy was clearly so excited that the words were completely lost on him.

"But," Bronson continued, thinking that more than anything he wanted his son out of his hair right about now, "if I were you, I'd take our plates to the trash...before your father changes his mind."

Tommy cleared the plates and left the table before Bronson even had a chance to blink, and finally he found himself alone with Peachy. The dress had really done him in. He could not take his eyes from her bare rounded shoulders.

Her skin was freckled but creamy, the color of fresh country milk. She not only looked beautiful but he had to admit she was passing the country life-style test. Not that he had really meant the evening as a test, of course, but he had been surprised at how many people had obviously liked her. Neighbors had invited her to stop for coffee, for a slice of their best pound cake and the like. Even Virginia, clearly wowed by Peachy's outfit, had suggested that the two of them go shopping together.

Peachy had been looking into his eyes. Why did a man like Bronson West have to come into her life at a time like this? The timing could not be worse. She wanted to get out of her engagement fair and square...if she got out of it at all.

She smiled and fished again in her pocketbook. "So what's your lotto number, sugar?"

"So you're calling me sugar, now." Bronson's gaze traveled slowly over her face while he fished in his own pocket. All at once, it sunk in that he had agreed to buy Tommy a car and that there was no backing out now. He knew good and well that his decision had nothing to do with Peachy's education. It had everything to do with the thin straps of her dress. One move on his part, he knew, and that dress would fall from her shoulders and completely free.

Then there was the fact that for some strange reason he did not want her to think he was guilty of having an overprotective attitude toward his son. Said son who now, he reflected, thought Peachy was the greatest thing since sliced bread. Still, he had somehow wanted to prove to her that he was not controlling, the way she said her own mother was.

"Are you just going to stare at me?" Peachy teased. "Or are you going to tell me your secret number?"

"Fourteen," he said. His gray eyes stirred from their contemplative reverie and came fully alive with a sparkle. He caught her wrist playfully and unbent her fingers one by one. "And you are—" he rested his own fingers on her palm "—twenty-one." Bronson winced. "Last year, I got Mrs. Cranzenberry. I don't so much mind that she's twice my age, but she has a tiny mustache and she's just not my type."

Peachy had to fight not to move her wrist. Her pulse had gone wildly out of control and she could even feel it in her throat. Bronson's fingers still rested lightly on her palm, lightly caressing it. "And what is your type?" she finally returned archly.

"Well," he said with a lightness meant to belie his true seriousness. "Red-haired vixens in distress..." He let his eyes travel over the front of her dress. "Lithe-bodied but with luscious curves that—"

"Well, it's a shame I'm not distressed, then." Peachy laughed even though his downward gaze made her feel more distressed than she'd ever been. Every inch of the man seemed to be saying that they were going to become lovers; that it was inevitable. Another of his fingers moved gently on her palm. "Well," she continued, striving for a light tone, "maybe next year you'll be lucky enough to get my number. Even I sound preferable to Mrs. Cranzenberry." Next year? What was she saying?

"If I really wanted to kiss you, I'd hardly need a number, now would I?" Bronson's eyes traveled down the long, even plane of Peachy's naked throat. He was well aware that their few shared kisses would never be enough. He wanted to make love to her. He *had* to. To hell with her New York roots and to double hell with her New York fiancé.

Bronson's eyes, Peachy saw, were sending her very clear signals of invitation and there was a hard, purposeful edge to the look. He was definitely not the kind of man who would back down, not once he was sure he wanted something. And it was her that he wanted. She was sure of that.

"I suppose you wouldn't," she said lightly.

"Guess not," he said, and smiled. Suddenly the fact of their circumstances hit him full-force. Although he was telling himself that her engagement meant nothing to him, thinking of it certainly darkened his mood. "Are you really going to marry a guy for his money?"

"I know how it sounds. But it's really not like that." She started to take her hand out from beneath Bronson's but when she moved to do so, he caught it more forcefully in his own.

"Then what's it like?" He lowered his voice to a husky whisper. His gray eyes reminded her of the sun shining through the clouds on a hazy morning.

Their faces were only inches apart. "I don't know," Peachy said weakly. She glanced around the room as if for an escape.

He knew he was making her uncomfortable, but he couldn't stop himself. "So, when's his lucky day?"

"June first," she managed.

His mouth dropped, but he still held her hand. "That soon?"

She looked back into his face. "Yes." Her voice was almost a whisper. "It is soon, isn't it?"

"Damn soon," he said.

Fortunately, people were now engaged in a full cleanup campaign. "I think we're supposed to fold chairs."

"Yeah," he said, still not taking his eyes from her face.

Peachy shifted uncomfortably in her seat. "Look, Bron," she said, grasping his hand more tightly. "Let's just have a good time. I really need—" she sighed "—to cut loose and have fun and not worry."

His lips curled into one of his naughty smiles. "Well, honey bunch," he said, "I'm all for that." He watched as she got up, her slinky black dress falling open at the slit. She folded her chair. He followed suit. Then he put his arm around her tightly. "Don't worry, sweetheart, I intend to show you the time of your life."

"Thanks, sweetheart," she whispered in her most con spiratorial tone.

Once the chairs and tables had all been put away, the two looked on as musicians appeared from every corner.

"You sure did clean your plate," Bronson remarked conversationally. She was very glad he had decided to let their earlier conversation drop. Now he waved at the gui tarists and fiddle players, and introduced her to Ellen Lo gan, who had a tamborine.

"I've always had a big appetite," Peachy said, following his gaze. She saw there was also a washboard player and a few men with spoons. She listened to the pleasant click-clack as the men warmed up, tapping the spoons against their thighs.

He shot her a long glance, then wiggled his brows. "I've got quite an appetite myself," he said.

"Is that so?" she teased.

"Yeah . . . and for a city woman, you're doing pretty well here," he continued. He still couldn't believe how everyone had taken to her. Hell, she'd eaten more onions than he had.

"For a city girl?"

"I said woman." Bronson couldn't help but notice that she was, indeed, all woman. She had a trim waistline and wide, full hips that were in definite proportion to her breasts. And before the night was over, he fully intended to take that womanly body in his arms again.

Peachy chose to ignore the remark about her woman hood. "What is this? Some kind of test?"

"Absolutely," he said candidly. "I hate snobs. And there's one test left." He grabbed her hand and pulled her onto the makeshift dance floor as the music began.

"Do-si-do?" Peachy found herself yelling at Bronson moments later.

Not only Bronson, but everyone present, helped Peachy through the square-dance moves, and she found herself breathless and whirling, time and time again, into Bronson's arms. Somehow, in the process, she lost hold of her pocketbook. In a particularly expert spin, she threw off her hat. Her shoes followed. She was sure she'd never laughed so much in her entire life.

Bronson was more than stingy when it came to relinquishing her to other dance partners for the slow numbers. So much so, that his complete possession of her soon became the object of a few sly winks. The only time they parted was for the kissing lotto.

"Mrs. Cranzenberry again!" Bronson groaned when he managed to get Peachy back into his arms.

"I think your Mrs. Cranzenberry is fixing the lotto," she responded during a promenade.

"Jealous?" he asked.

With pleasure, she noted that he sounded sincerely hopeful. "Oh, yes," she teased. "Very."

Bronson grinned, but still wished Peachy hadn't gotten Jessie Stewart. Jessie was twice Peachy's age, too, but he was still kind of good-looking Bronson had decided when he saw old Jessie kissing Peachy's cheek.

"Who'd you put on your ballot for Ramp Queen?" Peachy asked.

Bronson opened his mouth in mock shock. "Why, you, of course."

"I, of course, put your name down for king," she said.

When they didn't win, they stared at each other in feigned disappointment. "Bernie and Helena *would* win," Peachy said, watching the two oldsters kiss.

"Don't worry," he said, running his fingers lightly through her hair. "I'll make up for it."

"I just bet you will," Peachy said, returning his smile.

"Now!" he said. He grabbed her hand and tugged her, protesting, through the open door and into the cooling night air. When they were behind the door, he backed her up against the wall and placed one hand on either side of her.

He'd pulled her outside so quickly that Peachy couldn' quit laughing. "So are you going to kiss me or not?"

He leaned forward, letting his lips hover above hers for just a fraction of a second, then brought them down in a quick, wet, playful kiss.

Peachy reached up, putting her arms around his shoulders, but no sooner had she begun to lean into him than he broke the kiss and shot her another of his wide grins.

"Enough is enough," he teased. And before she could protest, he pulled her back inside.

Each time the square dancing was interrupted for a slow, everybody-get-your-breath-back Tammy Wynette song, she felt the perfect way her body fit and moved with Bronson's.

"Did you happen to wear this practically dressless dress just for me, sugar?" he murmured at one point, moving his hands slowly over her bare shoulders. He could feel the damp perspiration on her skin from the exertion of their dancing, and could smell the scent of her body beneath her perfume. He kept thinking that this was how she'd feel and smell when they made love. And he knew now it was a definite *when* . . . not an *if*.

"I sure did," Peachy whispered. She leaned closer to him, her forehead resting on his throat. She clasped her arms more tightly around his neck and let her fingers twine in the softness of his hair. "Like it?" she murmured.

He leaned over, so that he was whispering right in her ear. "I don't like it," he said. "I love it."

She smiled and nuzzled against him. They were dancing so slowly they were barely moving. Throughout the evening, she'd held him every way she could get away with . . . she'd danced, touching his broad shoulders, his chest, his back and his waist. He loved her dress, she thought, but she loved the way he felt against her . . . the way he smelled, the color and sparkle of his eyes and his teasing nature.

Bronson slowly pulled her hand downward, then caught it and held it to his heart. The way she moved against him, their hips and cheeks touching, made him long for the festival to end. He wanted to be somewhere far, far away from the well-lit parish house. To kiss her quickly and playfully was one thing—and he did want that, too—but the way he wanted to kiss her now deserved the absolute cover of complete darkness.

Any brassy New York confidence Peachy had felt at the crowded festival completely evaporated on the walk home. She could not forget the way Bronson had turned and twisted her body, as if it were something he had long since known how to hold. Now, Bronson kept his arm locked tightly around her waist on the way up Helena's driveway while Peachy found herself rambling about her work at Fancy Foods.

"We really need to find someone to paint the downstairs," she began. "I'd really like it to be a pale pink, or no, a pink-cream, almost eggshell kind of color..." She knew she sounded foolish, but talking relieved the tension she felt radiating from Bronson's body in waves. "Yes, eggshell pink is nice. Do you like that color?"

Bronson suppressed a grin. "Fine color," he said. "And I'm a little handy with a paintbrush," he continued, but he didn't loosen his hold. His arm was still possessively wrapped around her waist.

Was he willing to do the painting? She didn't want to ask him directly, since he might not have meant to offer.

The conversation fell flat. "I really am a snob," she said, noting they were coming closer and closer to the dark porch. "I was appalled when I found out Bernie and Helena were getting married."

She told him how embarrassed she'd been at the wedding; that it was just the kind of attitude her own mother

would have had and that she was ashamed of it now. She
said she was especially ashamed since Bernie and Helena
had looked so sweet together tonight as this year's Ramp
King and Ramp Queen.

When they reached the porch, Bronson slowly turned her
around to face him. "You're no snob," he said. "And no
amount of talking is going to make you any less confused
about our situation. And no amount of talking is going to
stop what I'm about to do...and what you're about to do."

"I'm not ready to make love to you!" she exclaimed. *Had
she really said that?*

He smiled kindly. "I just want to kiss you, sugar." It
wasn't exactly true, but he was pretty pleased to hear that
her thoughts had been running along the same course as his.

"I didn't mean..." she said.

He pressed a finger to her lips. "I know what you mean."

"Oh," she managed, feeling herself being drawn into the
tight circle of his arms. And suddenly, she knew, feeling the
muscles of his arms against her back, that no matter how
wrong it was, she wanted him. She had been waiting all
night long for this kiss. And she had been waiting her entire life for a man like him to come along. "Then kiss me,"
she said.

"I'm glad you're feeling bold," he said, freeing one of his
hands. He moved his thumb over the line of her jaw and
down the soft skin of her long neck. He traced her collarbone. The warmth of his breath came closer and his lips just
grazed hers, touching hers as he continued to speak. "I'm
feeling a little bold myself," he whispered.

His thumb moved beneath the thin spaghetti strap of her
dress and she would have moaned if his mouth hadn't covered hers with increasing pressure at the same time. The
moan was lost, pressing itself against his lips. Almost
against her will, her tongue sought his. Any thoughts she'd
had about her family and her marriage were completely
gone. There was only this moment in time.

He felt her trembling against him and knew, deep down
n his soul, that this kiss would somehow decide everyhing. With this kiss, he wanted to give all of himself and
make her truly want him, need him even. And he had needs,
oo...to feel her tremble, as she was already trembling now.

If he'd wanted her before, the taste of her mouth now
urged him on. He thrust his tongue deeply between her lips.
He felt and heard another moan that couldn't fully escape
er, and with a jolt, felt her hands slide downward, rub-
)ing his back with increasing pressure.

"So bold," he whispered. He broke their kiss for a moment, long enough to fully feel her hands move with a
harder, more sure touch over his muscles. His mouth covered hers again, all his pent-up longing for her threatening
his control.

If he continued, he would not be able to stop. But his
hands, propelled by passion, not the logic of his mind,
moved to her back, too, and all the long way downward to
the soft rise and fall of her backside and her thighs.

"You've got an incredible body," he whispered, running
his tongue over her teeth and lips.

She could feel her silky dress rise with the movement of
his hand and felt where the slit of her dress fell open. More
than anything, she could sense the difference between soft
fabric and rough fabric, between where her silk-covered
thighs or her bare skin just touched his faded, well-worn
jeans. The muscles of his thighs strained against her.

His mouth moved from her lips down the line of her neck
and then back up again. He shifted, in such a way that she
could feel his response, while his tongue sought out hers.

She feathered kisses over his lips and then leaned back in
the circle of his arms.

"Some kiss," he whispered raggedly, his mouth still
touching hers.

Her heart was pounding so fast and hard that it frightened her. She thought it might leap from her chest, but she

continued to relax against the strength of the arms that held her. She could still feel the length of his arousal against her. "Oh, Bronson," she whispered.

His lips met hers again and in the dream-like waves that came over her consciousness with each new touch, she had no real energy with which to care about safety or her future.

"Don't stop kissing me, sugar," he whispered. He released a long, heated breath.

If this wasn't safe, then it was dangerous. And the danger and exciting newness of it, so unlike the familiar solidity of her New York world, coursed through her. "If I kiss you once more, if my mouth so much as touches yours again, I doubt I'll stop," she whispered. "And this was just meant to be a good-night kiss, after a church social."

She stared into his eyes. Heaven knew, she had never, ever, felt this bold before. Watching him, she ran her hands up through the thick soft mass of his black hair. Her heart was still beating wildly and no matter how she tried to control her breathing, it did not seem to be slowing down. "I think I should probably go in," she managed.

But she only found herself leaning toward his lips again. She kissed him softly, slowly, letting more small tiny kisses fall on his mouth one by one.

Bronson sought out the tiny lobe of her ear. He caught it between his teeth and he pulled at it lightly, feeling the pliable way her body bent toward his. Then he lightly kissed her cheek and simply held her.

After a moment she managed to step back a pace, schooling herself not to look down, hardly ready to actually see the effects of his response, which she had more than felt. She tried to find her voice, but all she could think of was that no man had ever aroused her this way. Certainly no kiss had ever made her lose total control with such speed. It was like a bolt of lightning. She would have slept with him, she was sure of it. Now, right now, tonight if she hadn't somehow held on to common sense.

"So did I pass the test?" she managed. She smiled into his face, which was half-lost in the dark shadows of the porch.

"Test?"

"The one where I prove I'm not too citified?" She couldn't help but let her eyes fall; she caught a glimpse of his jeans where the taut fabric bulged. She glanced quickly to his face with a sharp intake of breath.

He followed her glance, then his eyes met hers in a long, direct gaze. His mouth fell slightly open when he saw that a thin black strap had fallen from one of her shoulders. It had been so long since he'd had a woman he wanted the way he wanted her.... He slowly guided his thumb over her collarbone again.

She was glancing down at his hand, half hoping he meant to pull the strap farther down. "You never answered me," she whispered huskily. "Did I pass the test?"

His thumb slowly hooked beneath the strap. He pulled it upward until it rested in place on her shoulder. "With flying colors," he said in the slowest, softest voice. He stepped away from her, still looking at her kiss-swollen, red lips.

She turned to go inside.

"I'll see you soon," he said.

"Promise?"

"I promise," he whispered.

And that, Peachy thought, promised to upset her life and the life of her family. But it was still the very sweetest promise she had ever heard.

# Chapter Eight

"Hey, there, yourself," Bronson yelled in response to Bernie's greeting. He stopped loading his Blazer and ambled over to where Bernie had leaned his metal detector on the opposite side of the fence. "Find yourself any gold yet, Bernie?"

"Not a nugget," Bernie responded. "But looking for it sure is keeping me in shape. How ya doing?" Bernie pulled a handkerchief from his back pocket and wiped it across his forehead.

"Fine," Bronson said. His eyes flitted over the yard, as if he might see Peachy, even though he knew good and well she was at Fancy's today.

Bronson had half a mind to ask Bernie if she really intended to go back to New York. But what did that matter to him? *They were seeking pleasurable companionship.* His sole purpose was to make their time together something memorable.

"Looked like one hell of a kiss took place on our front porch last night," Bernie said. "Better get it while you're young. I sure wish I'd met Helena when I was your age. As much as I love her, I don't have that kind of energy left. She'll never really know the stuff I was once made of." Bernie grinned. "Don't worry, Bronson," Bernie continued, "I just happened to glance outside, but when I saw the goings-on I went right on back to minding my own business." Bernie paused. "Cat got your tongue?"

"Nope." Bronson sent Bernie a devilish grin. "I figure a man's got a right to steal a decent kiss every chance he can." But decent, he had to admit to himself, was an understatement when it came to the way that certain woman had felt in his arms. Why did there have to be so much that was right between them? Bronson knew he wanted more from her than she was prepared to give.

This morning, when he'd awakened, Bronson had rolled over in his giant, empty, king-size bed, somehow half expecting to see Peachy there, like a vision or a dream. Unfortunately, only Mittens had been there, warming the starchy cool cotton of the sheets.

Bernie threw his head back suddenly and laughed. "You look a little star-struck this morning."

"Are you kidding? She's engaged."

"So you mean to tell me you don't draw the line at engaged women? Dr. West, you're a regular Casanova."

Bronson smiled, taking it as a compliment.

"Well," said Bernie, "I hope you two tread with caution. To hear Helena tell it, her folks sunk their teeth deep in both their girls, Peachy and Christine, and they're not about to let go. Peachy's wedding's some kind of big deal up in New York."

"Bernie, the woman's thirty years old," Bronson said wryly. But Bernie only shrugged.

Bernie spoke of New York as if it were a strange, far-off land and Bernie's line of conversation was one Bronson recognized as pure country. It was all sugar on the outside, but Bernie's glance carried a warning Bronson couldn't help but resent.

How big a deal could Peachy's wedding be? All weddings were important of course, but Bernie made it sound as if Peachy's were far more so than average. Besides, it was hardly Bernie's place to tell him or Peachy what to do, even if he clearly had their best interests at heart. Bronson intended to show the woman a great time. And that was all. *Because that's all she wants.*

"Do you think she's going through with her wedding?" Bronson asked, trying to sound casual. After all, who would know better than Bernie? Peachy was staying with him and Helena.

Bernie shrugged. "Haven't the foggiest."

Bronson was ready to pump Bernie for additional information, but realized Tommy was now behind him. How long had *he* been standing there?

"Bernie," Tommy said, "I'm gonna get that truck this afternoon. Sure you won't mind helping me with it?"

"Not at all, son," Bernie said. He pointed up the hill.

Bronson realized Helena was standing in the open door of the farm house. He waved.

"I'll help you with the truck, but I've gotta go now," Bernie said. "Helena calls...."

Bronson tried to ignore the fact that Tommy simply assumed his own father didn't know anything about cars. There had been a time, after all, when Bronson had rebuilt his own engines. And where did Tommy think he had gotten his genes for mechanics? From Bernie?

"Let's finish loading the Blazer," Bronson said.

"Must have been a cool good-night kiss," Tommy said, echoing Bernie's words while the two headed back toward the porch, which was stacked with board games, old baseball gloves and the like. "I mean, you really kissed Peachy?"

Bronson arched his brow in his son's direction. "You shouldn't eavesdrop."

Tommy grinned. "Well," he continued, lowering the gate to the Blazer, "it sure is odd timing, anyway. These toys have been in the upstairs junk room ever since I can remember. In fact, ever since I quit playing with them."

"So, it's about time we got rid of them, don't you think?" Bronson stacked the board games inside, with Monopoly on top. "Personally, I'm sick of all that mess upstairs."

Tommy glanced up from where he was rummaging through a box of toy trucks. "Let's see," he said, giving his father a wry smile. "These toys have remained in our venerable house through the Mountainside Interdenominational's toy drive every single Christmas...."

"Just load the toys," Bronson said. "Okay?"

Tommy retrieved a shoe box full of cars from the porch and brought them to the Blazer. "And we Goodwill clothes every season and nary a toy has gone—"

"The toys," Bronson said. "I see a little phonograph still on the porch beside that stack of books. I'll get the Lego, the table and the chairs."

Tommy guffawed, but hustled to the porch again, returning with the items. He continued, "Remember when Joyce Ryan had a little boy and Virginia Hall suggested you give her all this stuff? And then there was the Toys for Tykes fund drive at my school...."

"Never mind," Bronson said. "I'll finish loading the toys. You get in the truck."

"Good idea." Tommy smirked good-naturedly. "But I just wanted to point out that you did have all those previous opportunities to do this, Dad. And that the minute Peachy Lofton opens a day care at Fancy's fast-food restaurant for five or six measly little tykes, that's when you force me—cool Tommy West—to go play Santa Claus in May." Tommy suddenly burst out laughing. "That's who we are!" he exclaimed. "The spring Santa and his elf."

"Oh," Bronson said absently after a moment. "Don't let me forget to stop at Perry Paints."

"For what?" Tommy asked, moving around to the passenger side of the Blazer.

"I've got to get some pink paint," Bronson said, slamming the Blazer's back gate. He came around to the driver's seat. "It has to be pale, almost white. Well, not really white, more like eggshell, but still clearly pink."

"Eggshell," Tommy muttered. "Pale pink. Whatever happened to Casanova?"

Bronson turned, faced his son, and gave him a long, assessing look. "Who do you want for a father?" Bronson teased. "James Dean?"

"Nope," said Tommy. "James Dean never got to kiss Peachy Lofton."

BRONSON LOOKED Peachy up and down. The new teal uniform was definitely better for her coloring, and in the morning sun, her hair looked as red as flames. Flames made him think of fire. And fire made him think again of how her slinky body in its slinky dress had clung to him, not a full twelve hours before.

"That uniform's a real improvement," he said. "Not that you didn't look great in the old one. It fit better."

She looked a little upset. "It did?"

He smiled and shrugged. "It was tighter." And she had looked great, he thought, unable to forget how the polyester had molded her curves. Fancy's was extremely busy—busier than he'd ever seen it to date—but he was glad she found the time to lean forward, with her elbows on the counter, and smile her dazzling smile, even if she wasn't supposed to fraternize.

"Oh," she said archly. "I see how your male mind works."

"Like most male minds, I'd imagine," he said.

She laughed, stepped back from the counter and spun, modeling her outfit. "Helena made them," she said excitedly. "For now, we all have to wash them every evening, but I'm hoping they're instituted soon, as a real, company-manufactured uniform."

"The management let you do this?" he asked, smiling ack. "Guess a looker like you would be bound to have ome pull."

Peachy schooled herself not to think of how different he ooked today. He seemed so calmly flirtatious. Last night he thought, with a short intake of breath, he'd been a little ut of control . . . and so had she. "I do have connections," he said. She realized, for the first time, that as far as Bronon was concerned, she was just another struggling Fancy ºoods worker. "Incredibly connected," she continued. 'You'd be surprised."

But really, she thought, it was she who was surprised not o find her heart pounding wildly in her chest again, as it ªad the previous evening. In the daylight and in the conïnes of Fancy's, she only felt glad that he had stopped to ʳisit. Thank heavens, she no longer had to wear the orange ɔolyester outfit, she thought now. Still, as tawdry a thought ιs it was, she half wished her new uniform fit like the old ɔne . . . tight.

She turned, sensing someone behind her. Before she could ʲee who it was she got a hearty kiss on the cheek. "My savor, my mentor, my very favorite person in the entire whole ʷide world," Tommy said, laughing at her shocked expresʲion. "Did you put in a good word for me?"

"I sure did," Peachy said. "Darrell's expecting you. Go ɔn back." Peachy pointed toward the office.

"Well," Bronson said when Tommy was gone, "consider me one of your connected admirers, sugar. I've got ʲome stuff out in the Blazer for you."

Unfortunately, the place was hopping. Peachy turned, anyway, and called over her shoulder, "Mind if I go on break?"

Darrell's face appeared from behind the food warmers ʈhat held the extra pre-made burgers and fries. Surpris‍ingly, Darrell responded, "Sure, Peach. Go ahead. I'm go‍ing to interview our new potential employee."

Tommy waved at Peachy and Bronson, saying, "Wish m
luck!"

Peachy let Bronson grasp her hand and pull her out to th
Blazer. He had that wicked look in his eyes.

"So what is it?" she asked, holding back.

He tugged her lightly forward. "You'll just have to wa
and see," he teased. "Don't you trust me?"

"I bet you just want to steal a moment alone with me."

He wiggled his brows and kept luring her toward th
truck. "Always," he said. "And, don't forget, I'm a mas
ter thief."

"Trying to steal my heart?"

"Of course." He paused, still smiling at her. "But if yo
let me steal it, I won't give it back."

She laughed. "Who says I'd want it?"

"My, oh, my," he teased, running his tongue over hi
teeth, "You're sure easy prey."

When they were halfway through the parking lot, he ca
sually looped his arm around her shoulder. It felt both goo
and right, and she wondered yet again what exactly she wa
going to do about it. There were, after all, only two shor
weeks left before she was scheduled to walk down the aisle

"Voilà!" he said, removing his arm and opening the Bla
zer's gate.

Peachy's eyes roved over the contents. The back of th
cab was cram-packed with toys. And, she saw, they wer
very nice, expensive toys that had been well cared for; man
were still in mint condition.

Given the meager salaries with which some of the em
ployees made do, and the fact that they had other financia
responsibilities, as well, some of the kids probably didn'
have so many nice toys to play with, Peachy thought. No
toys like these. She also noticed a small play table an
matching plastic chairs. "These are for our day care?" sh
finally managed.

"Yes, ma'am," Bronson said.

Impulsively, she flung her arms around his neck and gave im a bear hug Helena would have been proud of. "That's :ally sweet of you. I mean it." Her eyes moved again over ie toys. "How can I pay you back?"

He grinned. "That's easy."

She looked up at the sly way his mouth curved and at the :xy glint in his eyes.

"Cook me dinner," he said.

"Some hearty, big, fit-for-a-tough-guy kind of fixings?" eachy couldn't help but remember the neat, beautiful ar-ingement of fruits he'd served her the morning he'd found er asleep on his porch. And she couldn't even boil water! 'What about me planning a nice, long hike, instead?" she iggested.

"You like hikes?" he asked, leaning lazily against the lazer's open gate and crossing his well-muscled arms.

"Love them."

"Good," he said. "But this is my territory, so hikes are iy department."

"Dinner," she repeated, wondering how in the world she as going to weasel out of this one. "All right," she finally iid. But she knew, even with Helena's help, any dinner she ioked would be a total disaster. "I'll cook you a meal ou'll never forget," she finished. At least that much was ue.

"But now," she continued, "I've only got five minutes ft, so I better take some of these things inside."

He caught her wrist and drew her to him.

"I'm working," she managed.

"No," he said, his lips hovering above hers. "Techni-illy, you're on break."

Nonetheless, he didn't kiss her but pulled her around to ie passenger side of the Blazer and opened the door. With chuckle, he backed her inside, so she was sitting on the assenger seat, sideways. Then, in one quick move, he fol-

lowed her in. She found herself lying backward in the se
with him leaning over her.

"Let's see," he said with a playful smile. "If you're n
keen on fixing me dinner..."

"I'll cook you dinner," Peachy said. "Oh, I swear I will
He ran his hands through her hair. "Yes, but will you..

Peachy giggled. "Oh, okay," she said with mock resi
nation. "Kiss me if you must."

He leaned farther over her, his lips just grazing hers.
must," he said.

She placed her arms around his neck and pulled hi
downward, meeting his lips with a soft sigh. His mou
tasted of morning coffee and he smelled of after-shave. A
ter a moment, she nuzzled his neck.

He reached above her and held up a piece of cardboar
It was coated with paint.

"Is this the color?"

"It's perfect," she said, her arms still around his nec
She ruffled his hair. "A pale, eggshell pink." She w
amazed that from her rambling descriptions he'd manag
to find just exactly the right tint. It was as exactly right
the way he felt next to her.

Heat rushed to her face. In all their playfulness, she
barely registered the seriousness of their posture. He w
leaning in the Blazer, his torso lightly placed between h
legs.

"The color's good," he said softly.

She quickly moved to get up and he let her. When she w
standing again, she took a deep breath and smoothed h
uniform top. He was smiling at her as if he knew exact
what she was thinking...that they'd been in a near lov
making position.

"You can take these, sugar." He handed her some pai
pans and rollers.

"You're going to paint?" she managed. "Oh, Bronso
that's so much work—"

Bronson laughed. "Well, Tommy's willing to help, on the ondition that we car shop when we're done." He was close nough that he could see deep into her almost violet eyes. Besides, spending my day off, or even two if I can man- ge it, a floor below you is hardly hard work." He winked. Then there's the fact that the toys are only good in ex- ange for a dinner and kiss, but the paint job...well, that'll ost you."

"What if I don't pay up?" What was it about him that rought out the pure tease in her?

He grinned. "Rest assured, sugar, I'd never force you to do anything you didn't *desperately* want to."

Maybe not, she thought, and the sparkle in his slate eyes ertainly said that he thought she would want to pay, per- aps even pay double. "Well," she began, deciding to ange the subject before she was in too deep to get back out gain, "this is really great. Perfect timing. The kids aren't oming until tomorrow. I've got care duty then."

Peachy hoisted the pans and rollers into her arms and then oked carefully at Bronson. "I hope I didn't step on your es by working out a payment plan for Tommy," she said. When I get an idea, I start implementing it, without inking first. Late last night, I started thinking that my help ight not have really been welcome."

She didn't bother to add that late last night had found her ide awake for reasons that had nothing to do with Bron- n's son and everything to do with Bronson. Bronson aned now in the open passenger side door. He was wear- g yet another pair of those well-worn faded jeans that owed off every blessed contour.

He let his eyes rove over her face. Her nose was sprinkled ghtly with freckles that he was sure came out when she got n. But, he reflected sadly, how she looked with a suntan as something he'd probably never know, not if she was sincere enough to head back to New York.

"Are you kidding?" he managed to say good-natured. "I stand to make ten percent."

"But you really didn't want to buy him a car?" watched as her face fell and she shifted the paint rollers a pans to her hip. "Be honest."

"The way I see it," he said, "we have nothing to lose being completely honest. I mean, what we have now is meant to last, so..."

"I know what you mean," she said. "I think—becau you don't want to be involved, long-term, and because I' getting married—there really isn't anything to lose. In strange way, it makes you easier to talk to than anyone I' ever known."

"Yeah." Bronson paused. "So, I didn't have to say yes buying the car." He put his hands in his pockets in a wa that pulled his jeans more tightly across his thighs. smiled. "Even if that dress of yours *was* a pretty stro bargaining point." He shrugged. "I hold on to Tomn pretty tightly sometimes."

"It's understandable," she replied. "Besides, holdi tight also means you're probably a good guy to have in person's corner."

Bronson's eyes narrowed and sparkled. "Yeah," he sai wondering as he spoke how any one woman, even Peach could look so damn alluring in a fast-food uniform. If thought she looked good in that, he'd be attracted to her a potato sack. "When I love something—" he flashed h a grin "—I'll fight to the death for it."

Peachy couldn't help but wonder what it would be like be one of those things Bronson West would fight to t death for. If he had lived in another century, she was sur he would have probably managed to fight a few duels. A ter a moment she said, "C'mon, let's get this stuff inside.

She watched as Bronson leaned toward the largest bo "I'll go and get Darrell to help—" she began.

He shot her a sideways glance and his lips curled in a half smile. Then he effortlessly lifted the box onto his shoulder. He glanced down at her again. "And lose this opportunity to impress you with my he-man build?"

She rolled her eyes playfully. "Right."

"See," he continued. "A good-night kiss of the caliber you dole out goes a long way with a guy like me."

"I guess it does," she said, laughing. "I guess it really does."

WHEN PEACHY DESCENDED the stairs to the new day-care center, she had expected to see the paint-spattered drop cloths, the disarray of newspapers and the pink-coated coat hangers that had been turned into paint stirrers. But she had not expected to see Bronson up on a ladder and stripped to the waist.

Up close, he was lean, but his upper body was incredibly well-toned. She could see the sharp delineation of lines that accentuated the muscles she knew the names of, like biceps. He had a number of other neat, firm, cleanly formed muscles, too, and even if she didn't know the technical names for them all, she surely knew that she longed to touch them.

He had, she thought, just the kind of body that was the stuff of dreams and fantasies. The only imperfection was a very large glob of pink paint that had somehow landed on his shoulder. In spite of that, his thick mass of wavy black hair just touched between his shoulder blades and gleamed with a glossy shine that seemed to call out for a woman's touch. And when he half turned, all the seeming millions of small muscles moved.

"Do I sense a presence there?" he asked. Glancing downward, he found himself staring into the top of that flaming red hair. Said hair that his fingers still recalled as if they had a memory of their own. He made his way backward down the ladder. "I hope you know this visit's long

overdue, sugar," he said. "I've been painting for hours
He shot her a mock pout over his shoulder. "And it's be
so lonely...."

"Why, you poor little thing," she said in her best a
tempt at a Southern drawl. She glanced around and rea
ized that Tommy was nowhere in sight. When Bronso
turned to fully face her, she saw that his shirtless front w
every bit as enticing as his shirtless back. Soft-looking da
hairs curled on his chest and moved downward in a seer
ingly logical pattern toward his smooth flat stomach ar
then into a very nice vee.

The niceness of what lay below was hardly something sl
was going to guess at, but she could well remember how sl
had felt him touching against her while they'd kissed. Sl
swallowed suddenly. His jeans were unsnapped.

"Sorry," he said in apology, catching her gaze. "I thir
I'm getting a middle-aged gut and it was more comfor
able..."

Every fiber of her being wanted to protest with the obv
ous. His stomach was so flat that a woman could iron on i
But that, of course, would hurt and she couldn't imagir
any half-sane woman wanting to hurt Bronson. Any woma
in her right mind, she was sure, would have just exactly th
response she was having. And she was fighting the urge t
make him feel very, very good. She said nothing, but on
tried to tamp down the noticeable flush that rose to he
cheeks while she watched him snap his jeans.

"I really was hoping you'd visit," he said. He picked u
a damp rag from the drop cloth and wiped his hands as l
ambled toward where she stood on the lower step.

Visit? she thought nonsensically, still watching the eas
limber way his well-formed body moved through the roon
Somehow, having him in this close proximity had made he
forget momentarily why she had come downstairs.

"I thought you and Tommy might be hungry," she man-
ed. "And since whatever you want is on the house, I fig-
ed I'd come take your orders."

Unable to help herself, she took the damp cloth from his
nd and turned him so that his back was to her. Under her
gers, his skin felt as soft as a baby's, but the scent of him,
e knew, was all grown-up male. She forced herself to
ncentrate and dab at the pink splotch on his shoulder. "A
int goof," she explained when she was done.

Bronson smiled, took the cloth from her, and tossed it to
e drop cloth. "Thanks," he said. He glanced around the
om. "My worker disappeared. I think he wanted to pick
 his uniform—apparently he's getting stuck with one of
e old orange ones for now—and to ask Darrell some ad-
tional questions. And he had to fill out W-2s." He pulled
t a plastic kid-size chair and sat on it.

"I think you're just a little large for that," Peachy said.
e looked more than comical in the tiny blue chair.

"What do you want me to do? Shrink for you, sugar?"
 asked as he pulled up a second chair for her.

"That's all right," she said lightly. "I like you just the
ay you are."

He flashed her a grin. "My size and all?"

She sighed. "I suppose you'll have to do."

He arched a brow. "Do for what?"

She looked him up and down. "Just do," she said.

He chuckled. "I can't believe how different the upstairs
oks," he said conversationally. "I mean, in a week or so,
u've managed to get a salad and fruit bar and some new
ppings, not to mention catchy new names—" he threw
ck his head and laughed, exposing his wide mouth of
raight, white teeth "—like Fancy's Fishiest, for the sand-
iches. The place looks cleaner, better cared for and the
lvertising banner outside does catch your attention."

Peachy somehow managed to seat herself on the under-
ze chair. "The one that says, Fancy's Is Fastest?"

"Yeah," he said. "It's not the words, so much as the fa
that it's lettered in that neon lime green."

She gave a smile of acknowledgement. Soon, she knew
she was going to need to document the changes and draw u
a finished portfolio for her father and the board. The ba
ner itself had been responsible for practically doublir
business, as simple a thing as it was.

She glanced around the room and surveyed the paint jo
The ceiling was done in white, and the eggshell pink, whic
now covered two walls, was drying nicely. "It looks great,
she said.

"It's not bad," he responded, shaking his head agre
ably. "But it's not done and—" He shot her a giant grir
"Well, I guess I'll just have to come back tomorrow."

Her eyes flickered over his shoulders and chest. "Wh
about your job?"

"I generally give myself two days off a week," he saic
"And I'd just as soon spend them doing something to he!
you out."

"You've already done so much..." she began. And, sh
thought, she didn't want to feel indebted to him. It was ba
enough that she'd kissed him the way she had the previot
night, given the fact that she was still very engaged. If th
kept up, she would feel she was setting him up. She did no
want him to expect things from her that she couldn't de
liver. She felt so drawn to him and so comfortable in h
company that the last thing she ever wanted was to see hir
hurt.

His arm swept over the room. "It's no big deal. I like
paint."

"I appreciate it," she said. "I really do." But in the cool
light of day, she knew she couldn't do anything that coul
be construed as leading him on. No matter how good tha
kiss had felt, no matter how good he looked, cramped an
shirtless in a kid's chair, and no matter how kind he was.

"But what?" he asked. "What's the matter?"

"Nothing," she said, rising from the chair. "I had better get back to work." She couldn't help it, but a coldness had crept into her tone where previously it had been warm. "Just let me know what you want for lunch."

Bronson caught her at the stairs. How could her tone change in just a heartbeat? Damn it, he'd seen the way she'd looked at him when she had come downstairs. He grabbed her wrist lightly and turned her to face him. "Why the sudden cold shoulder?"

She realized that he was standing very close to her...close enough that she could smell the sweet masculine scent of his body and feel where the bare skin of his chest was warm from physical labor. And she also realized that she, herself, was backed against the wall.

She felt that way both literally and figuratively. Yes, she wanted Bronson to be her friend, and yes, if she were the least bit honest about it, she wanted even more than that. But not now, today, or at this time in her life.

"Did I do something wrong?"

"No, Bronson," she said. "You didn't do anything wrong." That much was true. He hadn't. It was she who was creating havoc, fooling both him and herself into thinking they could date now.

Suddenly she felt as if she might burst into tears, which was hardly the kind of thing she was prone to do. But it was just too much to take. Only a few weeks before, she'd been happy. Or no, she amended mentally, she hadn't been, but then she hadn't known—hadn't had the faintest of clues—that she was unhappy with her upcoming marriage. Not until she'd met Bronson.

"I—I'm engaged," she said. "You know that."

"And?" he asked. He couldn't bring himself to move back, away from her. Yet again, he thought of how she had kissed him. Even if she was going to marry for money, it didn't mean, couldn't mean, that they should not see one another now. He *had* to see her.

"I'm not looking to get married," he said huskily, his eyes roving over her lowered eyes and her mouth. "After I lost my wife, I pretty much didn't look. I didn't look..." His voice trailed off and he leaned forward, until his forehead touched hers.

Almost against her will, Peachy found her arms moving around Bronson's waist, as if that might somehow help her better explain herself. The skin beneath her fingers felt very warm and smooth and soft. "Do you like confusing me?" she whispered.

He brought his lips close to hers. "If kissing you confuses you," he said, "then yes, I admit it, I do like it. I more than like it."

Before she knew what was happening, his lips were on hers again. The kiss was quick, without preliminaries. There was no grazing of lips, no soft warmup, just a fast and furious kiss. His tongue entered her mouth and the sensation seemed to touch her everywhere at once. Immediately, she pulled him closer, wrapping her arms tightly around his waist.

Time seemed to stop. It felt as if their kiss could go on forever. Peachy wasn't sure how much time was passing, but could only keep her mind fixed on the soft sensations of his lips and the warm spicy coffee taste of his mouth. She fought back a moan when he pressed hard against her and she felt the stirrings of his arousal.

For the brief second that Bronson opened his eyes, he saw Tommy poised at the top of the stairs. Fortunately, one glare sent Tommy packing. Bronson pulled Peachy against him, holding her as tightly as he could, and thrust his lips deeply between hers again. He wasn't about to let go of her now. He wanted her...all of her. And if he couldn't have all, then he wanted everything he could get.

"When you go back to New York, Peachy, I'll let you go. But right now, you're here...and I'm here...and you're in *my* arms." Bronson released her and stepped back.

She blew out a shaky breath. "Just for the time I'm here," she said. "I just don't know—I..."

"No strings," he said, his voice a soft, persuasive drawl.

"I'd have to hold you to that."

"I never break my word," he whispered.

They gazed deep into each other's eyes for a long moment. When Tommy reappeared, Bronson glanced up at him. "Peachy was just coming down to take our orders for lunch." He looked at Peachy again.

"That new Fancy's Fishiest would be good," Tommy said.

"Fancy's Fishiest sounds fine," Bronson said, still staring deeply into her eyes.

"Sounds good," Peachy said, and then headed back upstairs. Bronson watched her go, feeling half-ashamed of himself for pursuing her. He didn't want to confuse her... but he wasn't about to stop seeing her, either.

"We've still got a lot of painting to do," Bronson said, picking up his brush again and reinstating himself on the ladder. With each solid, even stroke, he found himself trying to remember where exactly his hands had been when Tommy had stopped at the door. Had they really been moving downward, toward Peachy's thighs? Or was that just his imagination? And had her fingers just begun to almost dig into the flesh of his lower back? Or was that just his imagination, too?

"Well, Dad, getting that pink paint worked pretty good," said Tommy after a moment. He laughed.

Bronson glanced down. "What?" he asked innocently, noting that Tommy's laugh was nearly a giggle. And he knew his son had quit giggling at about age eleven.

"You sure were going for it."

From his son's assessing look, Bronson might as well have just hopped ten cars on a motorcycle.

"The older you get," Bronson finally said, "the better it gets. And pink paint always helps." He thought briefly of his past marriage, then about Peachy. And he really hoped that older did mean better.

"I guess so," Tommy said. He shot his father a look that could only be construed as envious.

## Chapter Nine

Peachy wondered how she had managed to avoid Bronson through the rest of her shift, only to find herself now, the following day, standing in his office. She'd even let him feed her one of his fabulous, perfectly arranged fruit and cheese plate breakfasts this morning, and he'd shown her his house. It was larger than it looked from the outside, with a special breakfast nook, screened-in back patio, and six extra, spacious bedrooms besides the ones he and Tommy occupied. She smiled now, thinking of the way he'd only paused at the doorway to his own room, as if he hardly trusted himself to take her anywhere near the bed.

The house was so lovely that Peachy had spent much of the tour imagining herself living there with Bronson. And when he was reminded that Peachy had the day-care kids for part of the afternoon, he'd asked Tommy to clean up the paint cans and arrange the day-care furniture, before his shift. Then Bronson suggested that he turn his clinic into a petting zoo for the kids. She'd driven to Fancy's, to pick up the kids, while Bronson readied the barn, but when the kids weren't ready, Bronson had picked her up and taken her to his office. Darrell had said he'd bring the kids out to them later.

"C'mon," he was saying now. "You might as well meet the rest of the family."

Peachy squinted around the office. "You have invisible relatives?" she finally teased. She shot him a wry glance. "And you looked so normal, at first...." She watched him lean back, then sit on the top of his desk, and thought she'd never seen a man fit a pair of Levi's quite the way he did.

He moved his head slowly to the side, as if to survey her from another angle. "Oh, I don't know," he said, smiling. "Having genes for invisibility might come in handy."

"How's that?"

His smile widened to a grin. "You'll just have to come over here to find that out, sugar."

She walked toward him slowly, not taking her eyes from his, but she stopped right before she was in arm's reach. "Here I am," she said lightly, with a toss of her head.

He chuckled. "I don't think you're close enough yet," he said. The playful glints in his eyes deepened so that his eyes seemed to flash.

She took another step. He leaned, grasped her wrist and hauled her into his arms. When she glanced up, it was right into his gaze. "Am I close enough now?" she asked.

He leaned and kissed her lightly on the lips. "No," he said flatly.

She laughed. "I can't get much closer than this," she said.

He was silent for a long moment, his dark gray eyes still probing hers. "Bet you could," he said softly.

She leaned her head back, meaning to ask just how much he'd bet, but she changed her mind. Just the previous day she'd made a promise to herself not to see him and though she knew it was a promise she couldn't keep, she also knew she was only leading him on. "So how does having genes for invisibility come in handy?" she asked instead.

His answering smile looked a little lopsided and full of pure fun. "Why, that means you and I could disappear together, Peaches and cream."

Peachy wished they could. "And just where would we disappear to?"

"I don't know." He flashed her a grin. "You're the girl."

She looked him up and down, and sighed. "Well, some-where isolated..."

"Where we're alone..." he continued agreeably.

"With a shore, rolling surf..."

"But no surfers," Bronson put in.

"Please, no," said Peachy quickly. "But a quiet room, with French doors, billowing white curtains, sunsets all day long, a private masseuse..."

"I can do that," Bronson interjected.

She sighed again, thinking how wonderful it would be to have Bronson rubbing down her back and neck and thighs. "Okay," she said slowly. "And thick carpeting so soft that it feels like grass, no television or telephone." She chuckled. "No *tele* anything. And fresh flowers everywhere..."

"And a bed," Bronson said.

*A bed!* "There goes your male mind again," she teased, trying to keep her tone light, but thinking that it would be so wonderful....

His brows shot up then down again. "You mean you don't want one of those quarter beds that vibrates?"

She slapped his thigh playfully. "No!" she exclaimed.

He crossed his arms over his chest and sighed. "That's the thing about relationships," he said. "There's so much give and take." He scrutinized her face and finally continued. "I'll tell you what. I'll give up the vibrating bed if you promise to wear something lacy and green."

"Green? I thought your male mind would demand black... or maybe sheer white."

He shook his head, smiling his most genuine smile. "No, sugar," he said. "Green's definitely your best color."

"Deal," she said. She smiled, then glanced around the office. The creation of their private room was making her feel too sad to continue with the conversation. "So where's this invisible relative?"

"Whistle," Bronson said.

"What?" Peachy stared at him.

Bronson wiggled his brows. "Whistle."

She stuck her fingers in her mouth and blew.

When she pulled her fingers from her mouth, Bronson shook his head. "I never met a woman who could whistle like that."

"I could teach you how," Peachy said.

"I didn't say I couldn't do it," Bronson teased. "I said I never met a woman who could."

"So can you?"

He chuckled. "No."

"So I'll teach you," she said.

He nodded. "Sometime."

*Sometime. But there weren't going to be many sometimes.* Peachy suddenly felt something nuzzle her leg. When she realized it wasn't one of Bronson's booted calves, she squealed and jumped. Bronson's arms closed around her waist and he drew her close. "I'll protect you," he said. Then he threw his head back and laughed.

She glanced down into the face of the least lethal-looking mutt she'd ever seen. He had a bulldog's face, but watery, earnest-looking eyes.

"Watchdog," Bronson said, by way of introduction.

Peachy leaned and began to pet the dog while Bronson told about the wet, cold night he'd found the stray.

"Well, Watchdog," Bronson said, "this is the woman I've been telling you about. What do you think of her? Does she get the Watchdog stamp of approval?"

Peachy glanced up at Bronson with a wry smile. "He's hardly invisible."

"Well," Bronson said, as if considering, "he was under the desk."

"And it seems like he likes me," she said.

"Oh, he more than likes you," Bronson said, smiling down at her. "In fact, Watchdog says you're just about the prettiest woman he's ever met. Don't you, Watchdog?"

Peachy stood and put her hands on her hips. "Just about?"

Bronson glanced at Watchdog, then back at Peachy. "Oh, all right," he said after a moment, pulling her to him again. "The fairest of them all."

"ARE YOU Dr. Dolittle?" Jed, one of Darrell's sons, asked Bronson.

Peachy half listened to Bronson's teasing response while Brenda Smith, a solidly built seven-year-old with a long, tangled mass of blond curly hair skipped toward her. "Will you hold this? 'Cause I wanna pet Dr. West's lambs," Brenda said. Brenda looked so excited that Peachy wasn't at all surprised when the child suddenly hugged her after handing over a small blue hairbrush.

"Can we look at a horse, for real?" Brenda's equally sturdy brother, Tank, asked.

"Absolutely," said Bronson. "But first take a look around the barn."

Jed Stewart, Peachy thought, seemed the shiest of the children. He moved away from his brother Johnny and came to Peachy, placing his small hand in hers. Peachy squeezed Jed's hand and continued listening to the slow sound of Bronson's voice.

"Now, listen up," he was saying. "The lambs are the only things you can get close to without my help. Go ahead and pet them, if you want. Take a walk around, look at all the animals, but keep a safe distance—"

"Do pigs like to get petted?" Brenda interrupted.

Bronson threw back his head and laughed. Seeing his sheer enjoyment at being in his own environment, with the animals, and seeing how much he liked the kids—Peachy herself smiled.

"Pigs'll tolerate it, anyway," Bronson finally said. "But I'm not sure they exactly like it. However, I do have one spoiled little pig that will go so far as to eat out of your hand."

"Can he eat out of my hand?" Tank asked. "No pig ever ate out of my hand before."

"The he is a she, and yes she will," Bronson said. He glanced up at Peachy and smiled. "Ever feed a pig?"

Peachy shook her head and laughed. "No time in recent history," she said. "Actually, I'm with Tank. No time ever."

Peachy looked away from Bronson and squatted down to meet Jed at eye level. "Do you want me to go with you?"

Jed shook his head. "No."

"Do you want to go with the other kids?" She nodded toward the others who were already walking through the barn and peering inside the stalls and pens. "Mr. West and I are going to stand right here and watch."

Jed looked up into her face. "But I'm *afraid* of lions, Mrs. West," he finally said.

As shocked as she was at being called *Mrs. West,* she let go of that and concentrated on Jed, fighting back the smile that threatened to break through her now serious features. "Jed," she said, "there are no lions. I promise."

Jed stared at her for a long time and his face relaxed at the moment he apparently decided to trust her. "Oh."

"That's right," Bronson said, coming over to lean next to Peachy, against an empty horse stall. "I don't much care for lions, myself. They scare me a little."

"Really?" Jed asked, peering up at Bronson through his overly round brown eyes.

"Really," Bronson said with levity.

With that, Jed was off, following the other three children.

"You mean a tough, rifle-toting fellow like you is afraid of lions?" Peachy teased.

Bronson chuckled and shoved his hands deep into the pockets of his old Levi's. "Not nearly as much as I'm afraid of a tigress like you," he returned.

"Now how could you be afraid of a little old tigress like me?" she countered.

Bronson leaned into her and tugged the sleeve of her Western-style shirt. "Afraid isn't exactly the word, but every time you smile, I keep hoping you'll keep sinking your claws into me.''

She put her arm around his waist and smiled.

"I miss having kids," he said after a moment.

"You have kids," she said, glancing downward. She couldn't help but note that his Levi's, like every pair of jeans he seemed to own, fit snugly and accentuated all the contours of his lower body. "I mean, you have Tommy."

"Yeah," he said. "But the little ones say the damnedest things."

When Bronson had decided to try to spend the day with Peachy, he'd been afraid of pushing her, but now he was only glad to be with her. He let his eyes travel over her clean, white, cotton, Western shirt and jeans. This was one city girl, he thought, who wore country attire as though it had been made to order for her.

He turned and watched Brenda. In her somewhat bossy way, she was now taking the upper hand with Jed and teaching him how to commune with the lambs. Jed's previous bout with fear was apparently gone. He was petting the creatures' heads as if he would never stop.

"Now, don't get too close," Bronson called out to Johnny and Tank who were edging their way almost into the pig pen. "Want kids?" Bronson asked, turning back to Peachy. The moment the question left his mouth, he was sorry he had asked. It was too personal, and from the way she had expressed her confusion about her marriage the previous day, it was clear her engagement was serious. She was going back to New York, all right. "I mean, with your husband," Bronson qualified.

Peachy laughed. "Just who else would I have them with?"

"Me?" He flashed her a grin. When she looked a little shocked, he quickly said, "The handyman?" He watched as she raised her eyebrows, as if considering that proposition.

Staring into Bronson's face, Peachy recalled that that was exactly what she'd thought Bronson was when she'd first seen him. She thought about herself and Wellington, living together as parents. They'd discussed children, of course, assumed they'd have them, but beyond that she had no idea how actually living it through would feel. Perhaps it would be like living in the country had been for Bronson's wife, something that was better in theory than in fact.

"Still thinking about that handyman?" Bronson's flirtatious mode was something he just couldn't tamp down when he was around her. "Or are you just trying to make me jealous?"

She shot him a sideways glance. "I wasn't trying, but of course, I'm glad I did. Well," she continued, deciding to shift the course of the discussion, "I wouldn't wish *my* childhood on anyone."

He nodded in agreement. "I'd do things differently. I mean, I've done them differently from my parents already, and learned new things from raising Tommy." He dropped his arm casually over her shoulder. "What would you change?"

She thought for a long time, considering the many lessons that had been forced on her, even when she hadn't enjoyed them or wasn't good at the activity. It was a luxury problem to be sure, but a kid, she thought, should have more leeway to make her own decisions. If that had been the case with her, she realized, she might not be in the bind she was now.

"First, I think it's extremely important to let kids make their own mistakes, no matter how hard it is to do."

"Not my best suit," he said. "But in theory, I agree."

Suddenly, she laughed and Bronson found himself listening to the soft rise and fall of her voice. Her voice, he thought, was beautifully deep and had a ringing melodious quality to it. There was no cynicism or bitterness in it. It was as free and easy as the wind, and he liked hearing it.

"Little Princess School, for two," she finally said. "Little Princess School sums up everything I most disliked about my own childhood, especially the constant control exerted from my mother's corner. And that I always had to act so perfectly prissy."

"Little Princess School?" Anything called "Little Princess School" was bound to be a nightmare. He forced his attention away from her alluring face, checked the children, and then gazed back into her eyes.

"Yep. Every Saturday at Bergdorf Goodman. We—myself and all the other little princesses, who were about five—learned to walk, talk and act like regular ladies. We had fake lipsticks to work with, fake blushers and eye shadows. We had pocketbooks, wore white gloves and participated in posture classes.

"In the event of our future dates—and we were given to understand that we would have many—we learned to place our faux luggage on faux overhead luggage racks, so that when we were older and taking train rides to rendezvous with beaus in the Hamptons, we could deposit said bags overhead with extreme grace and absolutely no slumping. We had—"

"I get the picture," Bronson cut in, laughing. "And this doctor senses you still harbor a great deal of resentment."

"I thought you were a vet, not a psychiatrist, but I certainly have to admit that I'm repressing anger," Peachy said, feeling glad that Bronson was never going to meet her mother. The perfectly coiffed, manicured, waxed and wrapped Petulia was the living incarnation of pure femininity, at least as Petulia herself understood it.

Bronson, as mannerly as he was and as successful, had a physical presence and sexual energy that would give Petulia a real case of nerves. Peachy could almost see Bronson giving her mother one of his slow, lazy, even-toothed smiles and Petulia crumpling in a faint.

"When I was twenty," Bronson said, "I wanted to have six kids. That was my goal. And you'll be pleased to know that not one was to be scheduled to attend Little Princess School."

"Six?" Peachy watched their four charges who were now huddled together around the pig pen. She tried to imagine herself as a mother of six—or even four, as that's how many were present at the moment—and found she rather liked the idea of a big, warm, familial bunch of kids.

Kids always took to her and she herself had the kind of childish bent that allowed her to play with them on their level. Still, six was quite a lot. Nobody seemed to have families that large nowadays. "Do you just not believe in birth control or what?" she finally teased, cutting off her reverie.

Bronson grinned. "Generally I do, but in the heat of the moment . . ." He let his voice trail off, becoming as low and sexy as he could make it. He wondered yet again at how Peachy brought out his more rakish side. "In the heat of the moment, you just never know what might happen," he continued, drawing her closer.

"I have a pretty good idea," she managed, feeling her throat go dry.

He leaned so that his face was poised just above hers. "But ideas are nothing next to reality," he whispered huskily.

"Sometimes ideas are better," she said lightly. She tried to toss her head, but it only nuzzled into Bronson's shoulder.

"You think fantasies are better than realities?" he asked.

She shrugged. "Sometimes."

His smile widened and his eyes narrowed in a dare-you look. "Only in your past life, sugar," he said.

Peachy rolled her eyes, trying to ignore the implication that the reality of being with Bronson would more than fulfill her fantasies . . . and trying to ignore his hint, however subtle, that her fiancé didn't measure up. *Which he didn't.* "You're a shameless flirt," she finally managed. "Do you know that?"

Bronson laughed. "Yeah. Isn't it endearing?"

She smiled. "Sort of. You really want six kids?"

"Wanted," he qualified, then shrugged, wondering if he still had the same dreams now or *would* have if he found the right woman to share them with. "I've got eight bedrooms. One's mine, one's Tommy's. I've got six empty. It's completely logical. Six bedrooms besides mine and Tommy's equals six more kids. It has always made perfect sense to me. Besides, I grew up in a big family."

"You said that before."

He raised his brows in question.

She paused before responding to his glance. "When we were driving in the fog." Remembering that night, half of her wanted to relive it, and the other half wanted to curse it. And, she thought, the half that wanted to curse it was probably her better if not her more practical and cautious half.

After all, it was that night that Bronson's feelings toward her had clearly changed. And hers for him. That night had changed everything and now she had no idea where she was going. She only knew that unless she called off her wedding, she was going nowhere truly special. Unless she destroyed her father business-wise, she was headed for a life of second best.

"Of course, having all those kids wouldn't be nearly as fun as making them," Bronson was saying.

"Bronson—" she began, ignoring his teasing remarks.

"Yes?" His eyes fixed on hers. He had to fight not to reach out and touch her. As old hat as it was, nothing got him more than a woman dressed in a white blouse and jeans. Except, he mentally amended, when they dressed in particularly slinky black dresses. Or in a green lace underwear set, which was something he could only imagine.

"Yeah, sugar?" he prompted again.

She had started to bring up her engagement. Looking into his face now, she wanted to explain the situation to him fully, in a way that would make him really understand. At any other time, she would have more than welcomed his courtship. In another place and time she would have been able to give herself to him completely.

They were dating, plain and simple. They were standing in a barn, with their baby-sitting charges, talking about whether or not they wanted kids of their own. She had started to say all those things but had then decided it wasn't the right time. Was it really the fact that the children were here now that made the topic inappropriate? she asked herself. Or was it because she was afraid Bronson would take her words to heart and that she wouldn't see him again?

"You were going to say something?"

"It was nothing," she said. "Maybe we better join the kids. They look like they're about ready for the pig-petting segment of our tour." She smiled. "I'm kind of anxious to feed a pig myself."

"About dinner—" he said as they began to walk toward the children.

"Dinner?"

"You promised yesterday that you'd cook me dinner," he reminded.

He *would* remember that, she thought, wondering if she could manage to have a meal catered without getting caught. "Yes?"

He flashed her a wide grin. "I like ham," he said.

They had reached the pig pen and she couldn't help but say, "I hope not this one."

Bronson laughed, but otherwise didn't respond. He was already concentrating on doling out handfuls of pellet-like food. Watching the children's four pairs of glittering, excited eyes fix on Bronson, Peachy found herself wondering again about her future children. If there were any, that was.

She looked at Jed's small, lithe build and then at Tank, who was appropriately named, and then at Brenda's bright pink cheeks and pursed lips. Johnny, she noted, had the same huge dark brown eyes that belonged to his brother. And to Darrell, for that matter.

It certainly wasn't her usual line of thought, but she indulged herself for a moment. What would her children look like? What would their various interests be? It was difficult to imagine.

Suddenly she got a clear picture of a son in her mind's eye. And she wondered where in the world the vision of that little boy had come from—a little boy who liked to fish and play ball with his dog—and then she realized that the boy she was imagining wasn't blond and blue-eyed like Wellington, or even redheaded and blue-eyed as she was. And he didn't give a hoot about hot dogs, except for the fact that they were his favorite food.

That little boy was dark, with soft, glossy-black hair and a set of very gray, perceptive-seeming slate eyes. He was, to the T, the spitting image of Bronson.

'ARE WE AT Fancy's?'' Tank asked when Peachy gently nudged him from sleep. He was curled up in the back seat, with his head on Brenda's shoulder.

"I lost my jacket," Johnny said. "It's yellow with a Batman bat."

"Nope," Bronson said. "It's right here." He handed the jacket over the seat to Johnny.

"I think we managed to wear them out," Bronson remarked as he and Peachy helped the kids down from the Blazer and onto the sun-warmed concrete of the parking lot. They might be tired, he thought, but he felt invigorated. It had been years since he'd entertained a group of grade-schoolers and certainly as long since he'd done so in the company of a woman.

"It *was* some outing," she said, smiling back. "It must be about three. Tommy should already be hard at work on the very first shift of his life. Want to give him a hard time and then split a burger?"

"What about some real cuisine?"

Peachy found herself nodding agreeably, even though she'd done nothing but tell herself to back away from

Bronson for the past twenty-four hours. Or was it forty-eight? Or, she thought, had it really been weeks now? It was simply the wrong time for her to be with this man. Nonetheless, she didn't quit nodding.

If she weren't so attracted to him, it would be a different story. Then, she thought, there would be less confusion. Not only on her side, but on his, as well. Lord knew, she did want just another taste of the passion that had begun. Not to mention the fact that once she was past his more irascible nature, he was easy to be with. The time they'd spent with the kids had flown by as if it were mere minutes rather than the better part of an afternoon. But exactly how much could she take of his arms around her, of his mouth on hers, or even only of his company, without having an even deeper confusion set in?

Bronson rested his hands lightly on Brenda's and Tank's shoulders, marshaling them toward the squeaky-clean double doors of Fancy's. He noted the simple, natural way that Peachy moved her own charges; she held Johnny's and Jed's hands and walked at their pace. Bronson glanced around for Tommy when they reached the doors, but didn't see him anywhere. He realized that he was looking forward to seeing his son in his uniform and hard at paying work.

"Wonder where Tommy is?" Peachy asked. "He should be on his shift. It's too early for a break."

Darrell, Melissa and Jane were seated in a booth, waiting for their children.

"Oh, no!" Peachy exclaimed as she approached with Bronson and the kids. "I'm sorry we're late. We were just having such a great time...."

The three all looked toward Bronson with guarded expressions.

"It's only been an extra three minutes," Darrell said.

And it was clear, Bronson thought, from the way he said it that there was other news. Bad news.

Darrell caught Jed and Johnny in his arms when they ran up to embrace him. "Might as well just tell you straight ut," Darrell said, looking at Bronson. "Tommy had a car wreck."

Bronson's pulse raced. His mouth went fully dry and dropped, as if someone had just given him a gut-level blow. 'Oh, my God," he said.

"He's okay," Darrell said quickly, putting a hand on Bronson's arm to stop him from running out the door. "Just bruised up. But he went over to Children's Hospital."

"What?" How could he, Bronson, have been having such a good time? All while his only child was in danger... mortal danger. What kind of a father was he?

Peachy was too shocked to move. "Just bruised?" she asked Darrell. "Are you sure he's okay?"

"Children's Hospital," Bronson said gruffly.

His whole shocked body went into action at once. He turned on his heel, bolted back through the double doors, and across the parking lot.

"I'm coming with you," Peachy yelled, running after Bronson.

He half heard, but wasn't about to wait for anyone. He jumped in the Blazer and gunned the motor. Then he sped through the lot with his hand on the horn.

"Oh, my God," Peachy whispered, jumping in her convertible. She, too, sped out, trying her best to keep on Bronson's tail. She had no idea where exactly Children's Hospital was located. And, she thought, if Bronson didn't stop weaving through traffic, the two of them were bound to have wrecks, as well. She tried to concentrate fully on the signs, lights and other cars, but she was too scared.

She had a horrible, heart-wrenching gut feeling that she couldn't squelch. Why hadn't Bronson waited for her? Darrell had said Tommy was fine, and Peachy believed him, but how could Bronson want to face something like this on his own, without a friend for support? What if Tommy wasn't fine? And his own wife had died in a car wreck. Undoubtedly, that was what was running through the man's mind now.

Bronson was halfway to the hospital before he was even totally cognizant of the fact that he'd really put the keys in the ignition and turned them. Now, he half registered the fact that Helena's old convertible was in the traffic behind him. A jolt of anger went through him. Peachy Lofton was the last person he wanted to see. If she hadn't pressured him with her damnable attractiveness, and worked out a payment plan and gotten Tommy a job, none of this would be happening. Not to mention the fact that she'd upset his own damn life! What was he going to do when she got married? Couldn't she just leave him alone now? Let him find out what had happened, let him process it and let him recover his cool?

Jets of black air pushed from Bronson's exhaust pipe and Peachy was now close enough to see them. "Please, Bronson," she whispered. "Slow down." She hit her horn, passed yet another car, and just made it through an intersection on a yellow light. She wanted to be there for him now, no matter what might happen in the future.

Bronson sped right through a light, looking both ways with lightning speed. Glancing in the rearview mirror, he found himself wishing he'd lose Peachy in the traffic. He was blaming her, even though he knew there was absolutely no logic in it. But the thought had crossed his mind that if something happened to Tommy, she was all he had left. *And she wasn't even his.*

The tall glass-and-steel hospital complex came into sight. He sped toward the lot nearest the emergency entrance. It had never taken so long to get a ticket from an electronic box. It seemed like full years passed before the yellow wooden guardrail lifted so that the Blazer could enter the parking area.

He gunned the motor again and drove toward the emergency doors. As a vet, he was accustomed to sickness, accidents and grief, but it was sure different, he thought as he threw the gear into park and ran toward the doors, when it wasn't an animal, but a person. And it was very different when that person was *his* own only son.

Peachy watched Bronson disappear through the doors. She took the nearest parking space she could find and followed.

"It's a good thing I came," she muttered to herself when she realized that Bronson had only haphazardly parked the Blazer. He'd turned off the motor, but he'd left his keys in the ignition. She got in and drove around the crowded lot twice before finding a space for him that was fairly near the doors.

Inside, Bronson found himself swimming through red tape. "Tommy," he repeated to the duty nurse. "Tommy West. He was in a car accident." Couldn't the nurse check through her files any faster? Even though Bronson knew she was busy and that the waiting areas were all crowded, he still couldn't stop his impatient anger. Where in the world was his son?

He glanced over his shoulder, half-expecting to see Peachy materialize. He had absolutely no idea what he wanted to say to her. All he knew was that his anger was slowly moving out of control.

"Four-thirteen. Down the hall to your right."

"Thanks," he said, feeling suddenly washed out and numb.

"Bronson!"

It was Peachy. Bronson half turned and then simply continued walking.

"Wait, Bronson," she called. She wondered if he'd heard her. He was moving quickly down the hallway. He must not have heard her. Otherwise he would have waited. She jogged after him. When she was just a few steps behind, she said, 'I did my best to follow. And I parked the Blazer. I've got the keys.'

He turned into Room 413, his mouth going full dry again. Whether he wanted to admit it or not, he expected band-

ages and IVs. He didn't expect to see Tommy grinning an
pulling on his leather jacket.

Before he could even stop himself, Bronson said, "Wip
that smile off your face."

"Are you okay?" Peachy leaned against the doorjamb
hoping Bronson's angry words didn't mean a fight of som
sort was imminent. There was no need for it. Tommy, as fa
as she could see, looked right as rain. She started to ask
more specifically, what had happened, but Bronson sent he
a glance that stopped her cold. For the first time, she real
ized that he wasn't just angry, he was furious.

Tommy looked at Peachy. "I had to run home and I wa
on my way back into Fancy's lot. This guy ran a stop sign
He completely bashed in my left headlight." He shrugged
"It was basically just a fender bender, but my arm hit th
dash pretty hard, so I figured I better get it X-rayed befor
my shift."

"Why'd you have to go home?" Peachy asked. "
thought you were going to arrange the toys in the day car
and then just change and work your shift."

Tommy grinned at Peachy sheepishly. "Forgot my uni
form."

"Forgot your uniform?" Bronson leaned against the wal
and crossed his arms. He had been half-afraid to open hi
mouth a second time because he was just about to th
breaking point. He was sure he was going to blow in a wa
he would regret, in a way that nobody would want to forge
or forgive. "So you forgot your uniform and drove out in
hurry without, I suppose, watching where—"

"Dad," Tommy cut in, "*I* didn't run the damn sto
sign."

"You should have seen—"

"Dad, I know what you're saying, but I looked. There'
a trash bin—one of those big green numbers—at that inter
section and—"

"And nothing," Bronson said flatly.

"Fine," Tommy said. He stuck his hands deep into the pockets of his jacket. "Argue all you want, but I've now been pronounced fine, and I have to get to work. It's my first day and I'm late."

"You can't go to work, you just had a car—"

"Oh, but I am," Tommy said.

Peachy knew this was between Tommy and his father and she wasn't about to intervene, but the accident was clearly not Tommy's fault and she knew good and well that Bronson's anger came straight from his own guilt and his love for his son. The two were glaring at one another.

"Look," Peachy said. "I know the intersection Tommy's talking about—"

"I didn't ask you to follow me, sugar," Bronson said.

Peachy tried to stop her jaw from dropping without much success. "I'm just trying to help!"

In the past, she had felt the warm, slow, soft, assessing gaze of his oh-so-gray eyes, but now she knew exactly how it felt to have that gaze turn on her. His eyes were flashing and yet they were stony and cool. Cold, in fact. So cold that she almost felt the temperature in the room drop.

"Don't you think you've done enough damage?" Bronson asked. "And you're leaving here, anyway. Remember?"

Peachy clamped her mouth shut tight. "Maybe I am leaving," she finally said. "But if you hold the reins too tight, you'll lose the people who aren't...the ones you most love. Mark my words."

*But she was the one he could love most. With each passing day, he was more and more sure of it.*

Tommy brushed past her with a nod and headed through the door.

"Sorry," she said. "But things happen and this is just not my fault."

She reached into her pocket and tossed the Blazer keys onto the examining table. Tears welled up in her eyes, but she turned on her heel and left.

In the hall, she had to fight not to look over her shou der. She wished he would follow. That, at least, would l her know that he cared. But he hadn't even moved, hadn't even bothered to say goodbye, and he was not fo lowing her now. In Helena's car, she sat idly behind th wheel for a moment.

Oh, why did his hardheaded, cold unreasonableness ha to hurt her so much? she wondered. It was the defini downside to his strong personality. When she'd first m him, on his porch, those qualities had irked her, to be sur But now they seemed intolerable. How could they have future if he blamed her when things went wrong? Thinki that, she realized she *had* begun to imagine their future. Ar simultaneously, she was just as sure that there wasn't goir to be one.

# WEEK FOUR

## Coming to me...

## Chapter Ten

"I'm a damn fool, Watchdog," Bronson said. "It's been exactly twenty-one hours since I made a complete idiot of myself."

Watchdog didn't even wake up. He only rolled onto his back. "So I'm falling—or already fallen—for Peachy Lofton," Bronson continued. "And, Watchdog, I'm falling hard. I've got half a mind to try and convince her to elope in timely fashion. By the time her fiancé finds her, she'll already be married." Bronson smirked in Watchdog's direction. "Maybe even with child."

He seated himself at the swivel chair behind his desk, unbuttoned his lab coat, leaned back in his chair, put his feet up on the corner of his desk, then stared long moments at his own pointy-toed boots.

"Poor Watchdog," he muttered. "And poor me." He sighed. "Have I really been reduced to this? Unable to work, and talking to a mutt. And all because of a spat with a woman."

But it wasn't just any woman, it was Peachy Lofton. And it wasn't a silly spat, he told himself, no matter how much he might want to try to belittle the incident at the hospital. "From day one, I've been chasing her," he muttered. "And from day one, I've been pushing her away just as hard."

He stared through the squeaky-clean windows of his office and out into the brilliant late May sunshine and the soft

subtle shadows that moved in the leaves of the trees. "Now
Watchdog, what am I supposed to do? I'm not exactly ready
to propose. Hell, I've never even had the extreme pleasure
of making love to her."

He sighed, thinking of her warm, soft body, of the way it
pushed against his and yet yielded. Well, he thought wryly,
he very much doubted there'd be any kind of difficulty
whatsoever in that department. But he could hardly ask her
to call off her engagement so he could have time to see if he
wanted to propose. Could he?

"Well, there's only one way to correct this situation...
Are you even listening to me, Watchdog?" Watchdog
opened his eyes and barked. "That's right, buddy, I know
what I have to do."

Bronson stood, stretched his legs, and went out to the
front reception area. "Jilly?"

"Yeah?" His assistant glanced up from her place behind
the front desk.

"Would you mind canceling my appointments, today?"
he asked, knowing if Peachy understood how difficult it was
to raise a son that she'd forgive him.

His assistant's mouth dropped. "You're not sick, are
you?"

"Yeah," he said. "Lovesick."

WHY HADN'T SHE had the common sense to have sons? Petulia paced the thick carpeting of the plush, lower Manhattan office, waiting for her husband. He was to have lunch
with her and Christine. They were to meet Wellington at
Tavern on the Green.

"Coffee?" Petulia gracefully moved behind her husband's desk and poured herself a cup from a silver tea service.

"No, thank you." Christine rifled through papers in a file
on her lap. "According to this, Helena Lofton didn't RSVP
for the wedding reception. Who's she?"

"An absolute nightmare," Petulia said. "She and her husband became survivalist or something, in West Virginia, of all places. Can you imagine? We had to invite her, and I am not at all surprised she didn't have the decency to respond. She's only a Lofton by marriage."

"You're only a Lofton by marriage," Christine pointed out.

Petulia would have given Christine a small piece of her mind for that remark had her eyes not landed on a closed folder on her husband's desk. It was marked Confidential in bold red letters. Petulia opened it without hesitation.

At first the information hardly seemed interesting. The file contained sales information about activity in the West Virginia Fancy's over the past few weeks. Apparently there had been an unprecedented rise in profits. Her husband, she saw, was scheduled to fly down to find out why.

Petulia shrugged and almost closed the file. But her eyes ran down the list of employees and there she saw what she had been seeking for weeks. It was right there, in bold black and white. Unconcealed and clear as the day was long.

"Peachy—our long lost bride—is working at Fancy's," Petulia said.

"What?" Christine looked at her mother in disbelief. Then her jaw dropped another notch. "You're quite serious, aren't you?"

"Quite," Petulia said wryly. "And as mad as it sounds, I'll wager your runaway sister is staying with Helena Lofton."

"You'd think Peachy would at least insist that Helena Lofton RSVP, then," Christine said with irony. "After all, it's supposed to be her wedding. Unless, of course, after all the dances, parties, showers and note-writing, you expect me to stand in for her at the altar, as well?"

"Please do not plague me," Petulia said. "I'll see your sister in the aisle of Saint Patrick's if I have to—"

"Sorry I'm late!" Charles Lofton exclaimed, sweeping into his office. "How could I keep the two most beautiful women in the world waiting?'' He released a long breath and straightened his tie. ''I'm so sorry Peachy couldn' make it. I'm sure Wellington will be, too. She's had so many silly appointments lately! I know how important it is for her to look her best, but she has never cared so much about her hair and nails as she does now. Well, I suppose that's the way women are when they're in love....''

Charles stopped his rambling and glanced from Petulia to Christine and back to Petulia again. ''Is something happening that I should know about?''

Petulia stared at her husband a long time. Still behind his desk, she placed both her hands wide apart on the smooth mahogany surface and leaned forward. ''I'm sure you're aware of the trip you're to take to West Virginia?''

''Yes, dear,'' he said, seemingly perplexed.

''Well, you're not going.'' Petulia drew herself up to full stature. ''I am.'' She glanced down at her tailored suit. She supposed it would have to do. ''Today.''

''Now?'' her husband asked incredulously.

''Right now,'' she said, as if correcting him. Petulia headed straight for the door. Over her shoulder, she called, ''Enjoy the Tavern, as always, dear. And, Christine, please entertain Wellington to the best of your charming abilities.''

''That part of things is delightful, at least,'' Christine muttered.

Her tone with her husband had been pleasant, if a little cryptic, Petulia thought once she was in the hallway. But there was no mystery at all about what she was going to do when she found Peachy. She was going to haul her right back home and into that wedding dress, where she belonged. Working at Fancy Foods! How utterly shocking!

PEACHY WEIGHED one of Helena's vases in her hand, having every intention of breaking it against the far wall. *Don't be so immature.* She set down the vase and ran her hand over the tabletop, looking for something less lethal to throw.

The meditation book...the one she'd carried from New York to facilitate a peaceful attitude. "Meditate," she muttered. "All I've meditated on is Bronson West."

She picked up the book and heaved it through the open window with all her might. "I hate you," she yelled at the top of her lungs. The book wasn't even satisfying, she thought angrily. She wanted to hear something break.

She suddenly blinked. The book came flying back through the window. It landed with a dull thud on the floor. And then a soft voice called, "Just who do you hate, sugar?"

She went to the window, leaned out, and said, "You." As soon as she'd said it, she wanted to take the words back. He had an armful of long-stemmed white roses, even if he was holding them the way a mechanic might hold a wrench.

"Sorry, I'm just not musically inclined," Bronson continued through the open window. "Otherwise, I'd serenade an apology. But since I don't own a violin, why don't you put on your cute rubber boots and come out to play?"

She couldn't take her eyes off him. He was stripped to the waist, wearing yet another pair of those tight, well-worn jeans, and otherwise only a pair of boots and canvas gloves. A lightweight rope was coiled over his shoulder, Indiana Jones-style. He held a pair of miner's coveralls over his arm and two hard hats equipped with clip-on lights were on the ground. And then there were the flowers...white roses...her favorite.

More than anything, she wanted to tell him to leave her alone. If only she could do that, then she could just forget him, marry Wellington, make her family happy and get on with her own life and career. But she found herself tugging on high-topped rubber boots over her jeans, while he came inside to put the flowers in the vase that she'd nearly shattered to pieces.

"Come along, dear," he said in a mock-serious tone, hustling her out the door, across the yard and toward the woods. "By the look of uncertainty on your face, I'm getting the impression that you might not want to see me right now, but I'm going to try to convince you otherwise.

"See, I figure if I can just get you moving before you have a chance to unleash your anger, then maybe we can spend a glorious day together. And while we walk," he said hurriedly, "put on these wool sweaters." He shoved two sweaters into her arms and put a third on himself.

"What are we doing?" she asked, even as she pulled on the clothes. "It's too warm for these." Not to mention the fact that she would look ridiculous. The sweaters were old, mildewy-smelling and moth-eaten.

"Here," he suddenly said when they'd gone a ways. He stopped to grin at her. For the first time he allowed himself to come to a standstill and really look at her. "How do you manage to look so good, even in mismatched striped and plaid sweaters and muddy, oversize boots? You look even better in these than in a polyester uniform."

"I really don't know," Peachy muttered. She felt herself being half manhandled into a pair of clean coveralls. She realized the fabric had the outdoorsy, masculine scent that she had come to associate with Bronson. "You're crazy," she said when they were both in the odd getups. "Aren't you even going to tell me where we're going?"

Peachy half smiled when he only ignored her and strapped a hard hat to her head. He obviously had some adventure up his sleeve. "Don't you know you were kind of mean yesterday?" she ventured. "Aren't you even going to apologize?"

"Only when we're deep in this cave," he said, shooting her a wicked grin. She watched as he unscrewed one of the lamps he had brought. He placed dark pellets in the bottom half and filled the top half with water from a canteen. "Carbide," he explained, screwing the two parts of the lamp back together.

"Most people use electric lights now. These are old. I've had them since I was a kid." He adjusted the lamp so that water dripped into the carbide. A flame spurted outward from inside a reflector on top of the lamp. He clipped the lamp to her hard hat, then pointed to the hillside. "You're set, sugar," he said. "Go on in."

"Cave?" she finally managed.

"Sure," he said. "Didn't Helena tell you that this is limestone country? And where there's limestone, there're caves."

Certainly he wasn't pointing to the rocky sliver of a crack in the boulders in the grassy hill? If so, he really was crazy. She went toward the crack and once next to it could feel a cool rush of air. She sensed Bronson behind her and felt the length of his body press against her. "I can't fit through there!" She backed out, but only ran up against the solid, rock-hard wall of his body again.

"This is just the entrance," he said. "The cave opens out once you get farther inside. I'm right behind you. Don't worry."

"What's the rope for?"

"Just in case," he said.

That was hardly comforting, she thought. And given the fact that his proximity made her mouth go dry against her will, Peachy couldn't help but worry. But if she backed out, she was backing right into his tough, muscular, lean form. Suddenly she scurried forward, pressed now between two rocky walls. "Just *when* does this open out?"

"Soon," he said. "When you've gone in a little deeper."

"How deep?" she repeated, exasperated.

He chuckled, his voice low and throaty and very close by. "As deep as you want to go."

She was suddenly glad for the cool, dark dampness. Bronson, at least, wouldn't see her flush. In front of her, in the flickering flames from their lamps, she could still only see rock. She and Bronson were still moving side by side, flattened in the passageway.

"I bet no one's been in here for years," he remarked.

"Probably not many have the body for it," she said, wondering how Bronson managed to fit in the space. She was petite, but he was tall, with broad shoulders.

Angled next to her, Bronson had half a mind to tell her that spelunking wasn't all she had the body for. And he realized now, with her so close, that he'd forgotten how it felt to be deep in the earth, without much light, with a little fear pumping up his blood, and with another person. It was especially exciting when the person was one who sent his heart racing, even in the most mundane of environments. Perhaps, he thought, letting go of a sigh, bringing her here wasn't the best of ideas. "Are you doing okay, Peach?"

"I'm fine," she said. With relief, she saw that the space was widening now, so that the two could walk side by side, even if the rocky ceiling was becoming lower.

She glanced at Bronson, who was now beside her. Their faces were only inches apart and the tongue of flame from her lamp sent shadows moving across the angular planes of his face. How could it be so bright outside and so incredibly dark in here? She started to get that odd, otherworldly feeling she had gotten that night in the fog. Again, it seemed as if they were the only two people in the world.

West Virginia, she thought, with its fogs and caves and deep rustling woods, had a magical effect on her. And Bronson, as a part of this strange world, affected her like a sorcerer. "I can barely stand up," she said, ducking as the ceiling became even lower.

"I forgot to mention that there's also a very short—and I repeat, *very* short—belly crawl coming up."

She turned and looked at him in horror. "What?"

He shot her a grin, even though he was feeling a little cramped. Already he had bent his tall frame to nearly double. He took advantage of the dim light to scan the contours of her figure even though they were barely visible beneath the bulk of the heavy clothes. "I'll go first, if you like," he said.

"Please do," she said wryly, watching as he now flattened to his stomach.

She followed suit, but the passageway became tight again. Ahead, she could hear his heavy breathing. He was moving rocks aside, to make the going easier. She wondered just what in the world he had gotten her into, and yet the sheer physical exertion sent a thrill through her. She had to admit that the cool darkness was exciting.

The ground beneath her was cold and hard. It was as solid as Bronson's own body felt when against her. She shimmied too far too fast, and now found herself nearly between his moving legs. "Sorry," she said.

"No problem."

She backed away from his slightly splayed legs. Most of his weight rested on his knees and he dug the toes of his boots into the soil for traction. Watching his muscles work beneath the coveralls, she felt her pulse throb in her throat.

"I feel a little claustrophobic," she said. She told herself it was only the cave. The tight, moist, rock and mud-mossy walls were affecting her. So was the musty scent of earth that rose to her nostrils, smelling pungent and elemental. It was just the exciting rush of trying a new activity.

"We're here," he said.

His feet disappeared completely and for a moment she felt pure panic. Then she found herself in a large, cavernous, rocky room. "Wow," she said.

"Pretty neat, huh?" His eyes searched her face and then he smiled. A pile of rocks were in a corner of the cave and he seated himself on a large flat one. "Couldn't let you run off and get married before you had a good look at a West Virginia cave," he said with more jovial good humor than he really felt about that matter.

"What about bats?" she asked, stretching her legs and walking upright for the first time in what seemed like forever. She leaned against the cave wall.

He pointed to a space right by where she leaned and she turned but saw nothing.

"That round furry thing on the wall," he said.

She stared again. There was such a thing, but it looked like an oversize burr. She continued staring, long and hard then jumped back, a shiver running up her spine. The creature's wings were folded beneath it.

"They don't always hang from their ankles, you know."

His voice sounded calm to Peachy. It was slow and seductive-sounding. And it was right by her ear. In her preoccupation with the bat, she hadn't heard Bronson move.

If the bat had sent adrenaline coursing through her veins it was nothing compared to the effect of Bronson's voice o the effect of his hands when they encircled her waist. "I'm sorry I was so out of line yesterday," he said, not raising the soft sexy tone of his voice one decibel.

"That's all right," she said, moving from the circle of his arms. She turned and looked at him only to find that he was staring at her. God, was he staring at her! He immediately started, then dropped his gaze, but he'd been looking at her from the gray depths of his eyes with an intensity that almost frightened her. Feeling a little weak-kneed, she moved toward the flat rock where he had previously seated himself. Beneath her, the cold stone felt comforting. It felt solid and real, over and against the dizzying feeling she got when she looked at Bronson too long.

He seated himself next to her and couldn't help but note that the spark of desire was in her eyes. The lamps on their helmets sent out tiny sputtering jolts of flame. Her profile looked sharp and distinct to him; the curvature of her neck and the softness of her lips were near. "So what do you think of my secret cave?" he managed, looking at one of her long arms. It rested on her knee and dangled freely, nearly touching his thigh.

"It's amazing in here," she said. Still, it was difficult to hold casual conversation. Feeling his nearness, she thought for a moment that she wouldn't be able to continue breathing. She felt her chest constrict and caught her breath in an audible inhalation. She stood abruptly.

He stood, as well. Suddenly he laughed. "You've got a streak of dirt on your face."

She smiled and shrugged. Dirty or not, she had a clean, earthy feeling.

He pulled off one of his canvas gloves and slapped it hard against his thigh.

"Guess I better try to get it off," she said. As she reached up, attempting to locate the smudge on her own face, he caught her wrist. He moved to wipe away the mud streak but his fingers didn't reach their mark. She could feel the pulse point on the wrist he held beating wildly out of control.

It was his lips moving toward her mouth, not his hand, and before his mouth could even touch hers, she moaned. It wasn't a gasp for breath, and Bronson seemed to sense that. He stopped, as if teasing her, letting his lips only hover above hers. Waiting, she felt as though she were suspended in space, just floating.

"What is it that you do to me?" she whispered. Her own voice seemed like something outside herself and the words she uttered did not seem like her own. It was not the kind of thing she generally said to men. But then, things had changed, hadn't they? Bronson had changed everything.

"It's so primitive here, don't you think?" he whispered, leaning closer, over the inches that separated them. Oh, he thought, to have her here, deep in this cave, next to the elements and next to the earth, with the fire of their lanterns flickering in the hearty air and with the breeze tunneling past them. His tongue flickered between her lips.

She fought her impulse to gasp. Like the carbide flames, his tongue moved quickly, sending hot jolts through her body.

Why did this woman ignite his deepest desire? His lips explored hers slowly now, but he could feel want well up in him, almost like a physical hunger.

She felt him, moving her body, as if it were nothing, as if it were as light as a wisp of cloth, and she allowed herself to lean back. She no longer felt the hard solidity of the rocks behind her, but only the sweet softness of his lips. His tongue never left hers and she felt her own response rising, her mouth moving with equal force.

When she felt him draw back from her, she realized she didn't want him to move. She didn't want this kiss to end, not now, not yet. But he only led her gently toward the flat rock. Then the strength in his arms and his kiss drove her backward, until she was lying down. Even if she had wanted to escape, there was nowhere to go. She could only give herself over to her ever deepening feelings for him when he lay on top of her. Through the thin, worn jeans, she felt his arousal pressed against her. His hands slid between their two bodies, unzipped her coveralls, then moved beneath the layers of wool.

"I can't believe what you do to me, either," he whispered in the instant his mouth left hers. He sank his teeth lightly into her lower lip, meaning to stop any words. Then his tongue found hers, meaning to stop all thought.

Moving his cold hands over her bare skin, feeling the heat there warm him, he felt as if he were in some amazing place where he had never been before. He felt as if he were at the very core of the earth's center. He thought of stopping, to remove her hard hat. Her lamp's flame had been extinguished in their tussle and the hat only kept him from moving his hands through the luxurious softness of her hair. But he could not stop to remove the hat, not when his hands were already on the softness of her breasts.

"Oh, Bronson," she whispered. He had quit kissing her, she realized now. His lips still touched hers, but only barely. He moaned, his thumb and fingers touching her nipples with a pressure that sent heat down through her whole body only to soar back upward with a fast new rush of desire. His touches sent her hands flying downward, over his back, his buttocks, over the soft thin fabric of his jeans, to his thighs.

The sound of his breath catching made her want to cry out, but he kissed her again, increasing the pressure of his mouth on hers. She slid a hand between them boldly, wanting to touch the hard male part of him.

At the touch of her hand his breath caught in his throat again. "Ah, sugar," he whispered. In one swift motion, he moved fully on top of her. He reached upward, almost sporadically, to brace himself, and found a handhold on the rock. He moaned. Her hand was touching him lightly in the softest of caresses. She stroked him gently and then she moved on, to touch his thighs.

"Your hands feel so good on me," he whispered before he reclaimed her mouth and thrust his tongue deep inside it.

She arched her back against him and moaned, but broke the kiss. Very shakily, she said, "I think I want to make love to you." *She knew she did.*

"Just think?"

She nodded.

"Here?" he whispered.

"In your bed."

He rested his face against her chest, nuzzling his face into her breasts. "When you're good and sure, you just tell me, Peachy," he said huskily.

"I will," she said.

He shifted his handhold above her, so he could better relax. Before he registered what was happening, he had pulled one of the rocks above them free. And it started a small avalanche.

Something hard hit the side of her helmet with frightening force. "Bronson!"

"Damn," he said.

She felt herself rolling with him, hitting the ground. Dull thuds from the falling rocks sounded, hitting the earth around them. His lamp went out and then everything was black and silent.

"Are you all right?" His breathless voice was gruff.

She felt his hands running over her arms, pulling her sweaters down to cover her skin. She was panting, and when her breath evened, she said, "I think so." She mustered a half laugh. "We're dangerous together. I hope you realize that."

He chuckled. "But it's a good kind of dangerous."

In the dark, she felt the reassuring warm length of his body leaving hers and she reached out, catching him.

"I have to re-light our lamps," he said, his voice still sounding breathless and low. "I hit a rock and brought them all down. I should have had more common sense than to—" He had started to say "to try and make love to you here," but stopped himself. A hot flood of want hit him again, full force, while he fumbled for the lamps in the dark. He could still feel the way her hand had reached for him, touching him with the kind of abandon that only the deepest of passion could induce.

As her own desire diminished by degrees, she managed to sit up. She couldn't see, but sensed Bronson moving in the darkness. Regardless of what was to happen in the future, regardless of the fact that he said he had no intentions of marrying again, she wanted him still. In her heart of hearts, she knew she would always want him. No one's touch had ever moved her the way his did and no one's manner had ever annoyed and amused in quite that way.

"Bronson?"

"Trying to light these things in the dark is a pain," he responded. "Sorry." He was half-glad they were in the dark. He was hardly modest, but the absolute power with which he wanted her was something he would rather let subside a bit. "Here," he said.

One of the lamps flickered to life. Watching the shadows play on her face, he felt he could gaze at her forever. "You look—" he paused "—almost well-loved."

She smiled and stood, glancing for a moment at the rocks that had fallen. "Almost?"

"Well," he said as the second lamp flickered to life, "I didn't exactly finish."

"And I do want you to," she said, moving beside him. She kissed him lightly.

He lowered his voice. "Why are you getting married?"

"You know I don't really want to," she said.

"Then why are you?"

She gazed into his eyes. "You know my reasons."

"Yeah," he said. "Your father's damn business deal."

She nodded, feeling relieved, until she saw the hard look that crossed his features. It was a look of judgment.

"You're marrying for money," he suddenly spat out.

"You have to understand that it's very important to my father." *Please understand.*

He sighed, still unable to believe she'd really do such a thing and even more distressed now because he wanted her so desperately.

"Perhaps we better head back," she said, wishing he knew how excited the engagement had made her father and how much she loved her family. She tightened the strap on her hard hat and turned toward the direction of the belly crawl.

Bronson whistled softly. "Well, take a look at that!"

"What?" Peachy turned. The fallen rocks had exposed a crawl space. Something—she couldn't make out what—was inside. It looked like individual block-shaped boxes in cloth. She watched as Bronson threw the bits of cloth in every direction.

He glanced at her. "Come here!"

She came close and peered over his shoulder. Her mouth dropped. "Cans of soup?"

"Yeah, but look at—"

She couldn't believe her eyes. "Why, they're bars—"

"Of gold," he finished. "Your uncle really was rich!"

That information hardly came as any surprise to Peachy. She was still staring at the dull sheen that glinted off the stacks of bars. What did surprise her was that someone as crazy as Kyle had ever sprung from Lofton stock.

"Well," Bronson said after some time, in a still-shocked voice, "as good as it looks, I still wouldn't marry for it."

She caught his arm and turned him to face her. She stared deep into his eyes. "Don't judge me," she said. "Please."

His look softened. He glanced down at the ground and then back to her face. "For you," he finally said, "I'll really try."

## Chapter Eleven

"Hot dog!" Bernie said for the umpteenth time. He gave Helena a smacking kiss on the cheek. "I have to admit, though," he said, turning to Peachy and Bronson, "I'm a little jealous of the way you stumbled right onto the gold I've been looking for." He winked. "But I guess I forgive you."

Peachy nodded agreeably in Bernie's direction, even though the last thing she wanted to think about was hot dogs. She felt the loose friendly weight of Bronson's arm drape around her shoulders.

Helena kept an arm around Bernie's waist and with her free hand waved at the departing armored truck. She turned to Peachy. "Now, we can get that condo in Florida," she said.

"That's wonderful," Peachy said, feeling both the warmth of the late afternoon sun and Bronson's equally warm presence beside her. Her excitement over finding the gold and calling for the armored truck ebbed. Helena and Bernie's plans to leave pointed to the fact that she was supposed to leave, too. She realized she had harbored secret fantasies of coming back to West Virginia, ostensibly to visit Helena, but really to be with Bronson.

"And," Helena continued, "I suppose I can now give you a deal on my property."

Bronson forced himself to grin. His life-long dream of having his clinic right next door would come true. But really, there were two difficulties with that. First, of course, he had a few reasonable monetary reservations about taking the step toward expansion.

But more importantly, when he imagined that life now, it seemed oddly empty. Helena and Bernie were going to sell and move, and Peachy obviously intended to leave, as well. It just wouldn't be the same, not for a very long time. Not ever, he admitted to himself. It hit him full force that underneath it all, his dreams were what they had been seventeen years ago.

He wanted to be a vet, living in his family house, with his clinic next door, and yes, he wanted a wife who loved him, and not one but six children to fill his house with laughter and love. But the incredible find of the gold did not so much seem to mark the beginning of an era now. Instead it seemed to mark the end to an old one and herald the end of his relationship with Peachy.

"After trying to get this property for all these years, you haven't changed your mind, have you?" Helena prompted.

"We'll discuss it," Bronson said gruffly.

"Discuss it! You're taking this fool place if I have to give it to you!"

Without even realizing it, Bronson tightened his grip around Peachy's shoulders, almost as if both the property and this woman were now fully his. He shot Helena a grin. "Now there's an idea."

"Don't push your luck, son," Helena said.

"While you all discuss things, I'm gonna go start packing," Bernie said. He drew Helena into his arms once again, kissed her, and then headed for the house. Over his shoulder, he called, "It took me sixty-seven years to make the smartest move of my life."

"Which was?" Helena yelled after him.

"Marrying you!"

Peachy smiled at her great-aunt, wondering how she had ever disapproved of her marriage. Sure, it had been crazy, fast and unusual, but somehow, finding the gold seemed to portend the best of everything.

If only, she thought, she was meant to be with Bronson. She felt him release the arm that had so casually rested around her shoulder. She glanced at him, wishing he hadn't removed it. The perfect line of his jaw was hanging wide open.

"I thought we'd had enough excitement for one day," he finally said.

"What?" She followed his gaze. A long, sleek, black stretch limousine was making its way up Helena's driveway. And that could only mean one thing. "My mother," Peachy said slowly.

"You've got to be kidding," Bronson said.

"I'm afraid not," she said.

Once the car came to a halt, a driver in a black suit and black cap got out, slowly circled the car, and opened a rear door. Peachy's mother's set of slender legs peeked from the car. Then Petulia stepped out as daintily as one could onto such rugged terrain in high heels.

Peachy couldn't force herself to move. How had Petulia found her? As much as she wanted to go forward and greet her, she felt positively rooted to the spot. "Hello, Mother," she managed when Petulia stepped forward.

"Petulia!" Helena exclaimed, as if she were a long lost friend. "Welcome!"

Petulia's eyes remained riveted on Peachy.

"This is Bronson West," Peachy said.

Petulia sent Bronson a curt nod and the look in her eyes was, he thought, enough to make his blood run cold. He felt himself starting to get a little defensive. Just because Peachy's mother wore a powder blue power suit that made her look more suited to the cover of *Vogue* than to the West Virginia hills, did not mean she had to be rude.

"Get in the car, dear," Petulia finally said.

Peachy stepped forward, but felt Bronson catch her wrist. Did he really think she was going to get in the car, just like that? she wondered. Only when her mother nearly flew backward did Peachy realize that she was still dressed in the muddy coveralls. Her hair was filthy and, she was sure, the streak of mud still trekked right across her face. She was wearing rubber boots up to her knees. The only worse out-fit would have been her Fancy Foods' uniform.

"I said, get in the car." Petulia had regained a solid stance a few feet away.

"Now, Petulia—" Helena began reasonably.

"Please stay out of this," Petulia cut in. She glanced at Bronson. "You, too."

Bronson felt his anger rising, but it wasn't all directed at Peachy's mother. Why didn't Peachy stick up for herself? Since she allowed her mother to treat her like a ten-year-old—and she apparently did—it was no wonder she was headed for a lousy marriage with the New York jerk. How could Peachy, with all her gumption, hard-working nature and passionate fiery attitude, just stand there and not say a word? He sent her a meaningful glance, hoping to indicate that he would support her, whatever she said or did. Unless she got into the limousine with her mother, of course. That he didn't intend to allow.

"Mother," Peachy said, "I realize that you're worried about my wedding, but—"

"Worried?" Petulia burst out. "Christine has stood in for you at more functions than I can name. And I do appreci-ate that! At least she cares about Wellington's feelings! At least she cares about what happens to this family! Do you expect her to stand in for you at your rehearsal dinner? I would like to point out to you that that dinner is less than a week away now. My dear, do you expect her to stand in for you at the altar?"

Peachy waited while her mother let off steam. "Now there's an idea," Peachy couldn't help but say wryly.

Petulia sighed. "Are you coming back? After all, this is the most shocking turn of events I have ever witnessed. You're thirty years old, dear, and you had best grow up and face the music."

"Believe it or not, Mother," Peachy said, "I am really trying to do that."

Peachy realized that tears were glimmering in her mother's eyes and a wave of guilt washed over her. "I'll be back," she continued before she even fully realized what she was saying. How did her mother manage to make her feel so guilty? What she wanted to do was scream that she was never coming back. And that that, however hurtful, was the obviously mature thing to do.

"Your father has so much riding on this," Petulia continued. "I'll only feel all right if you come with me now."

That was one thing Peachy was not going to do. When she returned, it would be when she was ready. And she would return without Petulia. "I'll come back, but I'm not coming with you. Not now." She ventured a glance at Bronson. His eyes seemed to urge her on. His gaze was now strong and intense and clearly meant to communicate that if she really wanted any help from his corner, he would gladly give it. She felt a tiny rush of pleasure. Bronson was on her side.

"When, then?" Petulia opened her purse, took out a tissue and dabbed at her eyes. "There are only seven days until your final dinner. Eight until your wedding."

"Eight days!" Bronson exclaimed. He was sorry he had accidently spoken because now he felt the full power of Petulia's scrutinizing glance. She looked him up, down, and then every way but sideways. "Young man," she finally said. "My daughter is engaged. And she is going to be married."

In just eight days, Peachy thought, feeling as though she had just swallowed a weighty stone that was sinking to her gut. At first, she had counted the days, but lately she had completely lost track. She willfully ignored how close June first really was. If she could only have another month...just one more month to be on her own, to work and to be with Bronson. She had begun to build such a rewarding life in the country.

"I'll be in New York before the wedding," Peachy repeated. "But I am not coming now."

"So be it." Petulia's voice was full of resignation. "I can't carry you bodily. Though I suppose the driver would if I told him to."

Peachy hardly liked the thought of wrestling with her mother's driver. "I'll be there," she said again.

She watched as her mother turned on her heel and marched back to the limousine. The driver opened the door as she approached, his expression blank, as if driving such a car to such a place was the regular order of his business. Once Petulia had seated herself, he shut the door, circled the car, and got in. Peachy sighed with relief. Her mother was ensconced behind the tinted glass of the window so that Peachy no longer had to look at her.

As the car turned and made its way back down the drive, she felt Bronson's arm possessively encircle her waist. Somehow, it wasn't fair that she was in the wrong on all counts now. Bronson was judging her because she was to marry a man for his money and her mother was judging her because she no longer wanted to.

"I see what you mean about your mother," he finally said. "She sure knows how to throw a guilt trip."

Given their talk in the cave and the interchange he had just witnessed, Bronson was more sure than ever that Peachy was going to marry the Vanderlynden character. Perhaps there really was no way he could stop her. He wondered again if he could propose, in order to try to stop the marriage and to buy the two of them more time together. He hauled her close until she was tight against him and wrapped in his arms.

"We always have a good time together," he said, thinking that proposing was a truly crazy idea, given the amount of time they'd known each other. He sighed. "And we do

ave eight days left.'' Suddenly he found himself sending
uick hot kisses up and down the length of her neck. Then
e smiled. ''So, I propose...'' He drew in a short breath and
inished, ''that we go dancing.''

'WHEN YOU SAID dancing, I thought you meant on a dance
loor,'' Peachy said. Bronson's fingers were twined with hers
nd his free hand rested on her shoulder.

He stepped back and threw his arms wide apart with a
mile. It was dusk and they were high on the wooded hill
bove Helena's house. ''Sugar, if I had only known you
eeded an orchestra in the woods...'' he began.

She laughed and leaned forward to grab him, but he
urned and whisked his hand from beneath hers. ''Can't
atch me,'' he teased.

She pursed her lips, daring him with her eyes. ''You can't
atch *me*,'' she said.

He shot her one of his half smiles. ''That *is* more to the
oint now, isn't it?''

''Now don't start that—'' she began as he took a creep-
ng step toward her. She leaned forward, tugged the tail of
is denim shirt, shot him a teasing smile, and then turned
nd ran.

''Peachy,'' she heard him call in a low, deep bass, singsong voice. ''Oh, *Peach-ee-ee*.''

She had passed a few trees before reaching an old gnarled
oak, and now she pressed her back against it and panted
oreathlessly. She peeked around the tree. She saw just the
nerest flash of Bronson's black curls as he ducked behind
another tree.

''I'm going to catch you,'' he called.

''If you're lucky,'' she returned in a singsong voice that
echoed his own. She drew in a deep breath and then bolted
for another tree. The deep sunset had turned a smoky gray
with near nightfall and though it was warm, her cheeks felt
almost cool. It felt so good to run in the fresh country air
that she ran even farther than she'd meant to and only

stopped when her side began to ache. She doubled over, leaning against another tree, then turned, so that her face and hands pressed into the cool bark.

"I'm an expert tracker, sugar," came Bronson's teasing voice.

She giggled. Listening to the sound of her own voice, she couldn't quite believe it. In her New York world, at dinner parties and cocktail parties, she'd had a decent enough time, but she had never been the type to giggle. And Bronson always made her giggle, bringing out the more playful side of her nature.

"I'm coming for you," he called. His voice rose and fell on the soft breeze like chimes.

Listening to it, Peachy tried to fight the sadness she felt. It was such a whirlwind week. Bronson had taken time off working only while she was at Fancy's. The rest of the time they spent together. They were inseparable, even if they still had not made love. Even if every minute that passed she wondered if they would... if she could.

"You can't evade me for long."

She glanced around the tree, toward the voice, but didn't see Bronson. Where was he? She peeked again and when she didn't see him, ran for another tree.

"I'll chase you until the end of time, sugar," he called. His voice was fairly close and as soft as silk. Suddenly she wondered why she was running at all.

"I'll chase..." His voice was very, very close, seemingly on just the other side of the tree she leaned against.

He continued talking, lowering his voice to a whisper, making his way slowly around the trunk. "I'll hunt..."

She shut her eyes, wishing it was true. Wishing that he'd never let her go. She listened as twigs snapped beneath his boots.

"I'll track you down..." he whispered in her ear. "Until I find you," he said, raising his voice and drawing her into his arms.

"And now that you've found me," she said, managing to keep her voice light, "just what is it you intend to do with me?"

He backed her against the tree, bent his head, and kissed her, his lips just touching hers. Then he lifted her hand and squired her between two trees where pine needles had fallen and where the ground was soft.

He placed one hand on her hip and twined his fingers through one of her hands again. His lips curled into a teasing smile.

"But there's no music," she said, even though she began to follow his lead.

"Birds and crickets..." he said, grazing his lips over the top of her hair.

"Fireflies," she said, nuzzling his shoulder. All through the bramble bushes on the hillside, tiny lights began to blink one by one.

"They don't make any noise," he whispered, drawing her even closer.

"No," she whispered. "But we can make our own music."

"That's the point *I* was trying to make, sugar," he said, right before he lowered his mouth to kiss her again.

"HEY, PEACH," Tommy said, breezing into the kitchen where Peachy had made herself more than at home.

She turned and smiled weakly when Tommy stopped dead in his tracks. She had decided to make good on her deal and cook dinner for Bronson. Every recipe she had chosen had either the word easy or basic in front of it. Easy gazpacho, basic quiche plus, basic tossed salad with easy salad dressing... She'd decided against trying to make ham, since she couldn't find any recipes that looked easy enough.

"Thought you were spending the night with Larry," she finally managed. Without even looking, she knew she had flour in her hair from the not-so-easy-to-bake bread. Fortunately, she had found a frilly pink apron to cover her em-

erald green strapless dress. Her favorite shawl was fold
neatly on Bronson's living-room sofa, ready for her to wea

"I hate to tell you this," Tommy said, grinning. "But
the way to a man's heart is through his stomach, you're
big trouble."

Peachy glanced around Bronson's kitchen. It was a d
aster area. Pans were on kitchen chairs; the countertop he
more spills than she could even count. With a relief s
didn't voice, she watched Tommy whirl around the roo
beginning a general cleanup campaign.

Probably, she thought, she should have refused to coo
But it had turned out to be such a wonderful week . . . t
most wonderful of her life. Bronson had taken her dan
ing, not once but twice. Three times if she counted danci
in the woods.

And one afternoon, high on the hill, he had brushed h
short hair and then made her a wreath of wildflowers. S
had worn the floral cap all day, until the petals had wilte
and he begged her to allow him to remove it.

He'd taken her to all his favorite places, too. To resta
rants and a theatrical production . . . down narrow, twis
ing, unpaved roads that seemed to lead nowhere but alwa
led somewhere, even if only to an old high school make-o
spot or to a scenic overlook.

She had swung with Bronson on the porch, just sittin
silently, watching Bernie and Tommy work on Tommy
pickup. They'd looked at baby pictures and had gon
horseback riding. And now more than ever, she could n
bear the thought of leaving. So she had decided to do wha
she had never done for any man. She would attempt to coo
a decent meal. Oh, she thought now, she would give all th
money in the world to see her parent's cook, Alva.

"I forgot my toolbox and we're going to work on ou
cars," Tommy said. "But I can see you're going to fail mis
erably without my guiding hand." He was still flyin
through the kitchen, mopping here and scrubbing there.

Peachy realized Tommy was now kneading her wayward dough with something that looked like real expertise. Not only that but he actually began to roll the dough. He shrugged.

"My father sure can't cook," he said. "Someone had to learn."

Peachy's eyebrows arched upward. "I thought—he served me a beautiful breakfast after I fell asleep on your porch."

Tommy floured his hands, patted the dough and then began to braid it. He looked at Peachy and rolled his eyes. "Courtesy of every unmarried woman in the neighborhood."

Peachy felt a jolt of pure jealousy. "You mean, women bring all that—" She thought of the many nicely wrapped packages of goodies in the refrigerator.

Tommy laughed. "Believe me, since you've been around, the care packages are coming few and far between. However, they haven't stopped entirely. Virginia and Ellen know I'll starve to death without them."

"Virginia and Ellen?" Peachy followed Tommy to the oven, where he checked the temperature and inserted the loaf pan. She followed him back to the counter and watched him read over the recipes strewn across the counter. He tasted the gazpacho she had just finished and then began to grate carrots.

He turned, glancing at her over his shoulder. His eyes, she realized, were exactly like Bronson's. Both had an intense expression and a gaze that almost mesmerized.

"Jealous?"

She shrugged, trying not to let on that the fact of Virginia and Ellen did upset her. She had met them at the ramp festival, but now, even though she didn't know them well, they were making her feel inadequate. They could apparently make exquisite meats and breads....

"Are you in love with my dad?"

"What?" The question had come out of left field. Peach
reached behind her for a chair and sat down. "Well, it's n⟩
the kind of question that a strict yes or no really—"

"So you're sort of in love?" Tommy burst out laughing
Then he stopped and cocked his head. "It's Dad," he saic
He leaned forward and stared into Peachy's eyes.

"Listen to me carefully."

Peachy nodded.

"Put the gazpacho in the freezer for the next fiftee
minutes. Not the refrigerator, the freezer. Then put it in tl
fridge. You should have done this hours ago. Bread…forty
five more minutes. And use the bottled dressing in the r⟩
frigerator. Sorry, but that stuff you made is kind of gross."

With that, Tommy went flying through the back doo
Just at that exact moment Bronson came in the front.

"Smells like heaven in here, sugar," Bronson said. H⟩
leaned against the doorjamb, still wearing his lab coat. H⟩
took in a deep breath, as if to savor each scent. "Unfort⟩
nately," he continued, "I've got to shower." He move⟩
through the room, leaned down beside her and kissed her.

There was a sweet domesticity in his casual kiss and sh⟩
couldn't help but admit that having such a greeting ever
day of her life would be wonderful. "Go ahead," she saic
still feeling the softness of his lips on hers. "I'll set the t⟩
ble."

"You told me you loved to cook, but you didn't say yo⟩
were a culinary wizard," he said, glancing over his shoul
der.

"I have all sorts of hidden talents," she said smiling.

"And I do hope," he said, turning to face her fully, "tha⟩
you intend to demonstrate just a few more of them for me."
He gave her one of his slowest, sexiest smiles.

"I do," she returned with a smile that matched his.

But after he'd gone, she wondered how long they coul⟩
keep up the light banter…the pretense. It had been a week
full of good times. Five weeks, in fact. And they'd enjoye⟩
them in an attitude of complete denial, rarely alluding to

1at was to come. And now, the week was at its end. *To-orrow*, she thought, *is my wedding*. And it still seemed stant; an eternity away.

r THE DOWNSTAIRS bank of phones at the Plaza Hotel, etulia hid her face with a pair of sunglasses and turned her ıck to the coat-check employee. She hoped absolutely no 1e, her husband least of all, would realize that she had left r guests to their cocktails exactly nine times now. It was 1 minutes to seven and at precisely seven the waiters would scend the wide red staircase nearest a private banquet hall th dinner for all.

She found another quarter in the inner side pocket of her quined evening bag, deposited it, and called Helena Lof-n again.

"Four...five..." she muttered, listening to the unan-vered rings. Where was Peachy? She was not at Fancy's. etulia had tried there first, only to be told that Peachy was ot working. She also discovered that Peachy was sched-ed to work the following day, her wedding day.

Petulia let out a suffering sigh. Even if Peachy were go-g to do the most humiliating thing imaginable and jilt 'ellington—which she would not—her daughter would ardly have the nerve to work at a fast-food joint on her edding day. Or would she? Petulia was certainly begin-ng to wonder. "Seventeen...eighteen..."

Petulia was about to replace the phone receiver, but then 1shed herself flat against the wall. What had ever hap-ened to old-fashioned phone booths? The kind with doors .at afforded full privacy?

And what were Wellington and Christine doing down-airs? In an effort to hide herself, she stumbled into a dap-erly dressed gentleman with a cane who was positioned at .e next phone. She hoped his bulky figure would continue keep her hidden from view. She realized she was in trou-e if he finished his call, hung up, and moved on.

"Yes," she whispered into the still ringing phone. "
course, dear." She smiled at the man beside her.

Christine was only a few feet away and her voice had ri
to a pitch that anyone could hear. "My feelings, whate
they are, just don't matter. You're engaged to my sister!

"Right," Wellington said, his tone argumentative. "A
if she loved me, I suppose she'd attend our rehearsal d
ner, now wouldn't she?"

"I don't know," Christine said heatedly. "I suppose. I
how couldn't she love you? You're everything a wom
could ever want."

"Am I everything *you* want, Christine?"

Petulia stared at Wellington's tuxedo-clad form. He v
moving ever closer to her daughter. And, unfortunately,
was toward the wrong daughter. Petulia clapped her ha
over her mouth, half-afraid she might scream out loud.

"Hello? Hello?"

"Please be quiet," Petulia said into the receiver.

"This is Helena Lofton-Smith speaking. If you did
want me to talk, why did you call?"

Petulia continued to hold the receiver but pressed the di
tone button down.

"Well, am I?" Wellington now demanded. "Did y
think for a minute that I believed any of those trumped-
excuses about Peachy's absences? Do you really take me f
a fool?"

Petulia sighed at the exact moment that Wellington di
She glanced at the gentleman beside her. Fortunately,
seemed deep in conversation and was not going anywhe
soon.

"Well, no," Christine said. "Of course, you're no fool

"Well, I'm not," Wellington exploded. "But I've go
along with everything because . . ." His voice trailed off.

Petulia leaned forward, peered beneath the gentleman
elbow and strained her ears.

"Because these few weeks have been the best of my life," Wellington finished. "Even placating your mother, doing things like shopping continually, is fun when you're—"

"I won't listen!" Christine burst out. "Oh, it sounds good, but I won't and can't listen to you."

Petulia cringed, realizing that both the gentleman beside her and the coat-check clerk were watching the two now. What had Wellington meant by that business about "placating her"?

Suddenly, Christine fled past Wellington, the swirling skirt of her silver silk dress making the moment seem even more dramatic. Wellington caught Christine's wrist. It was his grasp on Christine as much as the running momentum of Christine's own flight that brought her in a single second right into his arms.

Petulia nearly doubled over in shock. She lifted one of the gentleman's elbows with her hand to get a better view. When she did so, she was more than sorry. Because the wrong daughter had gone more than weak-kneed. Wellington had lifted her completely off her feet and was kissing her in a way that Christine wouldn't likely forget. Petulia knew that she, herself, would remember it always.

"I won't! I can't!" Christine exclaimed again.

Petulia heaved a sigh of relief as she watched her youngest daughter escape. Wellington followed, but it was clear that Christine had every intention of putting him off.

Peachy would undoubtedly be back in Wellington's good graces in the morning. She could charm her way out of anything. Petulia found another quarter and dialed Helena again.

"Some drama," the gentleman next to her said. "I remember those sweet days of love-torn youth."

Petulia sent him a weak smile and listened to Helena's line. It rang and rang. Briefly she wondered if the social difficulties could be smoothed over if Christine did stand in for Peachy at the wedding, but nixed that idea immediately. What would people think? That Christine had stolen her older sister's husband-to-be? Christine would be ruined forever! To avoid such a thing, Peachy just had to marry Wellington.

MORE THAN THIRTY candles flickered in the room, the white-hot flames sparking and fluttering with the soft breeze. They turned orange and blue, and surrounding each flame was a soft yellow glow. Each candle deepened the shadows against the walls and curtains.

The candles had been Bronson's idea and he was very glad now that he had thought of them. He'd found every candle in the house, some decorative and ornamental, some merely of the practical white dime-store variety, the kind he kept in case of a power outage. They flickered from unused ashtrays, saucers and candle holders all around his dining room. They threw mysteriously sensual shadows into the hollows of Peachy's face.

"My dining room table never seemed overly long before now," Bronson said. He looked toward the opposite end where Peachy was seated. She leaned forward and smiled at him, while he continued to drink in the sight of her.

The shining emerald color of her strapless dress caught the light, so that that same light seemed to reflect in her eyes. A gold, loosely woven shawl rested on her shoulders. It gleamed and the whiteness of her bared shoulders and arms peeked through in swirling patterns that moved with the shadows.

"Your table seems suddenly long to me, too," she said, unable to help hearing the low huskiness of her own voice. She moved her shoulders gently to the soft music that came from the stereo in the living room. "The candles are wonderful," she said, and gave a soft, delighted laugh.

He tried to tamp down the thought that tonight was their last night. He wouldn't ever hear that laugh again, not in this way, alone with her, in his house, surrounded by candles. "What's so funny?"

She glanced over the table at the remains of the meal that with Tommy's help had turned out so beautifully. "I didn't realize until now that I pretty much recreated Helena and Bernie's honeymoon dinner."

"How so?" He didn't take his eyes from hers. He knew he couldn't, even if he had wanted to. He had never seen a woman look more like a vision. It was one of those nights when everything—the food, the wine, the company and the candles—was just right. All worked together, like a powerful symphony.

Peachy did not answer immediately, but took him in. He was freshly showered and shaved, and he had foregone his usual jeans for soft, dark, linen slacks and an almost blousy white silk shirt with heavy onyx cuff links. He looked as though he just stepped out of another century. It was a look that was timeless and romantic and had all the appeal in the world to her.

"If you're not going to answer, would you like to dance?"

Her breath caught as she watched him rise from his seat and make his way slowly down the length of the table toward her. Every lithe movement of his body sent a shocking, dizzying rush of desire through her. And it wasn't just the way he looked or how he affected her physically that moved her so, she thought now, but his steady and kind way. It was the light that came into his eyes when he talked of neighbors, the animals he tended, his son.

She took his hand, allowing him to lead her to the center of the floor. She had expected him to hold her tightly, but he placed one hand on her waist and clasped her hand with the other, holding it in the air. She rested a hand on his shoulder.

"I feel a bit like we're in dance school," she said, smiling. She liked dancing in an old-fashioned way, but she wanted him to enclose her completely in the circle of his arms. As much as they had danced together, it felt odd to be held this way now...tonight. "Now that we're alone..."

*Now that we're going to make love.* "Are you afraid come too close?" She'd tried a light, teasing tone, but failed

"Afraid of you?" His lips hovered above hers and remained there as she took his lead and followed his slow steps. He kissed her lightly, his lips only barely parting. His tongue flickered inside her mouth, making her want more but he drew back. "Never. The only thing you make me feel is desire." His mouth came close again, his tongue softly sensually, moving between her parted lips. He drew back ye again. "I want you."

He let his eyes rove over her face and fought back the rush of words that threatened to spill forth. He more than wanted her. He had no idea how he would manage when she was gone, and he wasn't sure he would be able to. He had shared so much with her. Somehow she had come into his life and with her he could show his more vulnerable side.

"You couldn't want me as much as I want you," she tried to say, but her voice was only a whisper.

She felt his arms tighten as he drew her closer, and now with a sharp intake of breath, she felt his thighs move against hers, the dark soft linen touching her bare legs. She moved forward almost in reflex.

Suddenly, with a force she could barely fight, she felt as if she might begin weeping. She could not bear the thought of this night ending. She didn't cry, but fought the feeling nuzzling her face into the slick softness of his shirt. Beneath the silk, the muscles of his chest moved, turning her in the dance.

"Your hair smells like apples," he whispered. He'd meant to just dance for a while, to draw the evening out as long a possible, but having her so close and in his arms again, created an arousal he couldn't control. He brought her hand to his chest, held it there for a moment, and then released it. He ran his hand through that sweet-smelling hair and rested his head on top of hers. Her hair was fine, and against his cheek it was, he thought, the softest thing he had ever felt.

He slowed his feet so that they moved in a small circular rhythm; her slender hips wedged ever inward, with each movement, toward his own.

"I was going to say..." Her voice trailed off as one of her hands moved to his back. She made small circles on the cloth of his shirt with her fingertips, then let her fingers drift downward with the lightest of touches. "I was going to say that Bernie and Helena had violets floating in bowls of water, too. And candles and baskets of warm braided bread."

"I could smell the violets all through dinner," Bronson whispered. "I can smell them still." And, he thought, they were the color of her eyes in the candlelight. He hummed a contented sigh, his head still resting on hers, his body feeling languid and yet taut with warmth that curled in his stomach and was moving down and outward, growing into more intense desire.

He pressed her even closer, willing her to feel his growing arousal. This was one night when he meant to hide nothing and hold nothing back. If he were only to be with her once, if once would have to last him the rest of his life, then he wanted all of her.

He realized that they had almost stopped moving. They were swaying in one another's arms, still gently turning in their ever-tightening circle. It was their circle alone, a circle so tight that nothing could come inside. Nothing else in the world mattered now.

"Oh, Bronson," she whispered. Her hands lowered on his back. She knew he had intentionally set a tone for this night that was slow, but for her it was almost painful. Every part of her wanted him, all of him, right now. And, indeed, forever. She held back, even though it meant trying to hide how her body sought to strain forward and how her hips undulated against him. No matter what happened, she knew she would never want to change anything about this night. Nothing at all.

"The night of Bernie and Helena's dinner..." she whispered. She wanted to finish what she'd been going to say, even though the hardening length of him was so near, straining against the loose folds of his linen slacks, stretching toward her.

Bronson bent his head, his cheek sliding over hers, skin to skin, before he drew back and flicked his tongue between her parted lips again. It was like the flame of a candle... hot and fluttering. He let go a ragged sigh. Then his mouth met hers with deeper pressure and her back arched toward him in spontaneous response. "Yes?" he whispered.

"I—" For a moment, she could not recall exactly what she had meant to say. "That night, I wandered down here..."

His lips brushed hers, just grazing them, and she increased the pressure of her hands on his thighs. Again, she wanted nothing more than to touch him in the most intimate way.

"The night you slept on my porch?" His voice was gruff and yet the sound of it sent a thrill straight through her as if she were a tuning fork vibrating against his sound. She felt his hands move upward, over the swells of her breasts. The emerald cloth that veiled his touch seemed like only an ever-so-thin bit of tissue through which she could feel every tremor of his fingertips.

Her shawl fell to the floor and his face now rested between her breasts. "It's nothing really," she said, her throaty voice catching as he kissed her breasts, one by one. He lifted his head and gazed into her eyes.

"It's just that that night, I watched Bernie and Helena dancing." *I watched you, too.* "It was dark and I could see them through the window. And I knew how special that night was for them. And I wanted..." She tried to fight it, but a tear fell down her cheek. "I wanted some night like that for me, just once in my lifetime, a night like their honeymoon night."

Bronson kissed away the tear that had fallen. And then he held her so tightly that she knew she had never felt more warm or more safe or more loved.

He pulled back and looked deeply into her eyes again. The sheer vulnerability he saw there nearly took all his remaining breath. "You wanted a night full of tenderness, a night of love that you would never want to end?"

She nodded, feeling the full heat of his desire against her, and she moved her hips as if they could catch and hold him near.

"I can't promise it, sweetheart," he whispered. "But I can try to give you that. This one night can be our honeymoon...a night you can carry with you always." He paused, wishing oh so many things were different. "A night you can take into your future." Swiftly he lifted her into his arms, cradling her warmth against him.

Never had any man's rougher exterior hidden more softness, she thought as he carried her toward the stairs. And she knew, even if he didn't, that he had already given her such a night and more. Even if the night came to its close now, that would still be true.

At any other moment he would have scorned the idea of carrying a woman up a flight of stairs, but he swore to himself that he would do anything in his power to win her now. Her reasons for marrying a man she didn't love no longer mattered. Tonight he would only demand what she could give.

If all he could do was bring beautiful memories to some lonelier night in her future, then he would. And it was hardly only for her. It was for him, too. He knew, with a surety of heart, that what she would give him she would never give to that other man, the man she didn't love.

The room was dark, with only the moonlight filtering in through the windows. He laid her on the large, king-size bed that had been empty for so long. The emerald green skirt of her dress flared over the covers like a waiting sea.

Bronson stood above her, wanting to tell her that he loved her, but he stopped himself because he was sure she loved him. If family pressures were urging her on to her marriage, such a vow from him would only make things more difficult. And to make things easy on those you loved was how you loved them, he thought now. No, he wouldn't say anything . . . only love her through his touch.

Above her, he looked large and powerful. She watched as he stripped to the waist, letting the light shirt drift breezily to the floor. His chest gleamed in the moonlight. She lifted her arms to pull him down on top of her and moaned when she felt the weight of him touching her down the length of her body.

Slowly he turned her to her side. The only sound in the room was their soft, shallow anticipatory breaths and the slow metallic sound of her zipper. Her hands had already moved downward, over the silken hairs of his chest and tentatively at first and then with more force, over the folds of the loose slacks. The cloth was nothing against the strength of his desire and the feel of the largeness of him in her hands made her tremble. Before now, she had felt him, but the denim had been more confining. Now she could truly feel him . . . his size, his strength, his growing need.

"You're so beautiful," Bronson whispered. He rolled the dress downward, running his fingers over and then inside the lace of her bra. "Green lace for me," he whispered as he touched her nipples. They were already hard and taut with her arousal. Her skin peeked through the nothingness of the fabric. He removed the bra quickly.

He sank his head down, against her breasts, touching and kissing, feeling her hands exploring him. As if from somewhere far away, he heard the sound of his belt unbuckling.

Bronson bit ever so lightly at her nipples, his teeth just grazing them, his hands moving downward. He caught her wrists, to stop the exploring movements of her hands. It took all his willpower. He wanted her to continue. He had felt her hands moving through the front opening of his shorts, her free hand pulling down his remaining clothes, but if he didn't stop her now, he knew this wouldn't last. And more than anything he had ever wanted, he wanted this time to go on forever.

Her hands almost fought his, not wanting to let go, but he moved them above her head and lightly encircled her wrists with the fingers of one hand. He kissed her mouth, her neck, her breasts, descending to her stomach and then moving back upward, while the fingers of his other hand trailed to the triangle of perfect hair, moving inside her. Her gasp alone, the complete abandon of desire he heard there, was enough to make him moan.

"I want you inside me," she whispered. She tried to pull him on top of her, but he remained by her side, his fingers moving in quickening circles. "Oh," she whispered, letting out another moan and only realizing then that she had been holding her breath.

"Not yet," Bronson said. His fingers were shooting inside her and out again, then moving in circles. His quick breathing was right next to her face, its heat blowing into her ear. Her hips arched forward, as if leaping toward his hand. She returned to the mattress with a force that sent her upper body forward, so that she was nearly sitting.

He laid her back down, still cupping the smallness of her and the heat of her in his hand, feeling the intensity of her climax gentle to tiny palpitations that felt, to him, like heartbeats... full of life... of love.

He moved fully on top of her, entering her with a slow force, each movement meant to take her farther and farther away. She would think only of him, the man who was loving her now.

"I can't take this," she whispered. She could still feel her climax, and she grasped wildly at him as he moved deeper inside her.

His eyes took in the sheen of perspiration glimmering on her breasts in the moonlight. He felt as if he were looking at moonlight itself.

He let himself go completely, giving in to the feel of her movements beneath him, until he forgot everything. The night, dinner, the moonlight, his son. Everything receded into an ever-graying haze, until all vestiges of control fled and for a brief moment even she, Peachy, the woman he loved, was gone.

"I couldn't feel if you—" he began. His arms that held him above her were trembling and he gently lowered himself, trying not to collapse his full weight on top of her.

"If I what?" She pulled him down, wanting his body to cover hers completely.

"Climaxed again," he whispered, turning so that he could gaze into her eyes. He ran his fingers over her cheek. "Sorry if I . . ."

"Sorry?" Staring into the gray depths of his eyes, she had never felt more moved. He looked suddenly very young and vulnerable and she knew that she was seeing him as no one else ever did. For a moment she felt she was staring right through his eyes and into his soul.

"Did I go slow enough for you?" he asked. "I want you so badly, sugar, that I got so caught up—that I—"

"Oh, yes," she whispered, pulling him close. "It was slow and perfect." She placed a hand at the back of his head and turned him so that his cheek lay on her breast. "It's never been like this before." She tilted his chin briefly toward her, so that she could see into his eyes again. "Never."

He nuzzled his face against her skin. "No regrets?"

"No," she said. She felt tears well in her eyes and though she did not allow them to fall, she knew that this night of lovemaking had changed everything about her life. "I just want you near me now, just like this."

He brushed his lips against her cooling skin and pressed his face against the softness of her breasts. How could he live, never holding her this way again? He simply could not. He knew it would be impossible. He had to force himself not to argue with her now, not to demand that she stay with him.

It was purely evil, but he hoped that when she made love to her husband, images of tonight would enter her mind. He hoped her husband could do nothing to please her, that she would realize only he, Bronson, knew her body because it was he who truly knew her mind. If only tonight had accomplished that, then she would return to him of her own accord.

# WEEK FIVE

*Pledged to my heart for
eternity...*

## Chapter Twelve

Bronson's hands moved slowly over the covers in caressing circles, but the sheets didn't even feel the least bit warm. And the bed felt just as big as it used to, back in the pre-Peachy era. Where was Peachy! And who the hell was banging at his door? He started, then managed to elbow his way to a sitting position. Whoever was knocking was not downstairs at his front door, as he had thought. The person was right outside his bedroom.

"Peachy?" Had the door somehow stuck? Was she locked outside in the hall? Or was it Tommy, returning early from Larry's?

Bronson still felt groggy and yet almost languid. His muscles felt sore from passionate exertion, but their tightness far from hurt. It only reminded him of how sweet his new love had felt in his arms. But really, he thought now, Peachy had not felt like a new love at all. He had grown to love her and, when she was in his arms, he felt as if she had been there always.

"Are you covered, young man?" The pounding sounded again.

Bronson pulled the sheet up to his waist. "Yes," he called. "Helena?" What was Helena Lofton doing at his bedroom door? He rarely locked his storm door and he supposed she had just walked inside and upstairs. But why?

She pounded once more before entering and standing at the foot of the bed. She wore one of her floral-print shifts and the frayed straps of an old out-of-style navy pocketbook rested over her arm. She flushed when she saw that his only clothing was a sheet, but otherwise held her ground.

"Good morning," Bronson finally managed. He glanced at the digital clock on his bedside table. It was nearly ten.

"She left!" Helena exclaimed.

"What?" Bronson's eyes traveled from Helena's face back to the clock. For the first time, he noticed a daintily folded sheet of paper. He opened it.

Dear Bronson,

I didn't want to wake you, and I had to go to New York today.

He paused, looking at the signature. Clearly she'd intended to write "Love, Peachy." But she had scratched out the L and settled for "Best, Peachy." Gone or not, that change in her stupidly perfunctory note rankled. He glanced at Helena.

She was looking at him with a shocked expression. "Well, aren't you going after her?" She continued to look at him as though he was the craziest man she had ever seen. "Her flight's at ten-thirty and Bernie's downstairs with Bessie."

"Bessie?" Bronson tried to gather his wits and tamp down his anger. He realized now that he had never really thought this would happen. To the very end, in his heart of hearts, he had expected her to call off the wedding. He had certainly expected her to tell him that she loved him.

"Bessie's Bernie's taxicab," Helena said, groaning in exasperation. "Now get up! You can't let her get married!" Helena threw up her arms in a gesture of despair. "What is wrong with the younger generation? I've been watching you two and I know good and well how you feel about each other. What in the world is wrong with you, Bronson?'' she repeated.

''Nothing!'' Bronson suddenly exclaimed. ''Of course I'm going after her!'' He found himself leaping out of bed, holding the sheet tightly around him. ''Well, at least let me dress,'' he managed. Running for the shower, he nearly tripped over the sheet. This was hardly an ordinary way to begin a morning. Nonetheless, from their kiss at first sight to that danged endangered deer in her car, had anything of or relating to Peachy Lofton ever been normal?

''Where's your travel bag?'' Helena yelled.

''Hall closet!'' he yelled, jumping under the shower spray, without giving the water time to warm. He soaped himself as quickly as possible. If Peachy really wanted to go through with her wedding, he knew there was no way he could stop her. But if she had the doubts he was sure she had, then maybe, just maybe, he would have a chance...her family be damned!

PEACHY FELT the increasing speed of the plane as it taxied down the runway and then the weightless release as its wheels left the tarmac. She tightened her seat belt and glanced down at the portfolio in her lap. It held Polaroid shots of the West Virginia Fancy Foods and papers documenting the changes she had made. She had also produced some effective, if crude drawings detailing changes she would have made if more money had been made available. If only she had sales figures to substantiate the effectiveness of the changes, everything would be a cinch. Unfortunately she didn't.

She opened the tie binding the portfolio, meaning to go over the pages and think of how she would address the board, but she simply could not concentrate. She'd had her share of bad days, but it had never been so difficult to leave a bed as it had been this morning.

She thought of Bronson, lying on his back in bed, and of his even, peaceful breathing, and of the way the sheet had twined around his waist. With all her heart, she wanted to be back there, curled beside him. She could have stayed there, lying next to him forever.

"Would you care for juice or coffee?"

She glanced up into the smiling face of an attendant. "I don't care for anything, thank you," she managed.

When the attendant had gone, she glanced through the window. Outside, the sky seemed grayish, the clouds thick. At moments, the sky was obscured altogether, reminding her of how she had driven through the fog with Bronson.

It looked like rain and, she thought, rain was supposed to be good luck on a wedding day. She had heard that before, where she couldn't remember. And yet she knew this was going to be one of the worst days of her life. Even looking at Wellington now, after her time with Bronson, seemed pure sacrilege. She belonged in the country with Bronson and she knew it.

Not that she was going to marry Wellington. If knowing and spending time with Bronson had not been enough to make her decide to call off her wedding, his lovemaking had certainly erased anyone but him from her heart. But she knew it would have been terribly wrong to tell him that. Bronson would think he had broken up her marriage. If he had any idea how much she had come to deeply love him, he would feel responsible.

She knew him well enough to know that his was a fine, upstanding country sensibility. If he thought he had anything to do with her broken engagement, he would feel obligated to be with her. And that she wouldn't have. If he were to ever pursue her, it would have to be solely because he wanted her, needed her and loved her. Not because the change in her feelings meant she wanted to be with him. That could never make for a lasting relationship.

Still staring through the window, over the wing of the plane, she wondered how in the world it could rain today. How could the sky portend the best of luck when what lay before her was most probably a failed merger, a furious

Wellington, a family battle and no Bronson...at least not until she had made herself her own woman, free and clear, and until no question remained about him feeling obligated or duty-bound toward her.

"YOU MEAN *that* plane, sir?"

Bronson had watched silently as the New York–bound plane lifted off. He'd watched it zoom through the ever-thickening clouds of the lousy day.

He leaned forward in an effort to stare at the clerk's computer terminal. "What else do you have?" He half registered the fact that Bernie and Helena had followed him inside the tiny Chuck Yeager International Airport.

"We have a direct flight, but it's not until this evening." The clerk glanced at him apologetically. "Sorry, sir."

Bronson tried his best to wait patiently while the clerk described umpteen-trillion routes that were all circuitous at best. He had to reach Peachy as soon as possible. He didn't even know the exact time of her wedding, for heaven's sake.

"Do you really mean to tell me that the quickest thing is to go to Charlotte, North Carolina?" he finally said. "That's a good four hundred miles out of my way!" Even though that was the case, Bronson found himself fumbling through his credit cards. He shoved one across the counter. "What time will I get to Charlotte?"

The clerk, as if sensing his distress, stabbed at her computer keys, checked the flight and ran his card through a machine in a flurry of motion. She hurriedly fixed his ticket. "Two-ten," she said, slapping the ticket into his hand. "The Charlotte flight's boarding now at gate two. Once you're there, you've got fifteen minutes to switch planes."

"Good luck!" Bernie and Helena yelled from somewhere behind him.

Bronson ran for the gate. He practically flung his carry-on through the metal detector, then skidded through himself. He arrived breathlessly at the boarding door. Suddenly he turned wildly and looked over his shoulder for Helena and Bernie. At first, he didn't spot them, but then saw with relief that they were waving from the other side of the metal detector.

"What time is her wedding?" he nearly screamed, hardly caring about the stares he got from people in the waiting areas.

"Three," Helena yelled. "And it's at Saint Patrick's."

Three? His flight was not even going to land until after two! He sent one last wave over his shoulder and bolted down the ramp and into the plane. He found his seat, tossed his carryon beneath the seat in front of him, then tried to fold himself small enough for the tiny space to which he had been so hastily assigned.

How in the world was he going to get from La Guardia to midtown Manhattan? He hadn't even been to New York in years and if it rained the way it looked like it was going to, there might well be flight delays. He glanced down at his clothes.

He was wearing his pointy-toed cowboy boots and he had been in such a hurry that he'd jumped into the first pair of jeans he'd grabbed. They were worn to the texture of thin paper and had a gaping hole in one of the knees. In some circles, he thought, that would undoubtedly be stylish. However, he'd had a close-up view of Peachy's mother's taste via her designer suit. And, somehow, he very much doubted she'd appreciate the outfit he'd chosen to wear to her daughter's wedding. The fact that he had worn a faded T-shirt and had no jacket, not even a sports coat, probably wouldn't help.

If he did manage to get there at all, it would be mere minutes before the church bells. And then, he wondered, just what exactly was he going to do?

"NOT ONE SINGLE WORD out of you," Petulia said. "I mean, do not even bother to part your lips."

"Mother—" Peachy felt her mother's grip tighten on her arm. She could also feel the strength of Christine's helping hand, not to mention that of her own old friend and bridesmaid, Julia Von Furstenburg. Regardless of which way she turned, or tried to fight all those oh-so-helpful fingers, yet another one of her flailing arms seemed to end up in the danged wedding dress.

"I know it's early," her mother rushed on. "But you haven't had any fittings for five weeks! And we just *must* see if last-minute stitching is required. But it's nothing to worry about, dear. Just remember that even Marilyn Monroe had to be sewn into her clothes occasionally!"

Peachy tried yet again to wrestle herself from the three sets of hands. She had never felt so mauled over in her entire thirty years. Her mother, Christine and Julia, she thought, might as well have been crazed women chasing a rock celebrity.

"Well, I'm not Marilyn Monroe," she finally managed.

"Oh, Peach, you've just got the usual case of the jitters," Julia said soothingly. "I had them, too, but please don't get so nervous you forget to toss the bouquet to Christine. After all, she is next in line." Julia rambled on. "I do hope you catch it, Christine."

"I'll be more than happy to give you the bouquet right now, if you want it," Peachy responded, glancing toward her sister. "And, Julia, contrary to what you think, I do not have any such thing as jitters. I'm not getting married." In fact, she now had less than a half hour to get to Wall Street and force her way into the Board of Directors meeting. She glanced at the wall nearest the door, where her portfolio rested. If anything was making her nervous, it was the merger agreement. "I am not getting married," she repeated. *Not even if it saves a merger my father needs.*

Julia laughed. "Too late now," she said.

Peachy realized that they simply would not believe what she was saying. She felt relieved when all three women stepped back.

"Now put on your shoes," her mother said.

Julia, she realized, was staring at her open-mouthed. "You look so beautiful."

Peachy allowed her mother to lift each of her feet and slip them into the satin slippers. She felt like the first urban Cinderella. And, oh, how she wished the ball was long over and done with!

"Now," Petulia was saying, "as soon as we're sure that everything fits, we'll undress you. Damion is coming here to do your hair. I think he intends to give it some loose curls, even though your headpiece covers it." Petulia stood, went toward the bed, and returned with the headpiece.

Even Peachy had to admit that the high white tiara with its long veil was beautiful. She stooped, allowing her mother to place it on her head. For just that moment, it seemed fair that she allow her mother to see her in the gown, even if she was not going to see her actually married in it.

"You look like a dream, darling," Petulia said slowly, stepping backward again.

"What's wrong, Christine?" Peachy noticed that tears were welling in her sister's eyes.

"Nothing," Christine managed. "You just look so perfect..." Her voice trailed off. "That's all." Christine hiccuped. "I—I'm just so...so happy for you."

Peachy smiled and impulsively gave her sister a tight hug. "Don't be too happy for me yet," she said. She thought of having it out with her mother now and trying to explain once and for all that there really was not going to be a wedding, but if she did so, she'd never make it to Wall Street.

Peachy glanced at the clock. How had fifteen minutes managed to pass? "You will all have to excuse me for a moment," she suddenly said.

"We must get you out of that dress first," Petulia said.

"Mother," Peachy said in her most convincing voice, "I have to go to the bathroom. All right?"

"Can't you just—"

"No!" Peachy exclaimed. She edged toward the doorway, allowing the wide skirt of her gown to obscure the portfolio that she discreetly lifted from the floor and placed in front of her. In the upstairs hallway, she grabbed her Anne Klein business bag. Then she twisted her train, flung it over her shoulder, and fled, full speed, wedding gown and all, down the staircase.

Once on the sidewalk, she suddenly realized she was an odd sight, even for New York. The business bag and portfolio hardly accessorized her wedding gown. "Taxi!" she yelled, raising her arm and waving it at the oncoming traffic. "Taxi!"

She shook her head in frustration. When an empty cab passed but did not stop, she stuck her thumb and fingers in her mouth and let go a whistle. "Taxi!"

With relief, she watched one pull up to the curb. Somehow, the orange color of the cab seemed fitting. She really was a crazed Cinderella and this was her pumpkin coach. But then, Cinderella had married the prince of her dreams, she thought, bringing herself back to the hard, cold reality of her situation. With an abrupt, practical motion, she tugged at the end of her train, got in the taxi, and slammed the door. Just as she did so, she saw her mother run outside.

"Stop that taxi!" Petulia shrieked, racing past doormen and dog walkers.

"Step on it," Peachy shouted. "Wall Street."

BRONSON HOPPED a turnstile on his way to what he hoped was terminal D. Just where *was* terminal D, anyway? he wondered. He half realized that his carryon was swinging wildly at his side. Every now and then he felt it make dull thuds of contact.

"Who do you think you are, buddy? The bionic man?"

"Why don't you look where you're going, mister?"

He barely registered the outbursts of complaint that he was creating in his wake. He passed a clock and without slowing from his full run, saw he had only seven minutes left before his next flight. It was just his luck that the rain had started and that turbulence had shaved precious minutes off his connecting time.

"You can't just go barreling through here like—"

"Wanna bet?" Bronson yelled over his shoulder. He ran at top speed over a moving, conveyor-type walkway, weaving in and around other travelers.

Four minutes, he thought, noting another clock. If he ran like this for another whole four minutes, he was fairly sure he'd internally combust! One day, he sure hoped he and Peachy were going to be laughing about this....

"YOU CAN'T GO in there!" Vivian Johnson, Charles Lofton's secretary, drew herself up to full stature and then ran toward the closed door. "Mr. Lofton is in a very important meeting."

Peachy puffed her cheeks to blow and took in Vivian's tight bun, sexless gray suit and white, starchy, high-necked blouse. She had forgotten about Vivian. And Vivian followed her father's orders to the death. Hoping for shock value, Peachy lifted the wedding veil that had fallen over her face during her fast and furious taxi ride. The tactic worked.

"Peachy!" Vivian exclaimed, her jaw dropping. She moved forward as if to double check that this was truly her employer's daughter. In the interim, Peachy dodged beneath one of Vivian's gray-suited elbows and ran inside her father's office.

Pappy Happy and her father, both already dressed in wedding tuxedos, were seated at either ends of a conference table. Four other men, none of whom Peachy recognized, were seated around the table's sides. She drew a deep breath, straightened her shoulders and took a stand next to her father.

"Peachy?"

In her tussle with Vivian, the veil had fallen again. Now, she raised it. "Hi, Dad."

Charles Lofton leaped up and embraced her. "It's been so long since I've seen you and nobody—not even your mother—will tell me what is really going on. Where have you been? Are you all right?"

"Good to see you, too, Dad," she said, kissing his cheek. She pushed him back into his chair and rushed on. "Gentlemen, I know this is irregular, but I'm Peachy Lofton." She paused to catch her breath.

"We're in the middle of a—" one of the men began.

"And that's exactly why I'm here," she finished. She suddenly felt self-conscious at having arrived in her wedding dress. Her father and Pappy Happy were dressed for her wedding, as well, but tuxedos hardly created the stir that a sea of shimmering organza did. Her gown definitely seemed to have sparked a whirring buzz of commentary. She swallowed and ignored the quizzical glances she was receiving from the men. "I've had the extreme pleasure of working at one of the West Virginia Fancy's over the past few weeks and—"

"Not the Charleston establishment!" one of the men exclaimed. "This is too good to be true."

"There's been a marked increase of sales there in the last few weeks," another of the men said.

"It's very unusual and we have been trying to pinpoint the source of the increased activity!" This remark was followed by a general low murmur of acquiescence.

"I'm scheduled to fly down there and your mother even . . ." her father began.

Peachy leaned forward, trying to curb her own excitement. She placed her hands on the conference table, palms down, in as much of a power stance as she could muster, given the way she was attired. "I, gentlemen," she said levelly, "am the source of the activity."

She realized she had their full attention now and had to fight back a grin. Quickly, she opened her portfolio and arranged the photographs and drawings, spreading them across the table. To her surprise, the men in the room listened carefully while she detailed the day-care system, the uniform changes, the new sandwiches that were being served

and the new fruit bar. She explained some of the promo
tional ideas that had proven beneficial and also discussed
equipment that she felt should be upgraded.

When she had finished her presentation, she was sur
prised to find that the men were not only receptive, but tha
they had a number of questions. She answered them in turn
addressing ways in which she felt employee productivit
could be increased and ways that consumers could best b
queried about services. She spoke for some time about ap
propriate forms of market analysis. She could hardly be
lieve the phrases that rolled from her tongue. After all, sh
hadn't given talks about market analysis since her colleg
days.

The men talked and nodded agreeably until Pappy Happ
finally raised a hand to silence them. Peachy smiled dow
the length of the table at him. He had silver gray hair and a
goatee, as well as a cane that he often kept in his hand, eve
while seated. Now he stood and nodded at Peachy.

"Well, young lady," he began. "You've saved me from
having to bring your father some bad news. As you may
know, the sales figures from the most recent fiscal quarte
have just been made available. In fact, it was just those fig
ures that drew your father's attention to the West Virgini
location. However, the new figures show that Fancy's ha
been taking losses. The location under question is the onl
one with promise. This was not the case a year ago, a
your—" Happy nodded toward Peachy "—engagemen
party, when talk of this merger commenced."

Happy cleared his throat and continued. "These busi
ness agreements, though only made verbally to this point
have, to some degree, been bound up with your weddin
plans. Mixing business with personal relationships is some
thing I have never done. In fact, I have always avoided it
And last night, looking over the new figures, I realized tha
I was going to have to decline from our deal today and re
fuse to sign our contract."

Peachy felt her jaw drop. Was Happy really going to back out on her father? She felt a rush of cold familial anger and glanced downward. Her father looked as calm and as dapper as ever in his tuxedo, but she could sense his disappointment under his well-trained businessman's facade.

Wasn't this what she wanted? she wondered. Not that she wanted her father's business to suffer, of course. But Happy was backing out of the deal, even though he still assumed she was marrying his son. That meant she was off the hook. She was scot-free.

"But all the figures are not down," she found herself saying. Could she possibly manage to save the deal for her father and not marry Wellington, either? She sent Happy a cool level glance.

"No," he said agreeably. "The ones in West Virginia are up."

Peachy's veil threatened to fall in her face. She brushed it back over her head with a sweep of her hand. "And doesn't that have any bearing on your decision?"

"No," he said. "It didn't."

"But it must." Even though she understood that Happy owed it to himself to make only profitable business deals, the merger agreement was, she was sure, going to become profitable for him.

She heaved a sigh and continued argumentatively, "I wholly agree that our business dealings must be separate from our personal relations—in fact, that is how it will have to be. I couldn't accept this deal going through just because of our personal relationship. Still, I have worked hard to make these changes and I have done so without any corporate knowledge or help. And I spent very little money. In my view, the interiors of our stores need to be redesigned!" Peachy knew she was rambling but, in her anger, she could not stop herself.

She had acted more than competently and the merger, she was sure, would be to the benefit of both parties. *And she would not have to marry Wellington in the bargain!*

"Just think what I could do with corporate backing!" sh
burst out. "And I need more than just Fancy's. What yo
have got over us is your menu, but we can provide you wit
better marketing. And that, sir, is something you do need.

"What do you think, Charles?" Happy asked.

Peachy glanced down at her father. He was staring at he
open-mouthed. He suddenly smiled, and then positivel
beamed with pride. "Well, as I have always said, m
daughter got all the business sense in the family."

Peachy had to fight to keep her composure. Looking int
her father's now-twinkling eyes, she knew his pridefu
glance in itself was payment enough for all the work she ha
done. She thought over the years, of how she had skiec
ridden horses, and gone to a good university and of how
after all that, she had produced nothing. Not until now.

"Would you be interested in overseeing these change
elsewhere?" Happy asked.

She thought of Bronson and of how she had missed him
even for these few hours. She wondered if she could poss
bly make her home base in the country, if she needed t
travel. The thought came unbidden that maternity leav
might be a problem, but she pushed the thought aside. I
such a thing ever happened, she was sure it could be worke
out. And who was to say that just because she had found th
career of her dreams that she would find the man of he
dreams, as well. "So, could I set myself up in West Virg
nia?" she finally asked hopefully.

"You could live anywhere, but I was thinking more i
terms of global changes," Happy said. "Beginning in th
United States."

She stared at Happy and then at her father.

"You have the background, the education and the train
ing," her father continued, picking up where Happy left of
"And, as you know, this has long been a family business
You just never showed any interest in it before now."

"If you begin to make these changes in the next si
months, I'm definitely still interested in a merger. We coul

sign this week but I want to jointly negotiate which changes will occur, where and when. And all that will have to be on paper, in black and white," Happy said.

She realized she wanted this. Oh, did she want this! "But I *can* live in West Virginia? That's where I've been for the past five weeks."

"You can't mean to tell me you actually like living in the country," her father said incredulously.

Peachy thought again of the beautiful early summer she had had, of the fireflies at night and the clear moonlit skies, and of Bronson who had made those things seem even better than they already were. "I love it." *And I'm in love, here.*

"But what about Wellington? His headquarters are going to have to be Wall Street for some time—" her father began.

"Wellington!" Happy exclaimed. "Dear God, it's twenty of three."

Peachy's gaze shot to a wall clock. It was indeed twenty minutes until her wedding. She ran for the door. She did not look back, but sensed that her father and Happy were close on her heels. She made it into an elevator. Just as the doors were closing, she managed to yell, "Don't rush yourselves. I'm not getting married."

As soon as the doors were fully shut, guilt assailed her. She had hardly meant to break the news that way, and she never should have told her father and Wellington's father the news before Wellington himself knew.

Nonetheless, she could not be hard on herself. She had flown a thousand miles, attended a business meeting, successfully accomplished what had turned out to be a job interview, and now she was trying to get herself out of a marriage. She was on a very tight schedule. She could hardly be expected to follow rules of etiquette, too!

EVERY NERVE and sinew in Petulia's petite body was wound as far as it would go. She glanced from a side door at her

fourteen hundred wedding guests while the eyes of th
bridesmaids bored into her back. It was fifteen past three
Peachy was nowhere to be found and Charles and Happ
had not arrived. She wrung her hands, listening to yet an
other impromptu organ piece. It was Bach. Petulia bit he
lower lip, fighting tears. The music was more suited to a fu
neral than a wedding.

Although the sea of guests was little more than a blur o
fine summery fabrics and exotic hats, Petulia could sens
their discomfort. She could feel the men glancing at thei
watches, and hear the rising murmurs of female voices, dis
cussing the lateness of the hour. A wedding running fiftee
minutes late! Had anyone ever heard of such a thing?

Petulia closed the door and turned. "You're not sup
posed to be here!" she exclaimed when she saw that Wel
lington had moved from his position near an altar door an
was now standing with the bridesmaids, next to Christine.

"Just forget it!"

Petulia's chest felt tight. "Forget what?" she managed.

"Sorry I'm late." Peachy flew through the doors. She wa
completely out of breath and felt self-conscious when al
eyes riveted on her. She leaned against a wall for a mo
ment, willing her heart to stop pounding, then she rushe
forward.

"Wellington," she began in a low, urgent tone. Sh
grabbed his elbow in an attempt to steer him clear of th
others. "We have to talk." Unfortunately, Wellington di
not budge.

"We certainly do—" he began.

"Please be quiet, Wellington," Petulia said. "The guest
can hear your every word."

"I don't care who hears me," Wellington said. He
stomped toward the door, opened it a crack, and said, "I
everybody listening?" as if to illustrate his point. Then he
stalked back to Peachy.

"Wellington," she began again, "I know I've been lousy.
I know I owe you every apology in the world—"

"I'm not marrying you!" he exclaimed.

Peachy was still concentrating on what to say. This was the most difficult thing she had ever had to do in her life. "I'm so sorry," she continued. "But I simply cannot follow through with my obliga—"

"Didn't you hear a word I said?" Wellington's voice had risen.

"I'm sorry that I cannot go through with our marriage," Peachy finished simply.

"*I* said *I* can't marry *you,*" Wellington said.

Peachy's mouth dropped. "Excuse me?"

"Oh, no," Petulia said, inserting herself into the conversation. "This just will not do at all."

"Given the way you've run out on me and the fact that I'm in love with someone else makes it wholly impossible," Wellington clarified.

For reasons of ego, Wellington's words rankled at the moment. That she was running out on him was fine. That he was running out on her was another matter entirely. "Well, I'm in love with someone else, too, if you must know," she couldn't help but say.

"Oh, yeah?" said Wellington.

"Yeah," she said.

"This is insane," Petulia suddenly cried. She ran forward, noting with satisfaction that her husband and Happy had arrived. She grabbed both Peachy and Wellington by the arms. "You two are getting married," she said. "You may well divorce tomorrow, but this has cost a small fortune and someone is getting married! Now, young lady, you're the one in the wedding dress and you, young man, are the one in the tuxedo. So, you'd best start preparing yourselves to march down that aisle."

"Mrs. Lofton," Wellington said, his tone now controlled and level, "with all due respect, I am in love with Christine. I'm fairly sure she is in love with me, as well, but the fact of my engagement to Peachy has complicated mat-

ters. Christine can hardly admit her feelings under the c
cumstances.''

"Peachy, I'm sorry!" Christine burst out. "I didn't me
to—oh, my God, I am so sorry!"

Peachy glanced at her sister in shock. "Don't worry," s
managed. "Things could not be working out better.''

"Please understand, Mrs. Lofton," Wellington conti
ued. "I absolutely cannot and will not marry Peachy. I w
not—"

"For heaven's sake," Petulia screamed. "Someone's g
to marry her.''

"Don't worry," a voice cut in. "I'll do it."

All eyes—those of the bridesmaids, Charles, Petuli
Happy, Wellington and Christine—turned toward the doo

For yet another time, Peachy's jaw dropped. He w
leaning against the door as calmly and casually as yo
please, with a surface cool that almost unnerved her. In h
taut, faded T-shirt, thick hand-tooled belt and worn jean
not to mention his pointy-toed cowboy boots, he looke
better than ever. And she had never been so glad to see an
one.

"Bronson?"

He was already moving toward Wellington. "Mind if
borrow your outfit, buddy?"

Peachy watched as Wellington gave Bronson a lon
thorough once-over. Then Wellington's whole body seeme
to go into fast motion. He started shrugging his way out
his tuxedo jacket. Bronson pushed him toward what looke
to be an empty choir room, for a pants exchange.

"Wait," Peachy muttered, starting to follow then
"Doesn't this require more thought? A few preliminaries
An engagement, for instance?" She stopped short at th
closed door. She hardly wanted to see her ex-fiancé and he
current fiancé of two minutes' duration trading trousers.

"Bronson," she began when he came back out in We
lington's tuxedo, which she noted was just a bit small, "ju

because I'm calling off my wedding doesn't necessarily mean you have anything to do with it.''

"But I do. Don't I?" His gray-eyed gaze roved over her face and then he touched her cheek and looked deep into her eyes. "Now, be honest, sugar," he whispered.

She glanced around, realizing that they had a rapt audience and that beyond the church door, the wedding guests' murmurs had risen to the level of outright talk. "Yes," she said. "But that just means we'll be free to get to know one another..."

"Somehow, I feel we're already past the dating stage. We know each other intimately, Peachy. And I want more. Like you said, I'm a man who knows what he wants. I know my heart and it's with yours.''

"But it's just so fast," she said. And yet she knew that was her mother's voice talking, not her own. It was the side of herself that believed too much in etiquette, rule books and propriety.

"Bernie and Helena got married too fast," he argued. "And now you think it's the best thing that could ever have happened to them.''

Peachy couldn't help but think of that honeymoon night, when she had watched the couple dancing. She had wanted that night for herself. And Bronson had given it to her tenfold.

She knew, with certainty, that if she did not marry him now, that she would in the future. After all, hadn't that been her plan? To move next door to him if he did not buy Helena's property and then to pursue her own life, while at the same time hoping that things would work out between them?

"It just seems so spur of the moment," she managed. Her insides felt jumpy and she felt a little faint.

He dropped to his knees in front of her. "Peachy Lofton," he said, "I love you. I think I've loved you since the first day we met, when I had to tell you that your house was inferior to mine. Now, I want you to move into my country home. I've loved you since that first day, when we first kissed...."

She took his hands in hers. "I started to love you when we drove that night in the fog and when you said you wanted a big family," she said.

Suddenly he smiled. "When you came careering up to my clinic door with that damn deer, I just—"

"Get off the floor!" Petulia thundered. "It's three-thirty!" She grabbed Bronson's elbow and hauled him to a standing position. "If you're proposing to my daughter, I have to at least ask what you do for a living," Petulia said. "I know it's a tacky question, but you'll have to forgive me. I can't help it. I'm a mother."

"I'm a veterinarian," said Bronson.

Petulia smiled. "Well," she said, "it looks like you're going to be the only vet ever married at Saint Patrick's in cowboy boots."

Peachy's mouth dropped. "I haven't said yes," she muttered. She stared at her mother. Was she really going to accept this turn of events with such grace?

"Wellington," Petulia was saying in a take-charge voice as she marched Bronson in Wellington's direction, "take this man where he's supposed to go. You know the ropes and he doesn't." Petulia leaned toward Bronson. "I've no idea who you are, but I'd like to thank you for this, from the bottom of my heart."

"Believe me, ma'am," said Bronson. "It would be my pleasure, but she hasn't actually said—"

"I guess I'm now a bona fide member of the backstage crew," Wellington said, sounding relieved. Peachy watched him give Christine a peck on the cheek. All the bridesmaids were talking again and no one seemed to be paying attention to her at all.

"I haven't said yes," Peachy yelled. "Doesn't anyone here care what the bride thinks?"

Bronson disentangled himself from Wellington and Petulia, and hauled her into his arms. "I do, sugar," he said as he pulled her close. "I never cared about anything more in my life."

Peachy glanced upward, into his eyes again. His beautiful gray eyes would be the first thing she saw every morning, every day, for the rest of her life. She half registered the fact that everyone had fallen silent again. "It's crazy," she whispered. "But..."

"But?"

"But nothing," she said.

His eyes sparkled. "Is that an 'I do,' sugar?"

"I do!" she suddenly exclaimed.

The next thing she knew his hands had nestled their way through the miles of organza and held her firmly by the waist. He lifted her so that she was poised above him, and then he swung her high in a circle in the air, until she was breathless with laughter. The fact that her mother muttered, "Thank heavens," and that the bridesmaids were all applauding barely entered her consciousness. There was only Bronson.

As he lowered her and brought her face close to his, he said, "I'm going to kiss you like there's no tomorrow."

"We have a lifetime of tomorrows," she whispered as his lips grazed hers.

"But, sugar," he said, as he increased the pressure of his lips against hers, "I just can't wait."

**Relive the romance...**
**Harlequin and Silhouette**
**are proud to present**

A program of collections of three complete novels by the most requested authors with the most requested themes. Be sure to look for one volume each month with three complete novels by top name authors.

In June: **NINE MONTHS** Penny Jordan
Stella Cameron
Janice Kaiser

**Three women pregnant and alone. But a lot can happen in nine months!**

In July: **DADDY'S HOME** Kristin James
Naomi Horton
Mary Lynn Baxter

**Daddy's Home... and his presence is long overdue!**

In August: **FORGOTTEN PAST** Barbara Kaye
Pamela Browning
Nancy Martin

**Do you dare to create a future if you've forgotten the past?**

Available at your favorite retail outlet.

HARLEQUIN      Silhouette

# Take 4 bestselling love stories FREE

## Plus get a FREE surprise gift!